TOUGH LUCK

THE SHAKEDOWN SERIES

ELIZABETH SAFLEUR

Elizabeth SaFleur LLC
PO Box 6395
Charlottesville, VA 22906
Elizabeth@ElizabethSaFleur.com
www.ElizabethSaFleur.com

Edited by Trenda Lundin
Cover design by LJ Designs
ISBN: 978-1-949076-23-3

1

———

"You did *what?*" Starr glared at her sister. Maybe the music at Shakedown had impacted her hearing. After all, she had been on stage for the last thirty minutes.

Luna shrugged delicately. "I didn't think he'd find Dad so fast. I mean it's been so many years, and we had no clues at all except for that last address and—"

"Behind our backs, you hired a private investigator to hunt for our lunatic, deadbeat father who dumped us in foster care sixteen years ago and hasn't been heard from since?" She swung her gaze to her other sister, Phoenix. "Did you know about this?"

Phee crossed her arms, flattening the red feathers sewn across the bodice of her costume. "Are you seriously asking me that right now?"

She supposed her sister was right. Of the three of them, Phoenix would be the last of them to look up the man who caused three eleven-year-olds to end up in a city office with Child Protective Services etched into the glass door. Protective her ass.

She placed her hands on her hips. "Luna, you broke our

rule." The triplets had sworn never to make life-changing plans without consulting each other. "Of all the promises to break, you had to choose this one."

She released the metal hooks of her corset and expanded her ribs. The tang of cigar smoke rose from her costume like an invisible cloud. No matter how much Woolite she invested in, the tobacco scent clung like a parasite. What was it about the burlesque club that made men light up like movie land gangsters?

"I brought it up a month ago, and you didn't say no."

"*We* didn't say yes." Starr dropped her corset and snatched her next costume off its hanger. "Why, Luna? We are finally in a good place, with steady work in a nice club, instead of those rat holes we'd spent years in. For the first time ever, we have a routine. We're settled."

"Well ... " Luna twisted her fingers together. "We have an appointment with the investigator. Monday."

Starr's forehead bunched. "No."

"It's just to learn where Dad is."

Was Luna really whining?

"I couldn't give a shit where he is," Phee scoffed and turned away.

Starr yanked the white sequin dress over her hips, snapped the straps over her shoulders, and shimmied the fabric down her thighs.

Luna, her face screwed into a frown, turned to Starr. "Please?"

Her sister had to be smoking something. Was Mercury in retrograde? Had the Earth's polar ends flipped and no one told her? "Where did you get the money for this anyway?"

Luna didn't look at them. Instead picked up a lipstick, stared into the mirror, and smeared more on her bottom lip.

Starr drew closer. "L, where?"

Her sister smacked her lips at her reflection and turned to face her. "Declan."

Phee spun, her eyes slanted, her mouth pursed into a grimace. "*What?* You did *not* just say that. You went to our boss?"

And, just like that, this situation went from bad to worse.

"Who has money and connections. He's always told us to come to him with anything at any time." Luna shook her boa free from its hanger, tiny black feathers peppering the air.

"Mix business with our personal shit?" Phee's mouth tightened further. "We don't do that. It's part of our deal, a deal we all swore to years ago when we'd been *fired* from a job because of a stupid break-up between you and the club owner."

"This is nothing like that."

Phee grasped the largest of her red fans. "You have gone mad. We're not done talking about this, L., but it'll have to wait until we get home. Now, we're due on stage." Phoenix yanked open the door and let it slam against the concrete wall. Blaring horn music spilled down the hallway.

Luna turned to Starr. "Guess she's really mad."

"You think?"

Her sister munched on her bottom lip. "And you?"

"Yes. I'm mad. Why would we want to find that man?" Her eyes threatened to spring tears, but no way was she going to cry. Tears spilled over men, especially those who messed up as royally as their father, never changed anything. "Going to Declan wasn't the smartest move, though I gotta hand it to ya, you've got balls of brass risking Phee's wrath. Greater men have fallen."

Luna swung her boa over her neck and tramped to the door. Pausing, she turned to Starr. "I'm sorry I didn't tell you both. I just wanted to ... I don't know. Anyway, sorry, but think about it?"

Starr should have said something right then. It's just she didn't know how to touch her sister's apology or what she'd done.

She slipped her feet into her heels, drew in a long cleansing breath, and checked her makeup. In this lighting, she almost looked like a teenager, which honestly, she'd never had the luxury of being—not really, not like other girls had. When your drunken lush of a father dumped you in a foster home, going straight from eleven years old to adulthood occurred overnight. What did Luna think finding him would resolve? They were twenty-seven years old. Too old to pine for a man who didn't want them.

She could not think about this right now. She had to get on stage. Later, she'd figure out how to stop Luna's quest. Peeling back a corner of their past would only lead to stuff they didn't want to know, like what a bastard their father really was. If she had anything to do with it, she and her sisters would head in one direction only—to the future.

Starr made it to the stage just as Cherry's voice boomed out their names. "I give you, Luna Belle ... " The dramatic pause was broken up by delighted applause. "Phoenix Rising ... " More applause. "And, Midnight Starr ... "

Starr split the heavy curtains with one hand and stepped into a bright wash of lights, smoke, and men's shouts hanging heavily in the air.

Cherry twirled her hands. "Boys! Be good to my girls ... " She stepped back to let the three of them take over the space.

God, Starr loved that first moment when the music started, when the pounding of the drums and the appreciative whoops and hollers rolled right over her. Instantly, life was better.

She pranced to the edge of her corner of the stage and launched into her signature move. She bent a little at the waist, put her finger to her lips, and made a quiet "shhh" sound. It had its usual effect: the noise abated a bit, and that smidge of control over the audience warmed her whole body.

The pounding of the bass drum grew more insistent, and she raised her fan high, shimmying her breasts in a clatter of beading. All thoughts of horrible fathers and their even more horrible childhood faded just like the crowd had on the dark main floor just feet away.

Male shouts close to the stage on her right egged her on, and she winked toward the darkened corner, only catching a glimpse of some handsome male features. She never could make out the men and women sitting at the cocktail rounds on Shakedown's floor unless she drew so close to the edge she could fall off—but she could hear them, and tonight, their enthusiastic shouts and applause nearly shook the floorboards under her heels.

Three young men had commandeered the cocktail round just off stage right, which had the best view. She drew closer and waved her fan toward them. They stood and hooted, their palms loudly slapping one another in an exaggerated clap. She began to back away.

Later she'd blame Luna for why things went so badly. Thanks to Luna's news, she was off her game. She spun on her heel, turning her back to the three twenty-somethings— the stupidest thing she could have done.

As soon as a warm grip on her ankle registered, she stopped.

Seriously?

"Get off me," she snapped at the inebriated frat brat who'd bellied onto the stage and wrapped his hand round her leg. He waved the other stuffed with dollar bills. She inwardly cursed her rookie move. She knew better than to turn her back on a crowd of drunken men, even at Club Shakedown.

His friends behind him whooped like the hormonal mob

they were, and his hand climbed further up her leg. Her feather fan slipped from her grasp, and the stave ends cracked hard on the stage. *No, no, no.* She glared down at McGrabby's cherubic face. With any luck, she'd freeze him like Medusa. Instead, her attention fired something in his eyes—a dark, brainless lust just like she'd seen in all those men at that strip club she and her sisters had abandoned years ago.

It wasn't hard to deduce how the kids commandeered the best seat in the house. A $1,500 bottle of Scotch lay on its side, empty. They were the progeny of a Daddy Warbucks, and tonight, Daddy's credit card was paying for a very expensive binge. Time to cut them off.

She grasped the thick velvet curtain to balance herself, lifted her other foot, and brought the heel of her shoe down on his marauding hand.

"You fucking bitch!" plus other expletives, ripped from his mouth.

She twisted her ankle to dig the end into skin, sinews, and bones. His contorted face was worth losing a crystal embellishment from the heel. Maybe her move would leave a scar, a reminder not to stick Daddy's money where it didn't belong. She was a dancer, not a sex doll.

A loud crash of chairs being overturned cut through the thumping backbeat and horns of the music. Bodyguards broke through the darkness of the main floor. So, the cavalry had finally arrived. As the kid was yanked off stage, his fingers dragged down her fishnets, shredding the entire side. She stumbled a little on her heels. Act over.

Man, tonight was one for the books. First, Luna's move, and now this?

She recoiled as another hand grasped her around the elbow. Nathan had shot through stage right, his huge frame towering over her. He pivoted her so his body shielded her from the growing mayhem a few feet away.

"You okay?" Fire blazed in his eyes, and his large hand squeezed her elbow.

"Cage the animals, and I'll be great."

"Max is on it." He scooped up the fan, thankfully by the staves and not the feathers, and steered her off the stage, just as a slew of indignant shouts and protests spewed from the three kids. In her periphery, she caught Max landing a blow on McGrabby's jaw. A sliver of sympathy arose for the boy, given he was half the bodyguard's size, but Shakedown's warnings were clear. *Grab the ladies? You get grabbed.*

"Oh, my, my, my," Cherry's voice boomed. "All this maleness, this testosterone—" she fanned her ample bosom "—has gotten me all aflutter." The crowd whistled and cheered. God bless emcee Cherry who loved nothing better than an opportunity to take over a crowd. The queen raised her voice even louder, "You know the only thing better than a man? *Lots* of men ... Oh, like you ... " Her words faded as Starr made her way down the stage steps behind the curtain.

Starr pulled her arm free of Nathan's clasp when they reached the hallway.

He handed her fan over. His eyes continued to throw sparks and a muscle twitched in his neck as if trying to swallow down his obvious anger. "That kid. When he reached for you—"

"Thanks. I'm fine, really. It happens." Though it usually didn't at Shakedown. Most of the burlesque club's clientele sat back and watched from a respectable distance. They were content with letting their imagination run wild but keeping their urges where they belonged—firmly tucked inside their minds. But these kids? Lying belly down on the stage like a flailing fish, offering a sweaty fistful of dollar bills? Save that gauche behavior for the strip clubs in West Virginia.

A quick inspection of her fan revealed the bamboo staves weren't cracked—thank all the burlesque gods and goddesses. Spending her weekend rewiring one of her fans was not on her Sunday docket. "Tell Max not to kill that kid, okay?"

"Not sure Max is open to negotiation there, and I agree." Nathan grasped her elbow again, and she flinched.

"I'm fine," she snapped.

He lifted his hands in surrender. "Not trying anything here."

"Sorry. I know. Reflexes from … " She stopped herself from going into her whole childhood abuse story. It wasn't the time or place.

He swung open the dressing room door for her.

Phee stepped in behind them and threw down her fans. "What was that?"

"Some frat boy was hallucinating. He thought the price of admission included me. He was drunk."

"Been cut off." Nathan filled the doorframe.

"A little late for that," Phee snarled and grabbed her water bottle.

Luna slipped by him and into the dressing room. "Cherry's covering. But, now what?" She plopped down in her makeup chair.

Starr rested her leg on her stool and studied her stockings. Yep, completely ruined. "Damn, I'm going to have to wear regular stockings for the closer."

"Won't happen again. We'll see to it." Nathan still hovered in the doorway, his right hand curling and uncurling as if he was shaking out a fist. "Need anything? Like from the bar? Luna, more water?"

"I'm Phoenix. That's Luna." Phoenix pointed at their sister. "And you can bring me a taser. Anyone who grabs me is going to get lit up."

Nathan smirked and nodded as if he agreed but stepped back and pulled the door close. Smart man. When her sister got rolling, nothing stopped her, and of the three of them, Phoenix hated the fact no one could tell them apart.

"Phee." Starr sighed. "He was just trying to help." He hadn't deserved her earlier snapping, either.

"You mean he was trying to impress." Luna raised her eyebrows up and down. "You should ask him for a drink later. Ya know, to thank him."

Phoenix blew out a breath. "She can't date Nathan. He killed a man."

"That would be half the men in this place," Luna stated.

Didn't Starr know it? Perhaps their childhood wasn't so far behind them after all.

2

Nathan had seen all kinds of stupid in life, but the baby-faced frat boy swaying on his feet defined a whole new level of moron. The brat spat blood at Declan's feet, barely missing the owner of Shakedown's swanky shoes.

"Fuck, man. Your monkey here started it." The kid lifted his chin toward Max, who sauntered up to them wearing a smug smile. The bodyguard had finally gotten to throw someone out on their ass, something Nathan hadn't seen much of at Shakedown. He, himself, would have loved to have tossed that kid who'd grabbed Starr into the river, watch him sink like a stone.

"Max ends fights. Doesn't start them." Declan's face, as usual, held loaded, restrained intensity.

Nathan parked himself just under the awning over the entranceway. "You need me to call the cops?" He'd like nothing more than to land the kid in jail for getting within a foot of Starr. He wouldn't last the night, which would be fine by him.

"No, we've got this."

"You mean you've got yourself a lawsuit." The kid cradled his jaw like he couldn't believe he got clocked while his other hand, mauled from Starr's heel, hung loosely by his side. Blood leaked through a linen napkin with Shakedown's logo scrolled on it. His two friends, who'd followed them outside to the parking lot, straightened, chests out, shoulders back, chins held high. Their ridiculous posturing made Nathan laugh. Had he acted with such bravado at that age? Yeah, he had.

The young guy sniffed. "This amusing to you, bar monkey? I'll sue you, too."

Whatever. Sure, he'd shoved the kid good, but when that idiot started half-crawling his scrawny body up toward Starr, well, his automatic pilot kicked on. Finally, he'd done something real other than stack liquor boxes and check I.D.'s, the only job he could get post-prison. He'd like nothing more than to show this kid what he'd learned *there.*

Declan held up the young man's driver's license to the streetlamp's light. "We have a strict policy here, Richard Blake Carter. That your real name? This I.D. legal?"

"Fuck, yeah, that's my name. My father, Edward Carter, *Esquire,* is going to love learning who you are. He knows people who can make your life and that of everyone you know, hell."

So outside prison walls wasn't much different from the inside. Things were supposed to be better out here, not filled with stand-offs with strutting peacocks.

"Did you see our sign?" Declan handed the I.D. back. "Hear the emcee point it out at the beginning of the show?"

Max's grin widened. "Touching any of our performers will result in the offender's permanent removal. Removal in one piece not guaranteed."

"Amen, brother," Nathan muttered under his breath.

"So what? I didn't hurt her." The kid swayed a little on his feet, his words running together. "Jesus, they shake their tits at us. They have to be used to it."

Nathan jerked straight, and Declan slapped his hand over Max's chest to prevent him from advancing, which probably saved the kid's life. He would have joined Max in showing the idiots how serious they were – that is, if they'd been alone and not being filmed.

Nathan's gaze flicked to the little circular hole where the awning hid the camera. Now the kid's stupidity was on video. Richard-the-simpleton's confirmation that he'd understood the club's restrictions would make Declan's job easier. CCTV cameras covered every hallway and parking lot space for exactly this reason.

Declan let out an exasperated sigh. "You assault our dancers and—"

"And what?"

One of his friends raised his iPhone, probably live-streaming this showdown. Man, life had changed in the nine years he'd been put away. Everyone's business was now available for the world to watch. It was like everyone had become mad voyeurs—everyone's business played out for the viewing pleasure of others.

Declan's jaw firmed. "You're banned. For life."

"Like I'd want to come back to this dump." He tucked his I.D. into his back pocket.

"Then, we've both won. Good night, gentlemen."

The kid holding the cell phone smirked and pocketed his expensive phone.

By the way Max clenched his fists by his sides, Nathan wasn't sure he should leave the man alone with the college brats, but the place was busy as shit tonight, and Jackie must have been calling him all kinds of new names for neglecting to haul dirty dishes back to the kitchen. He'd rather have followed those kids to whatever sports car daddy lent them, kicked their scrawny asses despite being filmed—a slight problem when a guy was on parole.

"Thanks for getting the ladies off stage safely, Nathan." Declan leaned against his cane. "You showed good restraint, not decking that kid."

"He wouldn't have been worth it." But, fuck, he'd have enjoyed every second it.

Declan gave him a half-smile. "They never are."

Clocking that kid would have felt good but his hard-ass parole officer barely tolerated him working at Shakedown. Something about the dangers of being around alcohol, women, and ex-cons like himself—as if he was a fucking twelve-year-old and not a 29 year-old man trying hard as hell to pay rent *and* not get hauled back to prison. But what'd she expect him to do? Live like a monk?

Still, he'd promised her and Declan, total, 24-7, sobriety, as a condition for his employment at the club. That last part wasn't so hard—kept him awake, aware of the hustle all around him just in case anyone got any bright ideas, like the delinquents now sauntering away as if the world belonged to them.

The frat boys threw themselves into a '65 Ford convertible. Probably didn't even realize the beauty of that iconic machine—the power and history they cruised around in thanks to Daddy's money. Some people just didn't get their own good fortune.

Max rejoined them. "Got to talk to you, Declan." His eyes darted to Nathan, and then back to Declan.

Nathan could get a clue. "See you both inside."

"Take Jackie some more Scotch, will you?" Declan asked.

Nathan nodded. He stepped inside, and the punch of cedar and orange scents from the ventilation system hit him in the face, so different from the stale beer and smoke of most bars, but then a lot had changed over the nine years he'd been behind bars. Nathan swiped the black curtain back at the other end of the vestibule. Loud trumpet music, catcalling, and bright stage lights barreled over him as he hustled down the hall to the storeroom at the back of the club.

By the time he returned, the O'Malley triplets were back on stage, throwing around those giant fans composed of feathers. Nathan ducked under the waitress stand and set the box down with a thud, bottles clanking against one another. He shouted to Jackie over the music. "Got you more Scotch. Need anything else?"

"Nah." Jackie vigorously shook a martini shaker. She jerked her chin toward the stage. "Girls are on fire tonight. Final act."

He leaned against the bar, focused on the stage. Flashes of light from all those crystals and bead things on the dancers' costumes practically dared the audience not to watch them—three identical knockouts. He'd finally reached the point where he could tell Starr from the haughtier Phoenix and shy Luna.

Midnight Starr was a perfect name for the woman who turned his tongue to knots the few times he'd run into her. All the burlesque dancers at Shakedown were good—some pretty, some exotic, some just so flamboyant you couldn't look away, but Starr was in a constellation by herself. Something about her energy just lit up the world around him. She should be modeling in New York, not having obnoxious kids treating her like a stripper.

He stretched his neck—damn stiffness crept up on him if he stayed still for too long—and scanned the room in case anyone else got the bright idea to breach the stage. No matter how civilized most of the crowd usually proved to be, Saturdays were a human zoo.

Starr threw herself into the shimmy move he loved and

cast her wide smile over the crowd. The horn beats grew louder until the crescendo, and the three girls struck an ending pose—each different, each as still and perfect as a Greek statue. Then Starr looked straight in his direction. She raised her fingers to her lips and blew a kiss to him—or to someone in his direction. She couldn't have intended that gesture for him. Wall Street suits and senators swept women like Starr off their feet, not grunts like him. Still, he had to swallow his heart back down into his chest.

"I knew you were into her." Jackie sidled up to him, her lips inching up.

"Not into anyone."

Cherry Noir strutted on stage to begin her nightly thank you to the audience who didn't look like they were interested in leaving anytime soon.

"By the way, some guy just asked for you. Expensive suit. Big tipper."

"Name?"

"Do I look like Western Union? He's over there." She jerked her head toward the back handicapped ramp that overlooked the main floor. A guy leaned between two oil paintings Declan had commissioned of Shakedown's dancers. Shadows hid his figure, but his silhouette was familiar. Just as Nathan's brain cells scrambled together a memory, the man stepped forward into the light. Tall, stocky, a head full of black hair, the man curled his large hands over the brass railing. Nathan stopped breathing until his diaphragm kicked into overdrive to force a sharp intake of air. *Fuck, no.*

The guy—his flesh and blood so familiar that every molecule in Nathan's body did a double-take—clasped the brass rail as if trying to crush it. Daniel MacKenna? No, he couldn't be. Daniel was six feet under. He should know. He put him there.

The guy shifted and locked eyes on him. He pushed off

and strode down the ramp toward him. Nathan's neck turned to stone, and his heartbeat took on its own rhythm. Those eyes: small, slanted, icy blue, *familiar*, bore down on him.

"Ruark MacKenna." Nathan steadied his voice as the spitting image of Ruark's very dead brother widened his stance in front of him. "What the fuck are you doing here?"

The man's eyes narrowed. "What do you think?"

"I did my time." And Daniel, along with this fucker, could roast in hell.

"Not good enough."

Not enough for him? "Your family rigged a jury and got me sent to prison for nine years." Not to mention what happened *inside* prison. Fuck him. "I owe you nothing." His fingers curled into themselves, and he clamped down every cell in his body that screamed to be let loose and wail on the son of a bitch now smirking down at him.

The last time he'd been this close to Ruark MacKenna was in a courtroom. He and half a dozen other MacKennas, had sat behind Nathan in the gallery, staring daggers into his back as he stood waiting for the judge to end life as he knew it. One minute he was a college student. The next he shared a prison cell with a man doing time for killing his whole family. That wasn't the worst of it. The MacKennas paid off his fellow inmates to regularly beat the shit out of him. His right shoulder, once dislocated, gave off a sharp pang of remembrance.

"You killed one of us. You think nine years was enough?" Ruark chuffed. "My *brother*—"

"Deserved it." And, more. "You left out the part where he was beating the shit out of Declan."

Ruark stepped so close the man's cheap aftershave assaulted his nose. One more millimeter and their chests would bump. Nathan straightened and stood his ground, though his skin crawled at the thought of touching any part of the man. Punching the smugness off Ruark's face would work, though. Nathan's heart thrashed and his fists tightened. His body was *all in* on that plan but he refused it. *Stand down*, he commanded.

The stage lights went black, and the house lights brightened, a not-so-subtle signal to the crowd that the club was closing. Their private conversation was about to become very public and brightly illuminated.

MacKenna's eyes slanted toward the dozens of people rising from their seats, and then faced Nathan. "This isn't over. Not by a long shot." The man turned and strutted away.

Nathan's heart continued to hammer against his ribs, and he began to move, even as his eyesight faltered, pricks of light getting in his way. *Fuck, not now.* He should go outside, help Max with crowd control. Instead, his hand swatted at black velvet curtain separating the public area from the back. The hallway was as still as a grave compared to the mayhem on the floor, and every movement he made, every boot stomp across the concrete, echoed too loudly. He slammed his body against the cinderblock wall and laid his palms against the gritty surface.

He wanted to smash something—or someone. He slapped his pec and told his heart to stand the ever-loving fuck down for just one goddamn second.

Women's laughter echoed further down the hallway. The dancers were getting off the stage, and he needed to move. He couldn't let Starr or any of the other dancers see him like this—coming unglued and ready to thrash the first person who looked sideways at him. Never again would he dissolve into the violence that rose up too fast, too hard, under his skin—a state he'd honed out of necessity in prison.

By now, Declan had to know who he'd seen. Little happened in his club that Declan didn't notice. The presence of a MacKenna would not have escaped him. Entering the man's office, Nathan didn't bother to knock. The general manager, Trick, was bent over Declan's desk, pointing at papers.

"I've got something to tell you. Now." For once, words rushed to him.

Declan's dark eyes moved from the paper he held in his hand to him. "Like Ruark MacKenna being here tonight?"

Nathan's head swung to Trick and back to Declan, whose stony face told him everything he needed to know. The man fucking *knew* a MacKenna was back to screw him over again. Even after nine years, the MacKennas had not forgotten that Nathan had killed their favorite son.

3

___

Starr tossed the last costume of the night over her stool. "I hate that thing." The red sequin corset was hell on her inner arms, leaving crimson scratches on her skin.

"It'll heal by Tuesday." Phee stuffed her shoes into her bag.

"You're only saying that because you love to wear red. Speaking of red … More roses? Third time this week." She fingered a silky red rosebud from a huge bouquet on her makeup stand.

Phee shrugged. "Max must have delivered them while we were on."

At least the roses beat the usual gifts, like chocolates, cheap bracelets from those accessory stores found in every mall around America, and grocery store bouquets of daisies and lilies peppered with baby's breath, most of which were down payments on something their giver hoped would happen. Like she'd crawl into some guy's lap because he deigned to spend twenty bucks? Think again.

"Where's Luna?" Starr plucked the little card off the pitchfork stand nestled inside the flowers.

"Retrieving paychecks. She's good at asking Declan for money."

"Phee—"

"I'm not doing it, you know."

She didn't need to ask what "it" was. "For the record, I don't want to see dear old Dad either, but you know L." Or at least she thought she did. "Once an idea gets in her head … "

"Well, she can forget this one."

Phee eyed the night's worth of costumes Starr had draped over one another on her makeup mirror and raised an eyebrow.

Starr huffed. "I know. I know." Phee's little neat freak self could chill. "I'll come in an hour early next week to clean up." For now, she just wanted bed, a big glass of wine, and to avoid the Big Talk they really should have about Luna's recent actions.

She slit open the little envelope and pulled out the note. "*And where two raging fires meet together, they do consume the thing that feeds their fury.* Huh."

"Romeo and Juliet."

Starr stared at Phee.

"What? Declan's got a lot of those books in his office. You know I read." Phee returned to stuffing bras and stockings into her bag as if she hadn't just referenced Shakespeare.

"I had no idea you liked Shakespeare. Well, whoever's sending these is a romantic, I guess. And rich. Hedge and Rose again." Baltimore's most hoity-toity florist shop was getting quite a workout from this secret admirer.

Bringing a bud to her nose, Starr inhaled the sweet scent. "Mmm, fresh." She did love flowers, their silky petals and soft scents reminding her of warm outside air, a rarity in her world these days. For one brief second, she imagined who might be sending them. Someone warm and wonderful and protective … Max maybe? Or perhaps Nathan, though she couldn't see him saying the word "roses" let alone sending them. Maybe her secret admirer would be like a movie romance—tough guy watches girl from afar, whisks her away from marauding frat kids, but is afraid to ask her out, and then one day, only for her ...

Luna flounced through the door, waving three envelopes in her hand. "Got them. By the way, Declan feels really bad about what happened, Starr. Oh, more flowers." She tossed the envelopes on Starr's makeup stand and leaned down to inhale a rose. "Your secret admirer again?"

"I wish I knew who was sending them. It's all too Phantom of the Opera-ish for me. Just say who you are."

Phoenix fluffed her hair in the mirror. "Some people are into secrets. Especially ones that involve going behind your sisters' backs." She glanced up at Luna with eyes that could have melted the paint off the walls.

"You'll forgive me someday." Luna drew a rose from the bouquet.

"You should be glad Maryland doesn't have a familial obligation law anymore because I'm not getting saddled with debt for whatever that P.I. finds." She waggled her cell phone at her. "Yeah, I looked it up as soon as the word 'dad' left your mouth."

"Money. That's all you can think about?"

"No, actually. Involving Declan? Bad move. The minute a man gives you money, they think they own you, and that, my dear sister, is something I won't tolerate. We don't owe Declan, or any other man, a thing. Especially Robert O'Malley, a man who is no father to me."

Starr really had had enough of this—at least for tonight. "Look, we all have good reason to hate the man—"

"I don't hate him. I don't think about him at all."

Luna's shoulders caved a little.

Starr sighed. "It's been a crappy night for everyone. We'll

talk about it tomorrow." She would not let them dissolve into another argument.

Luna's eyes brightened with hope. "So you'll consider going to meet with Stan? He's the investigator. He sounds really nice."

What was up with her sister's new stubborn streak about this father-daughter reconciliation? For the life of her, Starr couldn't understand why it had been so important to find him. The last time she'd seen him, all he'd cared about was the bottle in his hand and whatever cash she'd had in hers. He'd literally asked her for money, the fricking loser. Thank God for Declan. He gave them a chance six years ago to dance in a nice place that paid them well. She wouldn't let anything mess up their situation here.

She'd deal with it tomorrow. She pulled out a long-stem rose from the bunch and turned for the door. "You two go on. I'll Uber home. I need a drink." She'd ask Nathan to join her to thank him. Not many men came to their rescue, at least none that didn't want something in return.

4

———————

Nathan bolted up to Declan's desk and put both hands on the surface. "How long have you known Ruark MacKenna was coming to Shakedown?" He was beyond any small talk, never his strong suit anyway. They'd known each other a damn long time, long enough for Declan to have told him a former nemesis had shown up.

"A few months." Declan tapped his fingers against the edge of his desk.

Nathan just might crawl out of his skin. He rose to his full height and peered down at him. "And you didn't think to mention the older brother of the man I killed was in the club?"

Declan sighed.

Swear to God if Declan started to patronize him ... "How'd they find you? Us?"

"I'm not sure how they found us. Baltimore's a small place." Declan straightened his jacket and rounded the desk. "Thought we were done years ago, that we were off the radar screen, but they discovered I own Shakedown. Three months ago, I got a visit. He wants us back in business together."

"With you."

"Of course I turned him down."

"They deal in import-export. Now they want to go into entertainment?" Then again, the MacKenna family wanted in on anything successful up and down the East Coast, that much he'd learned from the newspapers. Not much to do in prison but read and workout and wait for the next surprise attack.

"If they want revenge, why'd they wait so long? I mean, I've been here for three months." Then again, they hadn't waited, had they? His joints ached at the memories—being dragged into a dark cell and pummeled by fists, being jumped in the men's room, his head rammed against porcelain and tiles. He'd learned to fight back in any way he could, but he'd always been outnumbered. No wonder he walked around with a case of what his counselor had blasély referred to as "the usual PTSD" —humiliating anxiety attacks that left him irrationally enraged and prone to violence.

Declan shrugged. "Ruark doesn't come often. We believe he hasn't seen you until tonight. Now ... "

"They want to take over Shakedown to punish you for giving me a job."

"Likely." Silence numbed his mind. It was a good trick, one he'd used in prison. He shook it off. He needed his brain working, hell, his feet working. He spun on his heel and ran smack into Trick, who laid his palm flat across Nathan's pec.

"We're not sure what is going on yet."

Trick would say that. He didn't know the MacKenna family. He didn't know Nathan had swung a crowbar at Daniel MacKenna so hard, he'd splattered the man's brains on the adjacent wall. Daniel threw punches like a professional MMA fighter—quick, hard, and lethal. That night, Daniel MacKenna had been intent on killing Declan. Had he not intervened, MacKenna would have.

It had gone down in Declan's old office in a run-down warehouse—a prosperous antiques business Declan had lost, thanks to those fucking MacKennas. At trial, his attorney had argued Nathan had defended Declan from mortal peril—that nothing short of lethal force would have stopped MacKenna. A jury—surely a paid-off jury—thought otherwise.

Nathan lowered his gaze to Trick's hand. The man wisely removed it. Good thing, as his manager could find himself without a few fingers, if not careful.

"We'll take care of it," Trick said.

Nathan chuffed. "Sure." He turned to Declan, who remained irritatingly calm, though a twitch in his jaw showed the frustration he hid. "You remember what they said? In the courtroom? Don't fuck with family."

"Nathan. I owe you. Let me handle this."

"You can't, Declan. One doesn't *handle* the MacKennas. I've gotta get out of here." Nathan spun, every fiber of his body needed out.

Never again would he be taken by surprise like he had been so many times behind bars. Nine years of regular beatings turned a man into something no one wanted—all rough edges and no impulse control to curb the savage energy that lived inside him. Prison had earned him nothing but a graduate degree in unfettered violence.

"You can't take on the MacKennas, either. Besides, where are you going to go?" Declan's voice had risen. "At least here, you've got friends."

His statement was a sucker punch to the gut. He had nowhere to go. He'd left prison with $20 bucks in his pocket and a pair of jeans and a shirt that no longer fit him. He had more now—thanks to Declan—but not enough to leave town.

He paused at the door and curled his hand around the

doorknob, wanting to crush it in his fist. "You're buying a lot of trouble."

"Like I said. I owe you."

"Consider the debt paid." He headed to the office he shared with Max, a ridiculous perk to begin with because what does the muscle need an office for? He'd think about his next step.

He yanked open the door. Starr leaned against the far wall, her nose buried in a rose. She cocked her head and lowered the flower. "Jackie said you were with Declan. Drink? I owe you one. For rescuing me earlier."

A drink? Nothing sounded better. Screw the moratorium on alcohol. If any night called for liquor, it was tonight.

5

Starr plunked her bag down and slid onto a stool at the bar. An image of her perfect ass surfaced so clearly in his brain he had to seal his lips in case his mouth proved as undisciplined as his imagination. Even having a MacKenna show up couldn't erase the effect she had on him. In fact, air moved better in his lungs, and his ribs unlocked a little, just by seeing her.

She placed the rose on the bar. "What's good for forgetting things?"

"Tequila." Tequila sounded real good right about now, but he wouldn't, despite his earlier momentary lapse in judgment. Alcohol wouldn't change his situation. He ducked under the waitress stand. While he poured himself a glass of water, he would play bartender.

"Somehow I knew you'd say that." She leaned her forearms on the bar and peered up at him. Her Rolling Stones t-shirt stretched tight across her breasts. It had seen better days. The material was thin enough to let him know the color of her bra. He'd give his life to be her t-shirt.

He pulled down the Don Julio 1942 while she pulled out her phone.

"Damn." She set it on the bar, face down. "Dead."

"Want me to charge her for you?"

"Oh, would you? Thanks."

He stuck the charger cord into her phone—a perk Declan had installed at the bar for patrons—then poured her a shot of the tequila.

"Your feathers okay?" He pushed the glass her way.

"My fans are fine. Hey, did you like the show?" She winked at him, a slow lowering of those long, thick lashes until they touched her porcelain cheek. Heat smeared every inch of his skin, and *thinking* wasn't possible.

"Perfect." A vision of her body twirling, the long strands of silvery fringe and sparkling beads shooting straight out and wrapping her perfect hips flashed in his brainpan. *Goddamn, to be a fucking piece of string.* Then, that slow air kiss —maybe offered to him? He hardened. His body really hadn't gotten the memo on respectful thoughts but then no one showed him respect in years.

She raised her shot toward him in a toast. Her smile was amazing. "To tonight being over."

He clinked the shot glass with his ice water. She shot her tequila back like a champ, and still looked like a cover model while doing it.

She pushed the empty shot glass toward him. "Can I have another?"

"Your wish is my command."

She laughed at his use of the cliché. "So, how do you like your new gig here?"

"It's good," he managed to spit out despite tonight's cluster. He filled her glass to the brim.

"Glad to hear it." She sipped the tequila this time and grinned at him anew. Yeah, he could fall into her smile if he let himself. "I hear you and Declan have known each other a long time."

"Yeah, worked for him when I was in school."

"College?" Her eyes brightened. "What'd you study?"

"Mechanical engineering." He hadn't thought about that in years.

"I almost went to college. To study arts management, but, well, you know how life changes … "

Did he ever. "Never got to finish, but here I am. Working for Declan again."

They were exchanging the most words since he'd started at Shakedown three months ago. Overall, the most words he'd spoken in days. Their conversation was casual, like normal people talk. Maybe all women were like this now? Hell, no. He'd met her sister Phoenix. She could freeze a man's nuts off with her eyes. Starr was different, easy and nice, but not all giggly like so many of the women at the club.

"I'm glad you're here. Declan's one of the good ones." She twisted the shot glass in her fingers. "He's a good boss, too. I trust those kids from tonight will never get in again."

"You got that right."

"I can't believe men think they can grab women like that." Her smile faded.

She shouldn't have to put up with that crap. "All men are idiots."

Sure, his own body lit up like a firecracker around her, but any man who flopped belly-first like a fish on stage to grab a woman was worse than an idiot. He'd seen how hard these girls worked, night after night, smiling down at customers like they were the most special people on the planet.

"Not all." Her lips arched up. In response, his heart did its skipping thing again, only this time for a better cause.

"Thanks for escorting me off the stage. That was real gentle-manly, and sorry for snapping at you."

He leaned his elbows on the bar top. "No problem, but, hey, sorry if I scared you … in the hallway when you got off stage." Of all people to throw his anger at, it shouldn't be her.

"Oh, you didn't. I just have these reflexes. My sisters and I had a bad father. He was the usual drunken abuser."

He straightened, and a trickle of heat ran down his spine. "Nothing usual about that."

"Yeah, well, I don't handle anger well, especially men with short fuses, and for a second there … " She trailed off.

"I reminded you of your dad?" Shit. He scrubbed his bicep and peered down at her. Had he gone off the rails that badly in front of her?

"No, not like that." Her blue eyes warmed toward him. "You just looked like you were going to lose it for a second."

"Let's just say I don't take well to men who put their hands on defenseless people. I get angry—fast." Something about this woman made him want to be honest. Perhaps it was the way her face was so open or the way her eyes fixed on him without hesitation. She deserved the same openness from him.

"Where does that come from?" she asked lightly.

"Prison. Got jumped, repeatedly. Beaten pretty badly. Makes a guy angry inside. But I control it, and I sure as hell would never lift a hand to any woman or child. I don't have it in me." It felt important to tell her that.

"Oh." She stared at him for a long time, and he couldn't find it in him to break her gaze. He could see the question in her eyes—what was he in for? He didn't want to have this conversation right now.

She suddenly raised the shot glass toward him. "Well. Here's to us. For overcoming."

"I can get behind that sentiment." He lifted his water, now

dripping with condensation, and slugged down a couple of swallows.

She gulped the last bit of tequila, slammed the shot glass upside down, and dabbed those pink lips with a cocktail napkin. Yeah, so now those lips were all his fricking mind could think of—so ungentlemanly. He couldn't have been more in fucking awe of her.

She cocked her head and assessed him. "You got family nearby?"

He sucked in air. Just like that, the conversation wasn't so normal.

"Sorry," she said quickly. "I tend to ask a lot of questions. I don't like mystery. My father said it would be the death of me someday." A sliver of sadness crossed her eyes. This woman should have had a father-of-the-year raising her, not a lush who'd abused her. Of course, it would have been nice if his own family had bothered to support him, instead of acting like he didn't exist.

He scratched at his beard. "That's okay. It's just hard sometimes to know what to say about family."

She murmured. "Tell me about it. Try being part of triplets. Sometimes I think my own head isn't my own."

"Finishing each other's sentences?"

"Even finishing each other's thoughts." She spun the glass under her fingers. "How about a girlfriend? Have one of those?" She cocked her head and sucked her bottom lip between her teeth.

Jesus, she was adorable *and* hot, and his heart hammered in his chest more than it should have for such an innocent question. He slowly shook his head, amazed she cared.

"Well, that's a shame. You'd make a good boyfriend. I mean, jumping on stage to rescue a girl."

She held his gaze for long seconds, long enough for him to memorize the darker ring of blue around her eyes. It reminded him of the water off Turks and Caicos during one of his college spring breaks. A splash of freckles decorated the bridge of her nose.

"Life's … complicated right now."

She sighed and leaned her chin against her hand. "Is it ever too complicated for love?"

Did she seriously want an answer because he had *nada*. Before he could cobble together some potential answer, she eased off the stool.

"Ya know what? This tequila is starting to do its job. I need my bed."

Wow, she changed subjects at lightning speed—so fast, he'd let his moment pass. Maybe if he'd asked her out, she'd have considered it. It didn't matter. His life was shit right now, and he would not let her get contaminated by it.

When he saw her reach for her wallet, he waved her off. "I got this." He unplugged her phone and handed it to her. "Only thirty percent, but it should get you home all right. I'll walk you to your car." No way was this woman going into a parking lot by herself at this hour.

She scrolled quickly through her phone and tapped the screen. "Uber will be here in two minutes."

"I can give you a lift."

"That's okay. Maybe next time?" She shrugged one shoulder.

"Still walking you to the parking lot."

"Thanks, Nathan. You really are a gentleman."

They didn't talk, but she hooked her arm through his as they crossed the short distance across the empty club floor, the vacuum cleaners humming over carpeting in the main hall the only other sound. Her impossibly soft hand against his skin was the best thing he'd touched in years. He inhaled her scent—spicy cinnamon laced with something familiar and earthy. Rosemary.

Once through the front door, a shiny gray SUV had already pulled up. He was disappointed at the driver's timeliness because he finally had an answer to her earlier question about love.

He opened the door for her. After she climbed in, she winked at him again. "Have a great night."

"You, too, Starr. And, no, it's never too complicated for that" —for some reason, the word "love" wouldn't come out of his mouth— "but maybe life can be too complicated to act on it."

She rolled her pink lips between her teeth, then released them in a soft smack, like she got where he was coming from. "Yeah." She pulled the door closed.

He knocked on the roof, and the car pulled away.

Man, what a missed opportunity, but his world was already too convoluted. Still, she was the kind of woman who gave a man something to aim for, like a life that was clean and violence-free.

His phone buzzed. The stupid thing was always yelling reminders at him. Erin Johanson's name flashed for a brief second. *Yeah, yeah.* He had another humiliating phone check-in with her on Thursday. Bitter resentment rode up his neck at how, now under parole, he had so little privacy. He already knew what Erin would say if he let her into his head, if he let her hear those thoughts he had about a certain redheaded burlesque dancer. *Getting involved with anyone new right now will be a challenge.* As if he didn't know that already. None of her business anyway, though, according to the great state of Maryland, if he took a crap, it was her business. He'd give anything to have a normal life where if he asked out a woman, it wasn't the business of Erin Johanson.

6

———

Stan, the P.I., turned out to be a regular guy in a regular office, behind a regular desk. Starr's well-honed radar told her he wasn't a creeper. Pictures of a woman and two little girls lined the credenza behind him. At least Luna had chosen wisely when she went behind their backs.

Of course, she couldn't believe she was here at all. Luna had begged her to come, and she'd capitulated on two conditions—it would be the end of her quest, and no telling Phee.

Stan laid his finger on a manila folder. "Seems he's in court-mandated rehab in Rockville, not too far from here. His name came up pretty easily, and that photo helped."

She glared at Luna, who flushed a little.

"He had to have a picture."

"Why did *you* have one? Didn't we burn all that?" She leaned forward, a trickle of sweat running between her breasts. The office was as hot as Hades, and the oscillating fan didn't unstick the tiny hairs on her neck one bit. "He's got debt, doesn't he? Loans?"

Luna sat back in her chair, the metal creaking a little. "How would you know?"

She shrugged. "A feeling." The last time she'd seen Robert O'Malley, he'd had a room in a foul hotel near the airport. He sat in a dirty, upholstered chair by the window, and slats of sunshine had cut through the broken blinds over his potbelly. He'd begged her for money because 'people' were after him. It didn't take an I.Q. of 200 to know what kind of people. So, she'd broken their sister deal, too, that one time, nine years ago, but it had been justified.

Stan tapped his middle fingertip on the folder. "He's got a record. Small-time stuff like bar brawls. Nothing serious, but it seems he finally wants to turn his life around. Of course … " He leaned back in his chair.

"There's more, isn't there?" She wished he'd just spit it out. "Just tell us."

"According to court records, this is his third attempt at rehab."

"Who paid for the first two?"

"His wife."

She and Luna looked at each other. Their mother had died when they were nine years old, so he'd moved on—without them. *More* betrayal. *More* pain. *More* anger. She wasn't sure what to feel first.

She turned back to Stan.

"This woman." He opened up the folder and showed a picture of a woman with flaming red hair holding up a police lineup photo template. The number across it was blurred. She scowled into the camera. A tattoo of green, red, and blue swirls crawled up her neck.

After they finished passing it between them, Starr tossed it on his desk. "His thirst for redheads hasn't waned." The roiling in her belly grew.

This was such a bad idea, but once Luna dug in her stiletto heels, nothing got in her way. Luna had suggested it might settle the question of "what happened," but instead, the P.I.'s results had only raised a hundred more.

Stan slipped the photo back into the file. "You ladies seem nice. You sure you want to know all of this because it doesn't sound like his life is one that" —his eyes skimmed over both of them— "fits you."

He held the file out to them. They stared at the thing, neither of them reaching for it. Finally, Starr grasped the edge and placed it in her lap.

He sighed. "Take it home. Go over it. But know, once debt collectors learn of relatives, well—"

"That's illegal." Luna's gaze fixed on the folder in Starr's lap.

"It's not illegal to start calling you, harassing you. And, these debts, well, they aren't exactly on the up and up."

"Loan sharks. Great."

"And those are the nice guys. You'll want to tread carefully. If you need some bodyguard assistance, I can arrange for it."

She shot to standing. "I'll kill him myself before I need that."

For long minutes, they stood in the hot parking lot, the folder spread out on the hood of their car. It didn't take long to go through it. Stan had been right. It'd been penny-ante crap, and his wife? She'd divorced Robert O'Malley last year and was currently in jail. So, now he was serving court-ordered alcohol rehabilitation? For the third time. And was loaded with debt? They needed to walk away.

"He's at a place called Sunset Home." Luna held up her phone. "I found it. It's not too far. A few hours drive."

"I don't care if it's next door." Starr shoved papers back into the folder and tromped to a garbage bin.

"Don't you dare!" Luna never shouted, but there it was. A couple across the parking lot stopped and stared at them.

She turned. "Why did *you* dare?" Luna couldn't be this naive and cruel, could she?

For once, their past, a life full of uncertainty and foster homes, had finally grown distant and dusty as if locked away somewhere. But then Luna had sprung open the box of betrayals by finding their father.

She marched back to her sister.

"How could *you*? How did you think it was going to go? Find him and go running into his arms? Start having family dinners every Sunday? Walks in the park?" Her chin quivered, and a shot of fear she might actually cry over this man bolted through her. She didn't break. None of them could afford to break.

Luna grasped the folder. "I'll take it. You don't need to see it again." Her face colored, and a sheen of wet formed in her eyes. "I'll go and see him by myself. You don't have to come."

"You need to stop this, and don't you dare cry, L."

"I won't." A tear escaped down her cheek.

For the life of her, Starr could not understand why Luna wanted this reunion. "Why? Just tell me why?"

"Because I don't want to be like him. I'm going to be better. And I want answers. Why did he leave us? Why was he so horrible? I want to know—" she glanced at the folder in her hands— "so I know how to help Phee."

Starr blinked. *Oh.* She bit her lip, hard, so she wouldn't say something stupid, like Luna could be right.

"Sisters forever, friends always," Luna whispered.

Damnit, to raise the mantra they'd crafted to recenter themselves when things turned ugly was a low blow. It was true, however, Luna *was* better, while Phee was still crippled inside. They had all been crippled in different ways, but Phee had suffered the most traumas. She'd borne the worst of their father's rages, ending up in the hospital. Then, at fourteen, when the system had kept the sisters split up, Phee'd been brutalized in one of her foster homes. She'd changed, had grown understandably cold, angry, distant, but she'd been allowed to stuff everything down for far too long. They'd enabled her to sweep everything under an iron rug.

Starr sucked in a long breath. Shit. Now she was going to have to give this idea a go because *sisters forever, friends always,* wasn't just a saying. "Phee will come around. We just can't push it too hard. In fact, it's downright cruel to make her face him again."

Luna's chin quivered. "The last thing I'm ever going to do is hurt Phee or you." She drew in a long breath.

This was the moment, wasn't it? Where Starr finally confessed her own secret. "I need to fill you in on something. When we were seventeen, I found him."

Luna blinked. "What?"

"Yeah. And it wasn't good. He was holed up in an airport hotel, drunk, broke—needing money."

"Tell me you didn't."

"I did. Three thousand dollars."

Luna gasped, her mouth formed an "O," but she quickly snapped it shut. "He needs to pay you back."

Starr snorted. "Yeah, right. The man is a deadbeat."

"Who owes us in every way. So, let's go and collect." She crossed her arms.

Starr arched her eyebrow.

"At the least, Phee is owed an apology, if nothing else." Luna lifted her arms and dropped them dramatically to her sides.

"Words would never—"

"I know, but she deserves to hear them anyway."

"She deserves for him to grovel on his hands and knees."

Luna squared herself to Starr, her face expectant and hopeful. "I agree. So you'll do it? Help me convince her to at least ask for it? Or even consider it?"

Truth was, could any of them move on by ignoring the fact they'd been abandoned not just once but twice—once by a mother gone too soon and next by a father, absent by choice? Forget the money. Could any of them ever have a healthy relationship if they didn't at least get *some* answers? She found herself saying words she never thought she would ever utter again when it came to their father. "Okay. I'll consider it — but this is for Phee, no one else."

7

Nathan's boots crunched over shattered glass as he rounded the concrete light pole to his car. The parking lot was dark, too dark, even for 2:00 a.m. on a Tuesday night. He peered up at the streetlight that should be shining down on his vehicle. Declan would be pissed that someone had used the overhead lamp for target practice.

A streak of black crossed his peripheral vision, and his back hit the driver's side door. He cursed. It was just a stupid cat that hung around the parking lot every night. He crouched down. One golden eye peered at him from underneath a bush. He straightened, opened his car door, and reached for a scrunched-up McDonald's bag on the floorboard. He found a few cold fries at the bottom.

"You like french fries, cat?" He squatted down and held one out.

The thing eyed him but took a tentative step from under the bush. It sniffed at the fry, then grasped it in its teeth, and backed away.

"Yeah, I guess you do." Heaviness filled his chest at the scrawny feline feasting on scraps, something he understood too well. He dumped the remaining leftovers under the bush. Maybe he'd get a good night's sleep now. He'd done his good deed for the day.

He'd hung around until closing hoping to see Starr again, but she must have slipped out of the back. He had a grand idea to maybe buy her another drink—something innocent, something a friend might do.

"Nathan, got a second?"

He bolted upright and raised his fists. His heart pounded so hard he thought his eardrums might explode.

"Didn't mean to scare you." Declan fingered a lit cigarette.

He dropped his arms to his side.

"Trying to quit, but well … " Declan stabbed it out on a small rock in his palm.

Damn, the man hadn't flinched at him readying himself for a fight. How the hell had he missed Declan being there? Man, he was off his game.

Declan pushed off the hood of his car and closed the few feet between them. His head fell back as he checked out the broken bulb overhead. "Looks like we've got a light out."

"Yeah."

"I'm glad you're here. Staying, I hope?"

"Yeah, well, I figure if you're not worried, and I keep my head down … " *And not beat the crap out of someone.* He still wasn't sure it was the best course of action, but the truth was, he didn't know what else to do about this newfound situation. Ruark MacKenna hadn't shown up tonight, but he was sure the bastard would crawl out from the sewer again. He wasn't about to leave Declan, or anyone for that matter, alone in Ruark's sights.

"There's something else I need to talk to you about." Declan lowered his gaze to stare directly at Nathan. "Not about Ruark, about the … other."

So now they were reverting to code? It wasn't like Declan. "What's up?"

"That kid from Saturday night. The one we threw out?"

"College kid? Vintage convertible?"

"That would be the one. We've been named in a civil suit. Assault charges. All bullshit. Nothing to worry about, but I wanted you to know."

He scrubbed his face. "That was fast."

"Having money means you can cut corners." Declan studied him. "Let your parole officer know. They dislike surprises."

"So, I'm named." He scratched under his chin. Of course, he was.

"I've got it, Nathan. Don't worry about it. Remember, we've got cameras all over this joint. A lawyer's going to take one look at the footage and know what's going on."

"And Starr? She got him good with her heel." So help him, if the justice system decided she didn't have a right to defend herself, he *was* going to punch something.

"Not involved. The kid's lawyers probably knew she had every right to defend herself."

"Good." So there was that, at least.

Declan fingered his cane, punched the ground with it a few times. "The kid's got no grounds. The truth will win out. But, tell Erin."

"Sure." When had the truth had anything to do with the legal system? It was more like which technicalities were violated or not. Or in this case, who had a record and who didn't, and what your parole officer wanted to do or not do. He'd only been meeting with Erin for a few months. He still didn't know if she was on his side or on the side of the checklist that always sat in front of her. He wouldn't be surprised if his welfare ran a distant second to the report she filled out after every meeting.

"See you tomorrow." Declan pushed off his car.

"You don't deserve this legal bullshit coming down." Declan had been convicted of vehicular manslaughter years ago. Then to get out and start a place like this—that hired ex-cons like him—the guy deserved a medal, not more difficulties.

"Yeah, well, we've been through worse." Declan got into his Jag, the thing creaking complaints.

Nathan strode to his car and lowered himself into the driver's side. Gulped in some air. Pushed it out of his lungs. Gripped his steering wheel so hard he could have snapped it in two. More air. More clenching and releasing his fists until the vinyl squeaked with sweat. Somehow, maybe by the grace of a God he barely believed in anymore, he tamped down his adrenaline over the news just delivered. He would not succumb to the PTSD bullshit that arose every time he let his guard down.

Declan's taillights disappeared down the street. The seconds ticked by as Nathan tuned into the distant traffic sounds, the lingering cigarette smoke scent from Declan's cig, and the shadows playing in the bushes swaying in the evening breeze. He didn't know why he hesitated, something just felt ... off.

He reached for the ignition just as he glimpsed a man emerging from behind the line of trees and scraggly bushes that hid a chain-link fence across the street. The man stood in half-shadow, the glow of a cigarette at the end of his hand.

Nathan wrapped both hands around the wheel again and stared right back at the figure. The man, who had to be Ruark, brought the cigarette to his lips and cocked his head. Still in silhouette, but shit, the family resemblance to Daniel MacKenna was right there.

He got out of the car, slammed the door hard, and marched toward Ruark. He was going to get some fucking answers. Instead, he found a pile of cigarette butts on the ground, one of them still smoking, and Ruark had vanished. The bushes and tree limbs swayed a little, and the lingering scent of smoke hung in the air. Ruark wasn't done harassing him or Declan. He rubbed his sternum and told his heart to get a grip.

Any thought of leaving Shakedown vanished. He wasn't going to leave the only people he called family. His boots pounded the pavement as he trudged back to his car. Let the MacKennas come for him. He wouldn't let them near Declan or anyone else at Shakedown.

8

———

Starr had never tripped on stage in her life, at least not until right then. The stupid strap on her favorite Capezios snapped and her shoe went flying into the crowd as she kicked her leg forward. Two guys in the front row fought over it as if Babe Ruth himself had come back from the grave and sent a flyball into the stands. Well, let them have it because her shoe was done. Damnit.

Oh, what the hell.

She perched on the edge of the lyra dangling from the ceiling, tonight decorated to resemble a glowing half-moon, and reached for her other shoe. She raised her leg, fingered the delicate buckle, letting her lashes rise and fall to signal the crowd they should be watching. Good boys—those front-row patrons had their eyes locked on her leg. She reached down, slipped the shoe off, and stood.

Bombs away, big boys.

She stepped back and then threw it as far as she could send it. Her heel sailed over the heads of the patrons and straight behind the bar, knocking into several liquor bottles.

Nothing broke, but the crowd went wild. Sunshine burst inside her at the crowd's roar.

At the end of the bar, Declan dipped his chin, and his eyebrows shot up like a scolding father. *Whatever.*

She shrugged at the front row of men in business suits and blinked. One of them blew her a kiss. How sweet. She granted him a return wink.

Throwing a shoe brought some much-needed fun to the sucky Wednesday, her least favorite night to dance. The mid-week gig brought out the hardcore alcoholics and the cheap bastards who showed up to sling back the half-price drinks. If she'd had another shoe on, she'd have slung it into the crowd as well, just to hear their delighted applause. It would be a pleasant diversion from stewing over the envelope filled with fifteen pages of "how to forgive" advice that arrived from Sunset House this afternoon. L. just could not stop her quest, could she? Screw the enforced reconciliation nonsense —for that's what it was—for the next five minutes anyway.

She pranced around on tiptoes, her toes spreading and stretching deliciously. She stripped off her skirt, leaving on a silver G-string and rhinestone bra. The bra would stay put. The pasties that matched this outfit were crackling a little from overuse, and showing nipple would earn more than a scolding look from Declan.

The music wound down, and Starr kicked her foot up in a parting move, split the thick red curtains, and disappeared into the darkened backstage. Another night down, another thousand dollars the three of them would split.

Starr stopped in her tracks at the bottom of the stairs.

A strange man, all dark hair and piercing blue eyes, pushed off the wall. "Nice throw." He dangled her shoe from his index finger.

"Keep it. Souvenir."

"I'll get you a new pair." With a slight smirk, he fingered the ruined heel.

"Oh, no need."

"Well, the restaurant requires shoes."

"Excuse me?"

"Where you'll have dinner with me."

By the look of this guy—broad shoulders that strained his suit coat, the intense set of his mouth—he was used to ordering people around.

"No, thanks." She smiled politely and tried to walk away, but he grasped her arm. Her breath caught in her chest. His smirk sent a chill down every limb.

"What does it take to get to a yes?"

Boots scraped on the concrete behind her. "You can start by letting go of her."

She welcomed the sound of Nathan's voice. He was next to them in a second. He circled her waist and pulled her nearly behind him. Jesus, the man was a protective beast. She kind of liked it.

"What the fuck are you doing back here?" he growled.

Starr's heart lurched a little at Nathan's tone.

The man shrugged and peered around Nathan. He whispered to Starr, "The muscle around here isn't very polite." He cocked his head and pointed at the camera trained on them from a corner. "Paranoid folks, huh?"

"MacKenna."

The guy's smirk didn't waver in the face of Nathan's scowl or size. Of course, if the guy's suit was an indication, the man packed as much muscle as Nathan, who had quite the biceps now that she clung to one of them.

"Got lost, that's all." His eyes trailed down her body, and she shivered as if she'd been splashed with ice chips. "I'll be at the bar if you change your mind, Miss Midnight." He then bent at the waist in an odd half-bow toward Starr and turned away.

Nathan's gaze followed the man sauntering down the hallway. Any fear she might have mustered up vanished. Who the hell did he think he was? Whoever that guy was, he pissed her off.

"Men." Starr scooted around Nathan, so she found herself in front of him. "Why do they always think their declarations work? *You'll do this. You'll do that.* Whatever happened to asking?"

What would it take for someone nice, like Nathan, to ask her out? The scar, high on his cheek, and the tats on both arms indicated he'd lived a rough life, but he had kind, warm eyes, and didn't push himself on her. The mix of having lived a hard life and yet being gentle gave him a subdued, quiet power. Well, except when his eyebrows bunched and his eyes fired like they did right now.

She gave his arm a squeeze. "Nathan? I'm okay, you know?"

A muscle in his jaw twitched, and the muscle ridges in his arms bulged a little as if he were caging something inside him. Maybe now wasn't the right time for an interrogation.

He finally gazed down at her. Without her heels, she lost a good five inches of height.

"That man—Ruark MacKenna—he's no good." He clenched and unclenched a fist.

She curled her hand around it, and a tiny shiver ran through her at the tension—and strength—she felt there. "He definitely was bossy."

Nathan's hand finally relaxed. "Tell me if he ever approaches you again, okay?"

She wasn't quite sure how to feel about Nathan's sudden defensiveness. "I doubt I'll ever see him again." Men like that came and went when they didn't get what they wanted.

"Oh, he'll be back," he spat. "We have a history."

Okay then. "What kind of history?"

"Hey, Nathan," Max called from down the hall. "A little help out here?"

"Coming." Nathan then glanced down at Starr. "I'll fill you in later. For now, you'll be careful, right?"

She shrugged. "Always. Thanks for rescuing me, again. Now I owe *you* a tequila shot." She winked, hoping maybe he'd lighten up a bit.

The tension in his shoulders remained, but the tiniest smile tried to form on his lips.

He sobered. "Seriously. Let me know."

"Okay," she drew out the word and turned toward the dressing room. How did she know his "history" with that guy wasn't going to be any good?

As soon as Starr entered the dressing room, Cherry Noir pounced.

"Ooo girl, you have got a secret admirer for sure." She raised a large glass bowl containing perfect white roses and yellow sunflowers. "The card says *I have seen roses damask'd, red and white, But no such roses see I in her cheeks*. Shakespeare. I googled it."

"Take them, especially since you opened a private note." Starr blew her a kiss and winked.

"Ain't nothing private in this dressing room, girl. And" □ she turned away with the arrangement□ "I don't mind if I do."

Starr threw on her robe, peeled off her false eyelashes, set them in their case, and went to work scrubbing off her makeup. "I swear there's something in the air here this week. A guy was waiting for me in the hallway. Nathan intervened." She dipped her fingers into the makeup remover cream.

"I've been in this life since I was fifteen, girl. There's always something going on, and *of course* some guy followed you. I mean, look at your fine self."

She swirled the emulsion over her cheek. "But something feels ... different." She'd been assaulted on stage, and then Luna had jerked her emotions around with her father-finding move. Follow that with the shoe guy in the hallway just now, the flowers that arrived every other day for the last two weeks, and she could only conclude the Universe was playing with her.

"And, Nathan swooping in?" Cherry asked from behind the mirror. "He is another fine-looking specimen."

That, he was. "He sure is strong."

Cherry peeked around her makeup mirror. "You get in a feel?"

Heat tickled at Starr's neck—and other places. "A little bit. His arms are frickin' huge."

"Mmmhmm. I've seen them." She disappeared behind the mirror again. "Maybe you and Nathan should take a little vacay. You could use one. And, besides, when did things feeling different become bad?"

"Good way to look at it, Cherry." And, great idea about a vacation with a strong guy like Nathan.

"Just call me Oprah. No, wait. On second thought, don't. Oprah should do Oprah, and Momma Cherry's gotta do Momma Cherry."

She swiped at her face with a cloth. "I love you, Momma."

"Love you more, daughter I'll never have." The pop of a lipstick tube being pulled off sounded from behind the mirror.

Starr's eyes pricked. She took a deep breath in and let it out, resettling a sudden emotional storm that began to whirl inside her. This week was too much, that was all. Time off to have a little fun would recharge her batteries. Or maybe a date with someone like Nathan.

She rolled her shoulders, a slight ache starting in the arm she'd used to pitch her shoe into the crowd. She shook out her hair, and glitter showered down—fairy dust they'd called it as kids.

Memories dropped all around her. They'd been doing so ever since the visit with the P.I. Visions popped into her mind at the oddest times, like when she'd picked up some dry cleaning. The scent of cotton brought the memory of Phoenix ironing her baby doll's clothes on the living room carpet and leaving iron-shaped burns. Just before she stepped out on stage tonight, another memory had squeezed her heart—Luna dusting her décolletage with pink glitter and getting sent home from fourth grade by the gym teacher who didn't like having her basketball court "decorated with sparkly crap."

That was it. Tomorrow, she would force the three of them to talk. The last few days of passing each other in their tiny apartment making small talk, sucked, and she hated keeping a secret from Phee. They weren't supposed to be doing that anymore, yet here they were.

Then she'd go and buy a new pair of shoes, maybe throw another pair another night because she had to do something to cast off this negativity.

After that? Maybe she'd try to get a date with Nathan.

9

———

Nathan glanced down at his cell phone. He had another few hours before he was due at his parole officer's. His brain ran through a list of time-wasting choices.

The Baltimore aquarium with kids screaming everywhere was out. Orioles game? That meant people he didn't know behind him, next to him, in front of him. After nine years of being perpetually on alert for physical attack, he didn't turn his back to strangers—ever. Maybe he'd walk more or just show up early.

He stretched his neck and sat his butt in the driver's seat of his car. Things could be worse—a helluva lot worse. He could be shuffling from an eight-by-ten-foot cell to a plate of dried out eggs in a mess hall where the only options were going to the gym, the yard, or the common room to watch reruns of *Law and Order*, all while keeping one eye on the other guys who lived in their own version of a 24/7 fight club.

His stomach growled just as he turned the ignition of his car. Okay, McDonald's it was. Twenty minutes later, after wolfing down the first of two quarter pounders and half his french fries, he rolled into the parking lot of the Parole and Probation Office of Regional Operations. Still early, but he ran through his speech to Erin about Saturday night's fight and the bullshit pending lawsuit. *Rich kids, hell-bent on showing off. It's my job to make sure people aren't attacked. The kid threw punches. Yada. Yada.*

"Just do it," he said to the windshield and cracked open his door. The news was pretty much going to light her hair on fire, so he might as well just march in, say the words, and get it over with.

As soon as he entered the building, the comforting scent of Elmer's glue and old leather, just like his elementary school days, hit him. Strange how one clung to the barest of pleasant memories in an attempt to calm the eff down. Nathan rounded the corner and walked the twenty-eight steps to her open office door.

Erin stood behind her desk, staring down at a stack of well-used folders. The one on top was his and bore a curling sticker because it overlaid some other guy's name. Every time he stepped across this threshold, the same questions arose in his mind. Did the guy whose name sat under his move on? Was he even still alive?

She didn't look up when he entered. "Nathan. On time as usual. I only want to hear good news today." She gestured for him to sit.

"I do have good news. I didn't start the fight." He lowered himself to the child-sized metal chair that could numb a man's butt in two minutes.

Her eyes shot to him. She sat and leaned back in her chair, her expression a pretty decent schoolmarm impression. "Oh?"

"A college kid got thrown out of Shakedown on Saturday night. Max got a punch in. Had to in order to stop the rich kid from assaulting one of the dancers."

She sighed. "Which one is Max again?"

"Head of security."

Didn't she have all this written down somewhere? Oh, wait, he was a number, a case file, a nobody to her.

"Yeah, yeah." She waved him off. "You know, working in a bar where fights—"

"Rarely occur."

"Mmhmm. You're not drinking, are you? Because my deal with Mr. Phillips was no alcohol, no drugs—"

"No, none of that."

"And? What else?"

"The kid that got clocked threatened legal action."

She slanted her eyes at him. "You named?"

"Apparently."

"But you didn't fight with him."

"I might have shoved him." He'd wanted to do a hell of a lot more than that.

"You know, I'm trying to save your ass. Do you understand this isn't good for you?"

No shit, Sherlock. He'd been convicted of second-degree murder. The great State of Maryland had him labeled, and he wouldn't be surprised if hitting a squirrel could get him life.

"Consider that strike one. No more trouble, Nathan." She sighed dramatically and leaned forward, resting her elbows on the scattered papers across her desk. "You get in touch with your family?"

Shit.

"You know, parolees who are in touch with loved ones … " she started, but he'd stopped listening. He let the buzzing in his ears rise, just like the cicadas in summer. When was the last time he'd heard that sound? So long ago. He searched his mind for something good to cling to, something other than the words she was throwing at him. *Family. Matters. Support.* They pinged inside his brain like gunfire. Family. What crap.

As soon as they'd heard the judge issue his sentence, they'd vanished. No sense in dredging up what he'd lost, who he'd lost.

His brain dislocated from his body—a blessed relief.

His mind conjured up all kinds of things instead, like the sound of tree frogs and birds at his family's farm. Chugging beer by the lake with his friends. Pulling on last night's tee shirt to go to class. Breathing in bright flower scents in a girl's hair. Imagining red hair, Starr's hair.

The room had grown still. Erin had stopped talking and was now staring at him with the what-the-fuck-is-wrong-with-you disdain he'd have to endure for another sixty-six times. Two years and eight months of these visits, and then maybe he'd feel some semblance of a future, because whatever this was—this not-being-in-prison-anymore—it wasn't freedom. It was limbo, one level removed from Hell. One word from her could put him right back there. *God... he couldn't go back there.*

He rose to leave, and she didn't stop him. He'd done what he'd come for. He wasn't going to sit one minute longer in this cesspool of realizations of how his life had gone to shit. He was an ex-con with a bounty on his head from a mob family who wouldn't leave him alone and a real family who wanted nothing to do with him.

On the way out, the hot air hit him like a sledgehammer —so hard, he couldn't breathe. He just needed a minute. He'd sit in his car; maybe listen to the radio for a bit. Only he didn't make it to his car. He doubled over the bushes on the lot's median and upchucked the gut bomb in his belly. At least his stomach calmed. He couldn't say so about any other part of him, and he was damn sick of it.

10

Starr placed her purse on the counter of the small coffee shop near the harbor. "I'll have an iced tea lemonade. Large."

"Hot or cold?"

She raised an eyebrow. "Iced?"

The young girl turned to make her drink, and Starr scanned the outdoor seating area. She had two hours, and the harbor's water glistened in the sunlight, calling her outside.

"They don't really listen, do they?" a male voice remarked behind her.

"What was that?" She turned to face the man. Ice blue eyes pierced the distance between them. It was the guy from the hallway at Shakedown, Mr. Shoe Catcher himself.

He chuckled. "Just heard you give your order. I'm a Chai Creme Frappuccino kind of guy myself."

"Oh?" Her arms hung at her sides. She couldn't pretend-flirt. There were two bachelor parties coming in tonight. She had no energy or time for anything that didn't make her smile without effort, and this guy had been downright rude to her.

"I know it's considered girly, but you should try it," he continued.

"Maybe I will sometime."

He handed a credit card over to the girl. "I'll get hers, Brenda."

Her insides bristled, though she smiled pleasantly. "Oh, no, thank you." She handed over a ten-dollar bill. The minute a man bought a woman something, they kept a running tally in their heads and knew exactly how they'd want to be repaid. "Keep the change."

She offered the guy a half-hearted smile and moved away from him to the other end of the counter to collect her drink. Without looking back, she headed outside. *Oh, score.* A couple was just leaving, and she quickly sat before anyone else could land the table. Metal scraped against the concrete as she positioned her chair toward the water. The heated iron was warm against her back and thighs, and the contrasting iced tea cooled her throat. She needed this moment, a break from thinking about what the hell to do about their father. She propped her feet up on the second chair, put on her sunglasses, and stared out over the choppy, dark gray harbor water.

A shadow fell across her lap. "Did you like my flowers?"

"Flowers?" So he'd sent the bouquets. Just great, because now she was going to have to deal with him. She looked up. Mr. Shoe Catcher eyed her up and down in the manner she'd grown far too accustomed to—like a poodle being assessed by Westminster dog show judges. Okay, ten minutes is what he'd get.

"I'm Ruark." He held out his hand. "Ruark MacKenna. We were rudely interrupted the other night."

"Thank you for the flowers. That was … kind." She returned his handshake. When she tried to pull back, he didn't let go.

"Oh, don't get super polite on me now, Starr. May I?" He finally let go of her hand and gestured to the chair.

God, she really didn't want to. Before she put her feet down, he yanked the chair back and settled in. Jesus, buddy.

"It's rare I get to have coffee with a beautiful woman. I've seen your act. You're good. Very sexy."

Her belly tightened a little. "Thanks." She swallowed what she wanted to say. Just because she was a dancer didn't mean she shouldn't be treated respectfully and not like a piece of meat.

"So, tell me, Starr. That your real name?" He placed his hand on hers.

And, there it was, the presumptuous attitude. "Maybe." She pulled her hand free. "Is Ruark yours?"

"Now, here I thought you had no sense of humor."

"What would give you that impression?"

"That fiery Irish look you're giving me. I recognize it well from my aunts, sisters, and cousins." He leaned back. "So, Miss Starr. Dinner. With me."

"I don't date customers."

He raised his Frappuccino to her in a toast. "Name your price."

"Price?" She scraped her chair backward and stood so rapidly the chair fell over. He appeared shocked. Good. "There is no price. There never has been. There never will be. I am not a prosti—"

"Whoa, whoa." He held up his hands. "Sit down. I wasn't proposing—"

"Weren't you?"

"No. I'm taking you to dinner. La Monde Joyeux, your next night off." The smile that stretched across his face only made him creepier.

"French food will make you fat." She tried to turn, but he grasped her forearm, and man, he had some grip.

"Let go of me," she ground out.

"This man bothering you?" A woman at the table next to them held up her cell phone. "Don't make me film this."

Starr nearly laughed, but the woman's backup was awesome ... and so appreciated.

He let go of her and leaned back in his chair. "It's just a miscommunication. Entirely my fault." He dipped his chin. "Please, sit. Enjoy your drink, and think of a hundred ways I can make it up to you. Let's just say your beauty brings out the beast in me."

She bit her tongue. He was a Shakedown customer, so she could be firm, but calling him all the beastly names for him that ran in her head wasn't appropriate.

"I know how to treat a woman." His gaze rested on her breasts. "Dinner is just the beginning."

The woman at the next table shrugged. "I'd go out with him."

Seriously lady? *Turncoat. With no taste.*

He turned his cold, blue eyes to the woman. "Thank you."

Confident and steady, Starr could tell this man was used to getting what he desired. He was handsome, but a quiet violence shimmered under his skin. She could practically scent it—the way his gaze now ran up and down her body, so slowly and with such intent, she'd felt violated.

"No." She picked up her drink and her purse.

"So it's a maybe."

"Oh, it's a no," she said without looking back.

There was no harm in getting to Shakedown early, especially since those eyes kept drinking her in like he was just assessing where to pounce first. Something was off about this guy. She could tell. Where men were concerned, she and her sisters always could. *Gee, thanks for that lesson, Dad.*

11

———

"Hey, Nathan, can you help me move this thing?"

"Fu ... me." Nathan's heart nearly leaped out of his chest at the female voice that came from nowhere.

Starr's head poked out from behind a long row of boxes in the back corner of the storeroom. "Sorry, didn't mean to take you off guard."

His heart skipped a few more beats, but he found his spine. "Just came to take some inventory. What do you need?" He stepped closer to where she stood. She wore no makeup, and her red curls were piled high on top of her head in a messy knot. She was still fricking gorgeous. It was a damn miracle his gaze didn't slide up and down her like a lecher every second he stood in her company, which now was exactly five times, with each time better than the last.

"I need to roll out this cage so I can get to the mannequins."

He pushed three heavy boxes out of the way. How the hell did she wedge herself between them and that giant, mock birdcage? The girl had some strength. It didn't take much for him, but he had at least seventy-five pounds on her.

She slapped dust from her hands. "Thanks for your help, Nathan. You always seem to be rescuing me."

Rescuing. How about he could bring her a load of danger if he wasn't careful. Seeing Ruark with her in the hallway yesterday just about made his arteries explode. He understood why any man would be attracted to her, but MacKenna was the worst sort of man. If he could build an invisible shield around Starr so Ruark didn't know she existed, he'd do it.

The cage squeaked as he rolled it off to the side to get to the industrial laundry cart. Hands, thighs, and three heads rested on top of a pile of other disembodied mannequin parts.

"Do I dare ask?"

"I'm not designing a murder scene, if that's what you're thinking." Her eyes flew open. "Oh, God, I'm sorry, Nathan."

Fuck him for real. She knew. He ripped his gaze from her sweet face. Seeing fear in another's eyes was one of the worst parts of having a record. How would she know she was safe back here with a convicted murderer?

He searched her face for horror, fear, or worse—curiosity—where he'd finally have to confess to her why he ended up in prison. He clung to the beat of silence between them, prayers lighting up his body from the inside that she wouldn't ask him anything. She said she didn't like mystery

...

Thank, hell. She clutched the edge of the cart, pulled, and *didn't* hit him with a barrage of questions, though they were sure to come soon. He should have never let his history with Ruark slip yesterday.

She wrestled with the squeaky cart for a few seconds so he yanked it out from under her quivering arms.

Her eyes widened. "Oh, you're strong."

Didn't that stoke his ego a little. "Moving boxes."

"I'll bet." She peered up at him. "Hey, can I run something by you?"

"Sure."

"We need a new group sister act. I'm so bored with everything we've got in the repertoire." She picked up a mannequin arm. "I want to put these together, put one in army fatigues, another in safari gear and another in ... something. Haven't gotten that far. Anyway, make them hunters. We're the rare birds that come out of the jungle. They're hunting us."

"So you're the prey?"

"Exactly. Except we best them. We blend in with the forest, and they can't see us. They end up dying in their own traps."

Her smile was adorable. So the girl had a macabre streak. Nice. "Gruesome."

"Too much?"

"It's original. You going to show the men dying?" He meant to be supportive, not provoke the slightly horrified look on her face. "Except, people don't want to see any violence," he added quickly. "Me, personally? I avoid it altogether, in case you're wondering."

"I wasn't wondering."

Sure she wasn't.

Her hand came down on his arm, and his eyes darted up to her. "I have an idea. We'll drop a mesh from the ceiling on them, and they'll be captured." She stepped closer, her lips quirking up. "Then maybe we'll have our way with them."

A blanket of stupid cloaked his mind. He didn't know what to do with her words or her sudden proximity. When she tried to pull back, however, his hand rested on hers to keep it there. Man, her skin was like nothing he'd ever touched—pure heaven. He wasn't going to be separated from it yet.

"Good plan," he said. "The audience will love it."

"Would you?"

He nodded. "Only if you're the star."

She smiled wide. "Most definitely." She pulled her hand free and picked up a mannequin arm. "But first, these need cleaning. They look like they've been through a jungle." She blew on it. A cloud of dust hovered between them for a few seconds, and she coughed. "Or a desert."

"There are some wipes back here." At least some part of his brain had reconnected. He headed to the cleaning supply area and pulled down a canister. "You shouldn't have to clean these, though. Or be back here by yourself." What if someone made their way back here? He'd have to talk to Declan about securing this room better. Cracks of sunlight streamed across the floor from under slightly-raised loading dock doors.

"I'm not alone. You're here."

That he was. He ran a finger over his lips. "So, need help?"

"Always. You wouldn't believe the things I've done for my art." She examined the arm.

"Is it tough being creative?"

"If people only knew..." She looked around. "It's quiet here." She leaned toward him. "I hear Trick and Rachel are back here frequently. Ya' know ... to do the deed." She did her flirty winking thing again and awoke the ever-present lust that flowed under his skin like a swollen river. Shit, he did not need an image of Trick and Rachel doing "the deed" in his head, which kept things in check in the sex fantasy department.

She laughed a little. "You're blushing."

"Am not," he grumbled. Great, he'd reverted to being twelve. He crossed his arms.

"What's this mean?" She touched the tattoo on his bicep, and he flinched. "Sorry. I shouldn't have pried."

He ran his hand over the gray and white design. "It's a dove. I got it for someone once." He ordered his brain to file the memory away—fast and hard.

"Oh." She didn't press, rather returned her attention to her cart of fake body parts.

She pushed on the cart with some effort. He immediately jumped in to help, because, damn, he just wanted to be next to her, do something for her. He gripped the side of the cart, taking it through the doorway.

She peered up at him. "You sure you have time for this?"

A lightness crept upon him at her smile. "Always got time to help you."

"I was hoping you'd say that."

12

One side of Nathan's mouth inched up, the scar on his cheek moving with it, and his eyes had softened. Oh, yeah, he liked her all right, and she liked *that*.

She didn't need help dousing a bunch of plastic legs and arms in the supply closet's laundry sink, but having him around made her relax. He didn't rush her, didn't assume she was easy like so many men—men like that ice-eyed Ruark. Nathan had a rare tough and gentle combination that touched her in the softest places of her heart—plus it didn't hurt he was one well-built, handsome man.

He rolled the cart to the small utility closet and opened the door. No way would the cart fit, so she picked up a plastic leg and arm and stepped inside.

Dirt dusted the front of her tee-shirt. "Wow, they're dirtier seen in the light." She cranked on the hot water and dumped them in. Nathan handed her three more.

As the water rose, she scanned the shelves for soap. "Can you reach that detergent for me?" She pointed at the bottle of dish soap.

He leaned over, his t-shirt riding up as he reached to the

highest shelf. Dark hair dusted his flat, hard abs, and she chewed the inside of her cheek. He really was a good-looking guy, the little gash on his cheek making him hotter. How was he single? Even if he did just re-enter the world, surely he was on some woman's radar screen.

Their fingers brushed when he handed her the bottle, his callouses only making him more interesting. This man worked with his hands—the direct opposite of those frat kids the other night. "Can you hand me the others, too?" She pointed at the cart.

He turned away, reached for the other body pieces. He had a nice butt. Checking him out so blatantly was hypocritical of her, but a quick glance couldn't be that bad, and it was fair play. She certainly got checked out enough. His t-shirt stretched thin over the ripped muscles in his back and shoulders, and those jeans fit him oh, so nicely. She cut her assessment of him short as soon as he righted and handed her a plastic male torso—a far cry from the real one standing in front of her.

After dumping the pieces in the sink, he didn't back up. In the small space, steam from the hot water clouded the air almost immediately. He stood so closely behind her, she could sense how their bodies might fit together, her butt against his crotch, his hard torso against her back, and her head, if she inclined it slightly, might nestle nicely into his neck, where his short beard would scratch against her.

"Where are you going to start?" His low rumble did little to switch off her rising libido.

"The legs." Like wrap hers around him. Instead, she plunged her hands into warm soapy water. She'd squeezed the plastic parts into the sink so tightly they would barely fit.

His arm brushed hers as he leaned around her and grabbed a leg part and started slapping a rag that'd been hanging on the side of the sink over it. She did the same.

They stood there, running the body parts under the water, wiping them down, rinsing them under the water again and again until they were clean. She tried not to watch how he handled the arms and legs, or how his large hands wrapped so thoroughly around the ankles and wrists. She failed at that attempt because *sweet lord on high* he was growing sexier by the minute. Those hands on her would feel so amazingly good. She could tell already.

She pulled the chain holding the stopper. "Let's leave them in here. Let them drain and dry." She shook water from her hands. He tore off some paper towels, captured her hands with one to dry them. The gesture was so protective and assured, a flood of warmth in her heart mixed in with all her rising physical interest.

He tossed the paper towel in the trash can.

"You got a little" —he wagged his finger toward his cheek — "dust there."

She crept closer. "I do?"

His rough fingertip brushed her skin, and more interest awoke between her legs. "Yeah."

Oh, why not? She leaned into him, let her breasts sink against his hard chest, and what do you know? He didn't pull back. Actually, he froze. She wasn't normally this aggressive, but he was just so … locked down. How was she going to get this guy to ask her out?

"Starr, I … " His words died, and he glanced down at where their bodies met.

Oh, damn. "You don't like me … like that."

"No. I do." He stepped backward. "Actually, I really do. It's just … "

"Your life is complicated. That doesn't scare me." It wouldn't, after all she'd seen – police showing up at her house as a little girl, guys slinging back cheap beer as they sat in lawn chairs in the garage, urging her to get closer, and later, bikers hanging out in the parking lot waiting for her after a dance show. And, God, what she'd seen at that strip club they'd had the great misfortune of working one year? He was the dead opposite of all that.

"Does your complicated life have anything to do with this history you mentioned? With that guy, Ruark? I ran into him at a coffee shop today, by the way."

He cursed, and shook his head at the floor.

"Nathan?" She bent her knees so she could look up into his eyes.

He looked up at her, and she straightened. His Adam's apple bobbed up and down, and his lips thinned. "It's a long story. But you gotta believe me, Starr—"

"I do. Ruark's a bully, and you're not. So, maybe you could fill me in sometime. Like over coffee … or dinner." She inched closer. "You know, Nathan, if you asked me out, I'd say yes."

He remained mute but swallowed hard again. He wanted to kiss her. She could see it—the way his eyes kept returning to her lips, and the way he now leaned toward her.

She licked her lips on purpose but didn't slither closer. Forcing his hand wasn't her intention, and maybe he didn't like such assertive women, though changing herself for a man wasn't happening.

Whistling sounded in the hallway, and then Max was standing in the doorway. "Oh, sorry, man." He held up his hands. "We got a major spill at the bar." He reached around the door jamb and grabbed the mop leaning there. He was gone, never looking back once.

When she turned back, Nathan hadn't moved.

"I better go and see if Max needs help." He cleared his throat. "And let me think about what we might do together."

Score. She stepped back to allow him room to leave, but not so far he couldn't brush against her again.

He glanced down and then back up at her as he scooted by. Oh, she earned a half smile as if he knew exactly what she'd been up to. Well, it was about fricking time the seal broke on their unspoken interest in one another. For once, she had something good to look forward to.

13

———

Nathan stared up at the night sky. Still no stars, but at least the Shakedown parking lot was quiet, just a few rumbling truck sounds in the distance mixed with a far-off siren. It was a beautiful night. It was a great fucking night. He had a date with Starr. So miracles did exist.

Maybe he'd go down to the water, eat the leftover chicken parmesan the cook let him snag, and figure out what to do about this newfound development. Jesus, he hadn't been on a date in over a decade. He'd have to give some thought as to where to take her—someplace fancy, someplace worthy of her.

He got in his car, turned on the ignition, and lowered all four windows. He turned his phone back on. The thing instantly pinged at him like a harpy with messages he'd missed. Every time he turned it on, all kinds of issues he talked about or had looked up on his phone just showed up. His belly jolted again, just thinking about how everything had changed since his forced vacation: self-check-outs in grocery stores, all that app stuff, ATM machines that talked to you. He'd about jumped out of his skin the first time he encountered one of those.

Raucous laughter echoed in the side alley around the corner. He put his car into drive and swung around to see who was loitering around the back entrance. His headlights spotlighted two kids who looked like they should be tucked into bed with Superman sheets under nightlights. One drew back his arm and released a beer bottle into the darkness. An animal screeched. *The cat.*

"Ha-ha. Nailed him." The kid high-fived his friend.

The other delinquent pulled out another bottle from the six-pack carton at his feet. "Ten bucks, I can hit it again."

Nathan hit the accelerator, stopping only a few inches from where the two punks stood. His bumper got so close, one of them slapped his hood. The shorter of the two—what was he, fourteen?—flipped him the finger. The other kid laughed before he picked up another bottle and hauled it into the dark again.

What had happened to the world? He wasn't allowed a single misstep, yet everyone around him could do whatever the hell they felt like. Nathan yanked open his door, his boots thudding onto the asphalt. He left the car running, lights shining on the two punk ass kids.

One of the kid's eyes grew wide as Nathan stomped closer, but he didn't lose his stupid grin as he spun on his heel and took off. The second one was slower on the uptake. Punk Ass Two startled at seeing him. Nathan got a hold of the kid's dirty burgundy sweatshirt and yanked him closer, which earned a satisfyingly loud rip of fabric.

The kid squirmed and bucked like a banshee. "Ow, get off me, man."

"What the fuck are you doing?"

The pounding of his friend's sneakers on the pavement grew distant. Kids had no loyalty either.

"Chill out, dude. We were just having some fun."

Nathan dragged him by the back of his sweatshirt into the alley. The mangy cat growled in the shadows, which only fueled his fury.

"Wha-what are you doing?" The kid's eyes grew larger.

"Apologize."

He had the audacity to stare at Nathan like he was the crazy one. "Fuck you."

Nathan hauled the kid up so their faces were separated by a millimeter. "Now."

"Jesus. You're crazy, man," he spat.

Nathan threw him to the ground. "Say it. To the cat."

"S-sorry." The kid scrambled backward, jumped to his feet, and ducked around Nathan, but only because he let him.

Nathan panted a little. Jesus. He'd almost pummeled that kid. For what? Going after a mangy cat? How about ruining the fricking good mood he'd been in.

The animal's growling had dropped an octave. Shit, was it that hurt? He returned to his car for the food carton. When he got back to where the cat's angry sounds continued, he crouched down, opened the pack, and held it out.

"Here, cat. We're not all bad."

One golden eye blinked from behind the dumpster. It hissed.

"Don't want it?" He shook the carton.

A small head peeked out. Then slowly, the body curled around the corner. It was limping. Shit, those kids.

He dropped the container to the ground, stood, and stepped backward to give the cat some room. It took less than a minute for the thing to give up its fear for food. It reached into the carton and pulled out a piece with its teeth and darted backward.

He turned to go home but then turned to retrieve the carton. He couldn't leave it sitting out like that, and did he see blood on the cat? He sat in his driver's seat and watched the mangy feline tear the piece of chicken bit by bit until it was gone. Yeah, this was one odd night. First his Starr encounter, and now it was just him, sitting with a one-eyed cat in an alley.

When the thing was done and had sniffed around the container to make sure he hadn't left anything behind, the cat settled on its haunches and licked his paw like nothing had gone down.

Okay, he was a tough guy. "See you tomorrow, cat."

A shadow moved to the side and then spoke. "Didn't know you had it in you." A stab of anger jolted his spine, and he half crouched for a fight. He swung his gaze down the alley. "Ruark."

The man stepped forward into the light. He fingered one of Shakedown's tumblers that he must have just sauntered outside with, like he owned the place. Such a damn MacKenna move.

No matter how hard Nathan tried, his body would not stand down. Sweat pricked over his skin, and his jaw ached. Damn body reflexes warred inside him.

"What do you want?" he ground out.

Ruark drew closer as if trying to scare him. *Too bad, asshole.* There was nothing this man could do to him that he couldn't deliver right back.

"I repeat. What the hell do you want, MacKenna? I did my time."

Cold blue eyes assessed him. "And, now you're here." He peered up the side of the building. "Checking I.D.s. Watching pretty girls strip."

"Dance," he corrected.

Ruark chuffed. "That what they call it now? You watch them. Closely. As if a loser like you could stand a shot?"

Plenty of barbed words had been slung at him in prison—

along with fists, pipes, shivs, and anything else the inmates could get their hands on—so MacKenna could go fuck himself if he thought anything he was lobbing would do damage.

Enough of this. Nathan angled toward his car. This guy didn't deserve another second of his night.

"Got to admit, the view every night here must help you jerk yourself to sleep easier," MacKenna called out. "Whores like that, shaking their goods all over the stage … "

Nathan stormed forward until he was a foot from Ruark's stone-cold face. The man's breath stunk like cheap whiskey and cigarettes.

MacKenna sneered. "There's the real guy. Jesus, you're easy, Nathan. Just like those girls. Especially the one they call Starr. She's the one you watch real close. And then there was that White Knight act you pulled when I was asking her out. And, believe me. She *will* go out with me, and then we'll see how easy she is once I get her alone."

Nathan curled his fists until his fingernails dug crescents in his palm, and he'd keep doing that until they broke the skin and bled if it meant not throwing the punch he desperately wanted to. One, this asshole wasn't getting near her. He'd see to it. Two, he also wasn't going to impact the direction of Nathan's life anymore—and a fight most certainly would. Starr was too smart to fall for this man, so Nathan would be too smart to fall for his bullshit.

"You aren't fit to be in the same room as her." Shit, and just like that, he'd given something away. He'd told the fucker exactly how he could wound him. "Leave all of them alone." His jaw locked hard.

"A parolee isn't in a position to tell me to do anything."

This MacKenna and the rest of his lawyering-up, silver-spoon family could kiss his ass. "Careful. You could be accused of stalking. That would be your modus operandi, now wouldn't it? Sticking your nose in where it doesn't belong. Why are you here, really?"

"You'll see." Ruark sauntered off in the cocky way only men who've never had their freedom taken from them did.

He'd given up on happiness long ago, but was it too much to ask for peace? Apparently so. For the first time in his life, he began to believe that saving Declan from being pummeled to death wasn't worth the price of never again having a normal life.

There was more coming from the MacKennas. Ruark MacKenna had just shown his hand. He would go after anyone Nathan got close to. Well, he would be prepared next time, not get caught in an alley with nothing but a cat as back up. As for Starr? She would be warned and watched.

14

Declan's antique executive chair creaked complaints as he leaned back. "Empty threats."

"Nothing the MacKennas do is empty." Nathan scratched his chin, his beard rough against his dried-out hands. He hadn't slept, instead, taking a run through Baltimore's streets until his lungs nearly burst and then showering for an hour as if hot water could wash away this mess. He'd stacked and restacked boxes in the back until Declan got to the club. *Don't try to go it alone when you're on the outside, they'd said.* The advice the two-timers he'd met in prison gave him better work.

"You just need to know Ruark was hanging around the club after hours." He stared down at the carpeting. "Nothing good can come from a MacKenna hanging around the club. He might be targeting some of our female employees."

Because that's what MacKennas did. They identified someone vulnerable, someone important to you, and took their revenge out on them. Jesus, if anything happened to Starr ...

"Glad you told me." Declan let his chair return to its

upright position in a loud thunk and steepled his fingers in front of him. "I know very well how they operate. So this is how this is going to go. Nathan, you're off the door. No buts. Trick ... " He turned to the man who'd been holding up the wall during this whole chat. "Call Amos. See if he can fill in for a while. I want you to help Max out front. One second of trouble and Ruark's tossed out on his ass. He, just like everyone else, has to abide by the rules here. No harassing my employees."

Trick finally pushed off the wall. "Been watching him for a while, like you asked, but I really thought we were done with him. Max caught him in the hallway once. Been delivering flowers to the girls. Starr mostly."

What? Ruark MacKenna had been sending flowers? Fuck, yeah, any man would want to woo Starr or any of the others, but the fact he'd singled her out was too much of a coincidence for him.

"He's got his eye on Starr." Nathan scrubbed his hair.

Declan at least looked concerned. "I'll nip that in the bud right away. If she wants, I'll get a restraining order."

That was it? "And then what? You know them. They're wealthy. Got connections. They're—"

"Used to getting what they want? Remember, I did business with them before ... " he trailed off.

Yeah, *before*. There were so many "befores," like before Declan discovered they were using his antiques to move drugs, and before Declan went to prison himself—a set-up that mysteriously got "solved" so he got out early. That last setup was a warning shot over the bow by the MacKennas, for sure. The man couldn't risk any more trouble.

"Nathan, trust me. We're going to handle this by the books. Now, does MacKenna know where you live?"

Nathan shrugged. "Probably. But I haven't caught any tails." After spending nine years staring at the same walls and a chain-link fence, he was just getting used to taking in the circus atmosphere of the world at large. He was bound to lose some details. "I think I've seen someone outside the club at times." Nathan scratched at his chin. "Might be Ruark ... but it was just a silhouette. Fuck, I don't know."

"Trick, pull up the camera feeds. Make sure everyone knows what Ruark looks like."

Nathan stiffened, and started to comment.

Declan held up his hand. "No details given as to why Ruark is here. It's no one's business but yours, Nathan."

He let out a puff of air. He trusted the man, but gossip about Ruark MacKenna would make the rounds. He'd just gotten an in with Starr. She was smart. She'd back off, and any possible chance with her would be off the table in a nano-second, just when he needed to stay close to her more than ever.

"Now go home." Declan stood. "Be back here tomorrow. For now, get what's running through your head sorted."

His temples pounded. Having a boss who'd also done time helped him understand the shit storm in Nathan's head on most days. But stop coming into work? That would put him at home, alone, with twenty-two hours to kill. Too much time to do nothing but let his brain run in circles.

Declan rounded his desk. "This could be good timing." He slapped Nathan on the shoulder, and he swerved out of habit. Declan ignored his response. "Starr asked for some time off. The girls have been working too hard as it is."

The man turned him toward the door. The conversation was over.

Once in the hallway, on instinct, he turned left instead of right. Starr needed to know everything so she could make up her own mind. Instead of finding her in the dressing room, it was Luna who told him she'd gone out to the main floor to pick up something. As soon as he stepped onto the floor and saw her standing at the bar, every muscle in his body seized. Ruark MacKenna leaned toward a grim-faced Starr, his arm in his gaudy suit coat reaching for her waist.

Nathan was going to disappoint his parole officer. No amount of deep breathing was going to counter his fury. It took every ounce of self-preservation he could muster to walk slowly up to them.

"Starr," he ground out. "Got a minute?"

She smiled up at him. "Of course."

MacKenna didn't so much as glance at him.

Nathan kept his arms by his side but took a wide stance. "I told you to stay away from her, now let her go."

Her jaw set, and she cocked her head at Nathan in warning. "We're in public," she sang between clenched teeth.

"I mean it, MacKenna."

Ruark's hand snaked to the back of the barstool, his fingers resting lightly against her back. Nathan's teeth ached from clenching them so hard. Yanking Ruark's hand to the bar, slapping it down, and taking a few of those fingers off with the lemon peeling knife just under the counter would feel really good right now. Maybe it'd take the edge off the nagging frustration that simmered under his skin every time he thought about how the system was so easily manipulated by a guy like Ruark—money, name-dropping. It took surprisingly little to make things go their way and go so wrong for him.

But not with Starr. He'd be damned if he'd let Ruark MacKenna use her.

Nathan stared down at the champagne flute in Starr's hand. "Starr, don't drink that." God knows what the guy had put in her drink.

The fucker's arm circled her waist, and he yanked her to him. Starr yelped a little and pushed against him. He let her go, but fuck, she trembled. A few people nearby started giving them worried glances—and moving away.

The guy laughed. "Guess I don't know my own strength. But don't worry, baby." He fingered a lock of her hair. "I'd never hurt a lady. But then maybe you're not a lady."

Nathan grabbed hold of Ruark's lapel and yanked him up, right off his stool.

The guy laughed. "Go ahead. Do it."

Nathan pushed him back down. "You're not worth the spit under my shoe."

Ruark re-adjusted his suit. "Don't mind him, Miss O'Malley. He lost his manners in prison. After he murdered my brother."

Her gaze shot to Nathan, her lips parting slightly as she spun herself free from Ruark, the bar, and him. If he could just get one fucking break already ...

MacKenna rose and held out his arm to Starr as if nothing had just happened. "I have a private booth, and we'll talk. I can fill you in on some things you might not know about Mr. Baldwin."

"Whatever you two have going on—" She lifted her hand in a stop sign gesture "—just, *no*." Thankfully, she left the drink on the bar top but turned away without so much as a glance back at either one of them. Shrugging him off, too? Well, too bad, sister. He was going to watch her back because Ruark MacKenna wouldn't get within five feet of her ever again.

"Ruark." Declan's voice wasn't welcomed.

"I got this, man," Nathan said to his boss.

"No one's got anything. This is my club, my guests, and my rules. Ruark. My office?"

The guy lifted his chin. "I don't answer your summons, Declan."

"Leave then."

Ruark huffed, turned to the bar and gestured for Jackie. "My tab. Close it." He then turned back to Declan. "For now."

Nathan didn't have time for this. Starr had marched off in a huff, and he wouldn't let Ruark MacKenna's words simmer in her consciousness for long. Damn, he didn't have her number, either.

Without another word, he spun and headed toward the exit. He caught Max in the hallway, who reported that Starr was headed to her car. As soon as he pushed through the exit door, he knew he was too late. A strange pang went off in his chest as he watched her car's taillights disappear down the street. He recognized that tug around his heart muscle. He cared for this woman—a lot.

The door slammed behind him. He wheeled around and slammed his fist into the metal casing. His knuckles stung like a bitch but it was good—so fucking good—to let out a punch.

God, he was in hot water—the kind that melted all defenses and made you grow even more obsessed with a certain redhead—and her safety and happiness. A man could get lost in a woman like her. It was going to be a problem, a real fucking big problem. He had to remain close, however. He just hadn't a clue how to do that now, given what she now knew about him.

15

Starr stared up at the Sunset Home sign in cheery yellow against an orange background as if the paint colors would elevate your mood about the place. She sighed and opened the car door. "Phee, what if he asks for you directly? What do you want us to say?"

"Tell him I've died."

The fact she'd come at all was amazing. Starr had come clean about her and Luna's trip to the P.I., and how she believed it might be good to confront their father, get some things off their chests. They'd had one hell of a fight about it, but by some miracle, Phee had agreed to go with them—and sit in the car.

Luna touched Starr's arm. "Just let her stay here."

Starr plunked the car keys in the console tray in case Phoenix needed to restart the air conditioning. As she and Luna crunched across the gravel parking lot, she swept her hair up into a hair tie, getting it off her damp neck. This summer's especially-heinous mugginess was going to kill her, or perhaps this visit would.

Blessed cool air washed over them as they stepped inside

the front entrance into a long hallway. By the looks of things, they could have been in a hospital. A woman in a nurse's uniform looked up from the reception desk and smiled.

"Hi, I'm Mimi. I think you're the O'Malleys. Is it true you're triplets?"

"We are. How is our father?" Luna's voice adopted the too-cheerful thing she did when nervous. Starr took her arm.

"He's having a good day. A real good day. Out of detox for two weeks." She inclined her head down the hall. "I'll show you where he is."

They followed her past individual rooms, some doors open, some closed. Through the doorways, Starr caught glimpses of the other residents. Some sat on their beds, staring into space. Another fingered a piece of a puzzle before snapping it down. A man in a wheelchair rocked back and forth before a window.

Posters lined the walls with bumper sticker sayings like *It Does Not Matter How Slow You Go So Long As You Do Not Stop* and *My Recovery Must Come First So That Everything I Love In Life Doesn't Have To Come Last.* If only that were true of their father.

"If you weren't depressed before arriving, you sure would be when you left," Starr muttered.

"They try." Luna furrowed her brows at her. "It's got nurses and counselors who graduated top of their class."

"You get that on Yelp?" Starr didn't care if Luna had poured over their website and every single document about family gatherings, in-home support, and more. All the forced cheer raised Starr's radar to high alert.

Luna yanked her arm. "Shhh, Mimi might hear you."

"Just kidding. You used to have a better sense of humor." Starr rubbed her forehead. Her head was killing her already.

Her sister glared at her. "You shouldn't kid about this."

Mimi led them through the maze of halls until they

reached a large room with nothing but a circle of chairs, the beige fabric stained on some, ripped on others. On the far side sat one haggard-faced man with grayed stubble on sunken cheeks. The man lifted his lids, revealing a wash of blue so familiar, except for the reddened capillaries.

A young woman in jeans and a yellow, flowered top rose and swept forward. "Hello. I'm Sharon, a counselor here at Sunset Home. Thanks for coming."

He stared across the circle of chairs at them, checking out Luna, moving to Starr, and then returning to Luna. So, this is what had become of their father.

Gone was the robust welder. There wasn't even a shadow of the man who could bench press his body weight. Instead, this stranger was hunched, wearing permanent pain on his face. The ravages of years of abusing a bottle had etched into his skin and yellowed his eyes. Madame Karma had done excellent work on this guy.

Luna jogged over to him as if the jolt of enthusiasm would mean something. The girl never gave up, did she? She took "wishing will make it so" to an award-winning level. Wishing or hoping didn't make crap happen. A woman had to go forth and conquer on her own.

"Hi." Luna crouched down and placed her hand on his. The guy hadn't even risen, but from the way his hands shook, and one of his legs jogged, he might not be able to.

Starr took the counselor's outstretched hand. "Where are the others? Isn't this a group therapy session?"

"For a first-time family visit, we thought it best it just be us." She peered around Starr. "There's a third sister"—she checked her clipboard—"isn't there?"

"Phee. She's not coming."

The woman nodded once. "I understand."

Did she? Did she have any concept of the emotional minefield she was about to enter?

Their father's eyes scrunched into slits as he assessed Luna. "Still so pretty." His face stretched into a grin that would make any car salesman proud. Luna looked so young at that moment, kneeling before him. The urge to run hit Starr so fast she shifted her weight from leg to leg.

"Dad," she sharpened her voice on purpose in an attempt to get his attention away from fawning over Luna.

He peered at Starr and, out of pure instinct or perhaps some long-lost sense of self-preservation, she stepped backward. God, she hated that. She hated that her instincts defaulted to flight if he looked her way.

He cleared his throat. "Thanks for coming." Then as if recognition sank in, his brow wrinkled even further. "I see one. I see two. Where's three?"

The familiar game immediately catapulted her to the memory of a warm day, a sprinkler making the grass slick under her feet. She was running, jumping, and her father growled like a lovable bear as he chased them through the spray.

"Where's my▯"

"She's not feeling well." Luna stood.

"That right?" He scrubbed the back of his neck.

"I heard you're out of detox. Good for you."

He reached out and grasped Luna's hand, gave it a squeeze as he stared up at her.

Starr's throat tightened, and a chill snaked under her skin. She blinked hard, gulped in air. What if she grabbed Luna, and they just left?

The counselor lowered herself to a chair, placed her elbows on her knees as if they were about to have a heart-to-heart chat. "Why don't we just sit for a minute? I realize it's been a long time since you've seen one another, and your father has some things he'd like to share."

Starr dropped her bag down on the chair so hard that it rattled items inside. "You don't say."

"I realize this is hard."

It wasn't Sharon's fault, but irritation made her spine tingle. God knows what lies her father had told his counselor. "Hard. Interesting word."

"Look, Cat—"

"Starr. I go by Starr now. That's Luna." She pointed at her sister. "And, Phoenix, well, she's feeling just fine. She simply didn't want to come in."

It was a petty thing to say, but she would protect her sister, even in the tiniest ways. This man would never be allowed to think his presence had any impact on her whatsoever—negative or positive. True, Phee had issues, but they were hers and hers alone.

Their father pushed his back into the chair and groaned a little as if moving hurt. "I didn't ask for this ... reunion, either. But I'm glad. I've thought about you girls. A lot." He ran a finger under his chin. The hard scratching sound of stubble sent a new shudder through her.

Luna rose and nestled into the chair next to their father. "You can blame it on me. I pushed for it. We have a lot to talk about." Her chest rose and fell fast, her eyes full of ridiculous hope.

Starr dropped herself into one of the chairs. It had unforgiving edges with curved arms as if it wanted to hug you into place. Well, she wouldn't be held in place by anything. She rose again and started to pace.

"Robert, why don't you go first? Tell us what this means to you. Luna and Starr being here, I mean."

He moved on to scrub his hair with a shaky hand. "A lot. Thanks for being here. I know what you all think of me. I get it. I just ... damn, I'm no good at this."

"Healing starts with one step. Why don't we all just say the first word that comes into our head?"

No one said anything, and Sharon let the silence stretch so long between them, Starr was sure a season changed outside. With each passing second, heat built inside her. Seeing him, looking right at this embodiment of evil, her insides hardened. He'd gotten away with so much. That was the bottom line, wasn't it? They bounced from family to family, split up most of the time, only together once in the end. Then, when they were "released from the State"—wasn't that the official word on their eighteenth birthday—they went on to receive more emotional and physical scars than any kid should ever bear. Did this man have any concept of what they'd had to do to survive—both *him* and after him?

The counselor tilted her head. "Starr? Perhaps you could start?"

"Sure. Abandonment. Neglect. Abuse. Starvation. Squalor. Terror. Drunkard. Addict." With each word, her father grew more still. He should be squirming in his seat, hanging his head, anything but hardening up.

"Starr, come on. One word." Luna's face reddened. "Mine is peace."

Her father's lips twitched up as he glanced at Luna. "That would be nice ... for a change." His voice cracked—actually cracked. He sniffed, shook his head.

There wasn't enough air in this room with no windows and nothing but industrial carpeting and uncomfortable seats. "I have another word," Starr said.

"Go on," urged Sharon.

"Agreement." She and her father had struck a deal years ago. Luna knew she'd handed over her life's savings to the man in secret. She didn't know about the promise he'd made for the money—to stay away from them forever. Starr would keep that part of their devil's bargain to herself. "Robert, remember the last time I saw you? Remember that."

Luna cocked her head. "Starr, come on. We don't need to go into it."

She didn't want to remember the last time she saw him? *Outside a government office.* It was the day they knew Phoenix was going to live, and she and L. were getting sent away. At least Luna had been spared Starr's last visit in that crappy motel.

His eyes cleared for one second as he sucked on his bottom lip. "Yeah. I remember."

Yeah? That's all he could say? She glared at her father. "Heard you got married again."

"Yeah, well, she wasn't good for me. We aren't together anymore."

"We know. Jail, huh?" Starr wasn't interested in pussy-footing around. If Luna wanted a reunion, it was at least going to be honest.

"Yes." He cleared his throat. "So, I'm sure you know I did a few stints, too."

"We do."

"You always were a straight shooter, Starr. I like the name Starr, by the way. It suits you."

A snake of ickiness trailed through her body. She didn't want this man to notice anything about her.

"You think?" Phoenix's voice startled her. Phee turned from the doorway—God knows how long she'd been standing there—and the sound of her jogging footfalls faded down the hall. Tears welled in Luna's eyes. They shouldn't have come. It was all too forced, too much too soon, and it wouldn't change a damn thing. There weren't any answers here.

Starr rose. Filling Luna's head with any more false hope that they'd suddenly become the perfect family was just "stuff and nonsense," as her mother used to say. *Stuff and nonsense.* Yeah, that was all they were left with. Oh, except for the nightmare memories. She'd be damned if she'd let this shriveled shell of a man force those on her or her sisters ever again.

She grasped her handbag. "I'll go and see Phee."

"Phee for Phoenix, huh?" Their father asked, his interest making her skin crawl.

"Phoenix Rising," Luna announced, like a proud mother.

Dear old Dad smiled, actually *beamed* at that, and she'd never wanted to punch someone so badly in her life. How could Luna think this would work? The man didn't deserve any more of their life, no matter what she'd promised her sister.

She shook her head and headed out to find her sister. Phee had probably been right all long—just stay away.

Outside, Phoenix, who hadn't lit up a cigarette in four years, leaned against their car, smoking. "Don't say a word."

She joined her sister and leaned her ass against the car. The metal nearly seared her skin through her jeans shorts. She pushed off and began to pace once more.

It was another thirty minutes before Luna came out to the car. None of them spoke the entire four-hour trip home. It was for the best. When they got home, they each retreated to their own rooms. Phoenix wouldn't come out, even after Luna had made Phee's favorite, lasagna. That's when she knew that reconciling with their father could be the death of them. No matter Luna's good intentions, some things couldn't be forced. They couldn't just forgive and forget the fact they all sported at least one scar on their skin from a belt, a stick, or anything else their father got his hands on. Phoenix had at least six.

16

Luna Belle peeled off her pink corset. The ensuing roar from the full-house crowd nearly took out Nathan's eardrums, but she didn't shrink back. How had he believed she was the shy one? More than two hundred sets of eyes remained riveted on her sparkling bra, but the crowd thankfully stayed in their chairs. He turned back to rounding up glasses and putting them in the bin. Luna was pretty, but she wasn't Starr, who he hadn't seen for the last two days. His mind kept drifting to images of her, and what she might be doing with her time off. He also stared at his apartment walls and had imaginary conversations with his parole officer about MacKenna. They usually ended with her seething mad for not being told of him last week.

Jackie ducked under the waitress stand. "Heard you had a little bit of trouble the other night."

The gossip about his run-in with MacKenna and their shared past had sure made the rounds quickly.

She cocked a hip. "Anything I can do to help?"

Was she kidding? "Nope. Thanks." No one was getting hurt because of him, especially not a woman, no matter how sexist that sounded even in his own head. Now how did he tell Starr that Ruark was only playing her to get to him?

Nathan threw the bar rag over the edge of the sink and turned to Jackie. "I'm going back for more Jack, and it looks like you could use some oranges. What else do we need?"

"Bombay. We'll be through with this bottle in no time." She lifted a half-empty gin bottle.

He made his way back to the storeroom, looking toward the dressing rooms for a glimpse of Starr. Nothing. He swiped back the black curtain separating the hall and the storeroom and jerked to a stop. Starr sat on a stool, scrolling through her phone. Her face, illuminated by the bluish light, could have passed for an ethereal being. *Like an angel.*

She looked up. "Oh, hi, Nathan."

"Starr." He swallowed.

She stood and stretched. "How are you doing?"

How was he doing? He was a goddamn mess. Imagining Starr with Ruark had occupied the better part of his days and nights, and now the speech he'd rehearsed abandoned him. "Fine. You?"

"Just waiting on Luna. Her car's broken down."

She tucked her phone into her bag and looked like she was ready to scoot past him.

Do it. "Heard you were off for a bit, and you might be rehearsing for a new show."

"Yep. We're tired of our old acts." Her brow wrinkled. "Hey, you okay?"

"You got a sec? It's about Ruark MacKenna. He's not a good man." Blurting out the truth for the second time seemed as good a plan as any.

"Oh?" She crossed her arms. "Did you meet him in prison?" Her tone was light, almost like she hadn't wanted to ask.

"No, but things happened between us a long time ago.

Lotta bad blood, and what he said … " God, he didn't want to tell her.

"About his brother?" She looked down at her hands, twisting around her phone.

"Yeah, I went to prison for killing his brother. It was an accident. Plain and simple. You gotta believe that." Or, not so simple, in reality, and she didn't have to believe him. She didn't *have* to do anything. "And, they… " Shit, he was no good at this talk-it-out-thing. He drew in a breath and blew it out.

She blinked up at him. "I believe you."

The tightness in his chest eased a little at hearing that, but Ruark wouldn't back off. She needed to know that. "It's just —he's not above physically hurting you to get to me. I don't want you to get—"

"Used? Hurt? Don't look so surprised. He doesn't really want *me*. Yeah, I know. I'm not stupid."

He raked his fingers through his hair. "Shit, I would never—"

"No, I know you're not calling me stupid, but I saw him coming from a mile away. The man wears a Rolex. He doesn't want someone like me."

Someone like her? What was she talking about?

"I know what men like him want. They just want to win." She pursed her lips. "And, he's not interested in winning me."

"He'd be lucky." Hell, he'd be blessed.

She lowered her lashes, a puff of air escaping her nose. "Yeah, I'm every man's dream. Every girl wants to be where I am."

"Angels envy you." Pretty words forced through his throat, but they were truth. This girl deserved nothing but flowers strewn at her feet.

She blinked at him as if she hadn't heard him right. "You don't have to say that, Nathan, really."

He looked down at her. "I never say things I don't mean."

She cocked her head as if still unsure what he meant. Her bottom lip quivered, and her gaze fell to his chin. "You shaved off your beard."

His hand went up to his skin, now clean of stubble and whiskers. "Uh, yeah, it's hot in the summer." Plus, he'd just wanted to—given his commitment to a clean slate and all.

She inched closer. He was so much taller, larger than Starr. He could engulf her entire body inside his arms. And, God, he needed to. He'd pull her into him, and inhale her unique scent until his lungs were full of it and her. Ruark— or any man—would have to cut off his limbs to get to her.

Her pink lips curled up, and her smattering of freckles stretched across her cheeks. Kissing her would be amazing. His hands itched to reach out, grasp her hips, and yank her flush to his body. The urge to do so rose so urgently that he had to step backward for fear of making a move too soon. He wouldn't scare her off.

"I liked your beard." She closed the distance he'd just put between them. The sweet scent of cinnamon and rosemary wafted between them. She was prettier up close, something he'd noticed that day in the utility room. How was that possible?

Jesus, she was doing that *thing* again—really looking at him. The pull to claim her obliterated all common sense. It didn't matter how many times he mentally flogged himself for his possessive lust. He'd spent years stamping out any want, any desire, for things he couldn't have. He was tougher than this. *Stop. Just stop.* He needed to resist her pull, stay strong, stay focused.

"The thing is, Nathan." She moved even closer, and his head swam with her perfume, his eyesight full of her face and hair. "If any man had a chance with me, despite your past, it would be someone like you."

God, she eviscerated his ability to resist. And, shit, he took the hint and his mouth just found hers. His hand reached out and wrapped itself around her neck, pulled her into him. The second his lips met her softness, shocking warmth filled him. He broke the contact. She hadn't asked him to kiss her. Had he offended her?

She curled her hand around the nape of his neck and brought him back to her lips. "I thought you'd never do that," she said into his mouth.

He kissed her again. This time when he released the contact, her eyes had softened toward him.

He should walk away; let her get on with her life without his kind of trouble. "I'm off tomorrow." His mouth clearly didn't agree.

Her fingers slid from his neck and her face drew back so he could get a full view of those sea-blue eyes and her freckles.

"Oh? Me, too." She tilted her head. "Hey, you ever been to Annapolis?"

If anyone knew how life could change on a dime, it was him. One moment, he'd been a married college student and much more—slinging back beers in a bar with friends and on the weekends helping Declan stack crates of shipments. The next, he'd sat in the backseat of a police cruiser, so fucking naïve, not realizing it'd be the last car ride he'd take before settling on the cracked vinyl seat of a bus taking him to prison. Even that memory couldn't shake his good mood— hell his fan-fucking-tastic mood—thanks to his date with Starr tomorrow.

A greasy burger scent arose as he opened his car door— time to stop at a service station and vacuum out all the crap left from too many fast-food meals.

A plaintive meow sounded at his feet. The stupid cat rubbed itself back and forth across his ankles.

"Sorry, cat. Got nothing for you." He slid into the driver's side. Before Nathan could close the door, the cat jumped onto his lap and crawled across to the passenger side. Like a queen, the thing lay down, and looking at him, let out another cry. What the eff?

He reached out to move the cat back to the ground, and it hissed. He drew his hand back. "Fuck. It's my car." Part of him was proud of the scrappy little thing. Just the other night, it got pummeled by two punk ass kids and he—she?—was still fighting. Still ...

"Get out." He hitched his thumb as if the thing could understand him.

With a long sigh, he hoisted himself out, moved to the passenger side, and opened the passenger door. The creature glared at him with its one good eye like he was the devil. After they stood staring at one another for at least two minutes in some strange human-feline showdown, Nathan gave up. He shut the door, went back to the driver's side, and started the engine.

"You piss in my car, and I'll throw you out."

The whole ride over, the stupid cat whined and moaned like it was being taken to a slaughterhouse. He pulled into his parking spot and opened the door. He scrambled out and held the door open.

"Well?" Now it went silent. "Fine. Spend the night here."

Just as Nathan was closing the door, the animal darted out and curled itself around his leg. Damn, the beast purred. If tonight couldn't grow any stranger, the critter followed him inside and silently leaped to his one and only chair like he/she owned the place. It circled twice and then laid down. If this cat had fleas ... Given the state of its fur, he was sure it did. When he got closer, the damn thing hissed at him, and then swished its tail and curled onto its side. Okay, the Queen or King or whatever it was wasn't going anywhere.

Shit. He stepped backward, almost afraid to turn his back on the cat. He closed the door behind him and shook his head in the empty hallway. He was losing his damn mind, or perhaps his good mood piqued a hidden Good Samaritan gene. The thing might try to claw one of his eyes out in his sleep, but he'd be damned if it crapped in his apartment. He sure as hell could have used a guardian angel himself while behind bars, so what the hell. He found himself back at his car. If 7-11 sold engine oil and pot scrubbers, surely they carried cat food and cat litter.

18

Nathan raised his face to the sunshine and tuned into the water slapping the side of the pier. A seagull cry mixed with the laugher and chatter from the café across "Ego Alley," the skinny channel way that separated the land and the pier he and Starr were sauntering down. Annapolis was one hopping place. By the size of the crowd, it was a wonder they'd snagged a spot in the parking lot.

Starr squealed. "Look at the size of that one." She pointed at a gleaming white yacht.

They'd watched at least a dozen schooners, yachts, and boats that cost more money than he'd make in a lifetime, sail by, tack at the end, and come around for another show-off sail by.

Her gaze followed its glide. "I bet you could sleep ten on that one."

"It'd be a tight squeeze. Looks can be deceiving. Six of us spent a week during spring break on one of those boats. I'm shocked we didn't throw each other overboard by the end."

He hadn't thought about that in so long. His life had been divided in two—before incarceration and after. "Before" was a blurred Monet painting, overwritten with the hard, disjointed lines of a Picasso.

"When was that?" She hooked her hand in his arm as they made their way down the long dock.

The touch was unexpected and genuine and lit up his insides like a Fourth of July celebration. "Long time ago. University of Maryland."

"Oh, right, mechanical engineering. Must have been nice there."

He liked that she remembered that detail about him. "Yeah. Hey, let's sit at the end." He held up the picnic she'd put together in a small duffel bag. Next time, he'd take her to one of those cafes across the thin waterway. She wore a pretty sundress, and she'd look good sitting in one of those little café chairs sipping an iced tea. Like a model.

"It must be ten degrees cooler here than Baltimore." Starr twisted her hair up into a messy knotted bun. "I swear I could live here, by the water. Baltimore's harbor is nice, but …"

"Nothing like this one, huh?"

They let their feet dangle off the edge of the dock and put the picnic stuff between them.

"Thanks for coming with me, Nathan." She threw him one of her signature smiles, and his chest threatened to bloom damn hearts and roses like those stupid cartoons. Since they'd kissed, he couldn't stop thinking about her lips, which, just like her hands, were softer than anything he'd touched in years.

She squinted out over the inlet. "I like watching the boats. Wondering where they've been, where they're going."

"Around the marina. Rich people don't want to be too far away from their assets."

She bumped his shoulder with her own. "So cynical."

"Nah, just been around."

"Well, if I had all the money in the world, I'd live on a sail-boat." She arched her back, her face raised to the sky.

He could see it. Starr wearing tight little shorts and a t-shirt, hoisting up a line with enthusiasm, the strands of her hair, red, now streaked with gold in the bright sun, twirling in the breeze—like it did now.

"With a lot of sunscreen, of course." She pressed a finger into her arm and watched the brief impression pink up.

"Need more?" He pulled out a bottle tucked into the side of the bag.

"Nope, I'm good. The SPF 100 is doing its job." She sighed. "I'll bet if I sailed around the world, I'd finally get a tan, though Phee says it'd just be my freckles blurring together."

A strange sound bubbled up in his throat. Oh, a laugh. "That's one thing I haven't had trouble with."

"See? Men get it all. They tan. They age better than we do." She pulled the bag closer and unzipped it. "And they can eat twice as much as we can. Hungry?"

"Starving."

"See what I mean?" She mock-punched him in the arm.

Being with her on a date wasn't exactly like he'd imag-ined. It was better, more relaxed. She handed him a sandwich on white bread with a telltale piece of yellow cheese and ham sticking out. Yeah, normal. None of those three-bean-quinoa-crap salads and artisanal bread he'd seen behind glass cases on his one-and-only trip to the Gourmet Foods Market.

He bit into the sandwich. "This is good."

"Not gourmet, but ... " She shrugged.

"I'm more of a white bread and Velveeta cheese guy anyway."

She pulled out a little Tupperware container. "You don't

like sweet relish in your potato salad, do you?" She raised an eyebrow at him as she handed over the container.

"Uh, no." Honestly, he couldn't remember. "Haven't had any in a while but it sounds great."

"Oh, good, then I can see you again. Why anyone wants to make potatoes sweet, I'll never know." She fished around for two forks and some napkins.

After the first spoonful, he decided to add potato salad to his food list and get off his fast-food diet. They ate in silence, gazing over the water. The slapping of the oily, salty water against the dock beams was calming—soothing even.

She brushed her hands together. "Can I tell you a secret?

The woman changed the subject like no one's business. "Sure."

"Promise not to tell Phee or Luna?"

"Promise." He barely talked to the girls anyway.

"Good. I feel like I need to tell someone. I got into the University of Maryland, but I didn't go, and I never told my sisters."

His mind whirled, trying to do the math. How old was Starr anyway? Could they have been there together? If he'd met her, would things have been different for both of them? "Why not?"

"If they'd known, they'd have made me go. I couldn't leave them."

"You're close."

"Yes." Her eyes softened as she gazed out at the horizon. "Our mom died young. Dad couldn't handle it, and he got abusive. We had to protect one another."

His protective instincts did what they always did around her—raised their fists.

"I've done a lot to keep us together. Even paid off my dad once to stay away."

His hands curled around the end of the dock so they'd

have something to do. If a woman had to pay a man to fuck off ... Well, he wasn't a man. He was a parasite. Nathan shook his head, not knowing what to say.

"Still can't believe he took it." Her legs swung off the edge. "They don't know all the details, and I need to keep it like that. They have enough on their shoulders with our history. But now Luna has gone and hired a private investigator—"

"She did what?" Man, that was one ballsy move.

"Yeah. And Stan—he's the P.I.—actually found him. He's in rehab in Rockville. We went to see him."

"You did what?"

She cringed because, of course, he'd practically yelled. "Sorry." He hung his head a little, curled his fingers into the wood even more. "You're not going back, are you?" It took some effort to soften his voice.

"No way. So, there, you have a secret of mine."

"Your secret is safe with me. Thanks for telling me." He meant it. Even knowing more about her past, it only made him want to curl her body into him more.

She looked over at him. "Would you tell me something? A secret, I mean."

He scratched at his beard, the one he hadn't shaved today because, hell, yeah, he was going to grow it back out. Starr liked it. "Sure."

"About you going to prison. I mean ... how it happened."

Just like that, his appetite and good mood deserted him because he liked this girl, and he was now going to have to tell her the worst about his life. Her anger he could handle. Hell, even hate. But, her fearing him?

He glanced over at her, read in her eyes that she really wanted an answer. Shit, his back began to ache, and he stretched his neck as if that would buy a few seconds. He ripped a piece of his sandwich off, threw it into the water, where two ducks paddled furiously to fight over the scrap.

"This stuff doesn't scare me." She stared at him so hard he felt it in his bones. "My father went to prison."

An invisible boa constrictor started on his ribs. This woman should be around good men, not guys like that.

"And, it's not like I haven't been friends with people who've landed there, too. For God's sake, Shakedown is … " her voice trailed off. She faced the water, shoulders nearly up to her ears.

"Shit," he muttered. "Starr … " What would he tell her? "I'm a murderer" didn't exactly roll off the tongue. He'd killed a man, for Christ's sake, and he, himself, might die given the stampede starting inside his chest. The scars on his skin he could live with, but these humiliating anxiety attacks? Worse.

She squinted in the sun. "You said Ruark MacKenna wasn't a good man, so that means the brother was—"

"Worse. They're … " Fuck, his heart thrashed inside his chest. "The worst kind of people," his throat managed to get out. "Look, I went to prison for a long time. I did something I wish didn't happen, and it was nine years of never being able to let my guard down, so I have trouble dealing with shit sometimes."

He threw his last bite of a sandwich into the water; his appetite vanished along with his earlier peaceful mood. He jumped to his feet, needing to stand.

She scrambled to her feet, her dress catching a slight breeze. "Maybe I could help."

Help. What could she do, really? He couldn't really take care of her, couldn't get her one of those boats that kept sailing by, which was exactly what she deserved.

"I only asked because Ruark MacKenna felt I should know. I understand how men work. Always trying to one-up one another. Well, I thought, you telling me, and me showing you it doesn't matter, sticks it to him a little, ya know?"

A stupid laugh broke from his throat. "You are one of a

kind, Starr." Because, honestly? It would feel better to be the one to tell her.

"I don't like being in the dark. That's all." She moved closer to him. "And, I want to help. I really like you."

He cleared his throat, more to punch down the rising tightness. "I've liked you since I first saw you."

"But?" She raised an eyebrow.

"But I couldn't act on it because I've still got stuff to deal with, stuff that makes it hard to see a way forward with someone as respectable as you. I get these anxiety attacks. And I want you safe …"

She inched even closer, her scent reaching his nostrils. "I just thought you were shy. But you should know I don't scare easily."

He huffed out a little air at that. "I won't involve you in my mess."

"Or you don't want to get involved at all."

No, he didn't, because the more she knew, the more she'd get drawn toward the darkness that the MacKennas brought.

She broke eye contact and gazed out at the water. "Sorry, Nathan. It's just been a crappy week, and I tend to push when I feel control slipping … I don't know. I'm sorry. Forget it."

He only wished he could forget. She helped there, reminding him of who he used to be—concerned more about passing grades and getting laid and how to get out of Sunday dinners at his folks. Stupid matters. Peaceful things.

Shit, he'd give anything to be that guy again—mostly for her.

Instead, he stood on a dock holding himself together, knowing he was just a few words away from unleashing a firestorm in him. He didn't want to admit this weakness—not to this woman who stood there all clean and full of sunshine and who, quite frankly, needed him to be strong. But truth was, if there ever was a time to man up, this was it.

So he just let it out. "I was working for Declan while at school. Daniel MacKenna, he … " There, he'd said his name.

She tilted her head at him.

"He and his family got into business with Declan. You know he used to sell antiques, high-end shit? He was kind of famous for it. I moved crates for him, basic stuff. One day, a crate busted open. The MacKennas did import-export, only what they were importing and exporting—"

"Drugs?"

She caught on quickly. "Declan just about blew a gasket when I told him. Using his precious vases and lamps as shipping containers for heroin wasn't exactly the partnership he had in mind. And, then … "

He was going to have to keep going, or he might never be able to tell this story again. "One Saturday night, I was in the back." He could almost smell the sawdust and raw wood crates in the air and feel the weight of the metal crowbar in his hand, cold and solid. "I was opening crates when I heard men shouting. It was Declan and Daniel. Fighting about something. Thought I should go and check it out. When I rounded the corner, Declan was on the floor."

He rubbed his sternum as if that would ease any of the tightness, and open up some room for more air. "Daniel stood over him, adjusting his cheap-ass suit coat." Just like Ruark's.

Nathan ran his fingers through his hair. The dock pitched, swayed. Starr's hand reached out as he tried to right himself. "I intervened. Daniel … "

God he needed to ground himself before the next part. He counted four ducks. Tuned into the rhythmic slap-slap-slap of the water mixed with the din of diners across the channel. Sucked in the salty air mixed with boat fuel. He would not dissolve into the out of control animal that took over his body and mind with ungoverned anger. He could do this—he could confide in this woman.

She squared herself to face him, her eyes wide, those red curls floating in the breeze. "Nathan." Her voice mixed with the slap of water against boats, seagulls, and wind rushing in his ears. "Nathan, don't. You don't have to talk about it." Her hand wrapped around his bicep.

Her touch was all it took for the past to break through.

Memories rained down so hard, he nearly drowned in them. Still, his damn mouth wouldn't stop. "Declan was on the floor unconscious, and Daniel just kept hitting him and hitting him. I tried to stop him. He fell and hit his head." Yeah, after the crowbar in his hand had done its work. "The MacKennas cried murder and … " A crazy laugh bubbled up in his throat.

There was so much blood on the concrete floor, he'd nearly slipped.

"A few weeks later, I was wearing orange in federal prison."

A hand tightened on his arm, and he stumbled backward. It's just Starr, he told himself. *Just Starr.* No one's about to jump his ass, and even if they did, he could take them. That had been the problem—he'd fought back every beat down he'd gotten in prison, and that only made them try harder to kill him.

"I spent a lot of time in the prison hospital because the MacKennas made sure I paid, even on the inside."

She sucked in a sharp breath. "Are they the Irish Mafia or something?" she asked lightly—awkwardly—as if trying to lighten up the mood.

"Worse." His arms and legs started to ache at the memory of the regular, surprise beatings, and sudden solitary confinements. "The MacKennas paid to have me beaten just short of death, gave me time to recover, and then did it again

—for nine years. Well, their plan to inflict as much damage as possible worked. I am damaged." Was he ever, his skin was laced with scars from knives, surgeries on his face, his shoulders, his knees, and his back.

She'd grown still, and her beautiful blue eyes shone in the sunlight. Look at those eyes, he told his brain. Forget the hammering in his heart, the rush in his blood drowning everything else out. Slow his breathing. He would not fall apart in front of this woman.

"You tried to stop him from beating up Declan, and they sent you to prison where you got beaten up? Those fuckers."

His chest ripped open, and with it, the truth. "Because, to them, I'm a murderer." Technically, what he'd done might have been classified as self-defense, and with a better lawyer, he might have made his case, but with the entire MacKenna family pushing for the murder charge ... Well, a man would have had to have been a Rockefeller to go up against that clan's attorneys.

"You saved Declan."

He swallowed hard. "I wasn't prepared and ... " How did he say *"I was too young and stupid to understand relying on a public defender only meant one thing—jail time"* because even thinking it fed the tornado twisting inside his body. He shrugged. "Hey, at least I didn't get the death sentence."

He turned away from her. The madness in his chest was trying to pull him down. He would not let it—not here, not with her.

"But Declan. Didn't he—"

"Try to turn it around? Yeah, except he was in a hospital. Medically induced coma."

"He could have saved you. Testified." Her voice was vehement, pained.

"No one could have saved me from the MacKennas."

"But when you were inside, Declan—"

"Never knew what went down on the inside." He didn't involve the man because what could he have done? Instead, he'd shut down, gone blank, and fought back as hard as he could. His bones had healed. His mind—not so much.

The boards under his feet creaked and groaned. He stood silently, fighting for control, as Starr hurriedly gathered sandwich wrappers and containers and stuffed them into the small bag.

"Let's go." She grasped his hand and tugged gently. She coaxed him away from the end of the pier, not really seeing where they were going. But did it really matter?

19

———

Starr climbed into the driver's seat. No way this man could drive. "Nathan, let's go to your place."

"Can't do that."

No one could breathe this hard and be okay, and his eyes —God, his eyes—glazed over with wild agony and fury. He shook with whole-body tremors, and sweat ran down his forehead as if he was fighting a battle with himself.

She'd caused this. She'd resurrected his pain because she couldn't stand a little mystery. She'd just had to push. She'd had a crappy week with her sisters, and she let it influence her judgment. She was too impatient, always wanting more, right now. Well, she did want something more. She wanted this man, this very good man, to have some peace.

She scooted over to his side and straddled him, cradled his face. "Nathan. Nathan. Is this an anxiety attack?"

He nodded stiffly as his fists curled into the seat edge. "Let me be."

"Hey, look at me. I'm right here." She didn't know if that would help, but he looked like he might explode. What did they say about people about to launch into anxiety? Touching could help, so she touched one of the parts of him she'd thought about the most.

She brought her lips to his, his five o'clock shadow roughening her skin. His breath pushed into her mouth. His lips didn't respond to her kiss, but what else could she do?

"What are ... you ... doing?" His voice halted, the ferocious thundercloud behind his eyes growing.

"If you say you don't want me, I won't believe you, and you promised you only say what you mean." She'd do anything to bring him back to the present, including stripping everything off, right here in daylight, in the middle of the marina parking lot. Make him feel whole—that's what he needed.

She picked up his hand, placed it on her ass. "Feel me. Just feel me."

She startled at a sharp crack against the passenger window and hit her head on the car ceiling. Nathan's fist rose, a line of tiny scars across each knuckle, and those beautiful, pain-filled, soulful eyes widened.

She leaned down and pushed open the car door, easing herself off Nathan's lap. "Officer, I can explain."

"Yeah, yeah. Listen, this is a family place. Just move it along." Could he look any more bored?

Thank God. "We will. Right now."

She circled the car and eased back into the driver's seat. "It's okay. We can go somewhere."

"Starr, I—"

She placed a finger over his lips and kissed him again. "I know what to do." She would fix this.

She eased her way through traffic until the cars thinned on a familiar, private two-lane road.

With any luck, Colonel Brookman, the owner—and longtime Shakedown customer—was traveling and would never see them slip into his private alcove. Her one visit had been an unwise decision, which she hadn't repeated. She turned down the dirt driveway. *Please let him be traveling. Please let him be on the other side of the planet.* She really didn't want to have to push the good Colonel off a dock again just to get away.

"It says private property." Nathan's voice cracked her concentration.

"It's okay. We'll be safe here. I come here a lot." It was worth the lie.

She eased the car slowly down the lane until the trees cleared, and a small area widened to a view of water that lapped gently against a wooden mooring. She yanked the car into park, clicked off her seat belt, and swung her leg over him until she straddled his hips. "Nathan—"

"Please, Starr … Can't talk anymore. Can't."

"No talk." She yanked open the buttons that ran the length of her sundress.

The lines in his forehead deepened. "Why are you doing this?"

"Because you shouldn't have gone to prison, Nathan." *And my father should still be there.* She'd open herself up to this man, a good man who'd lost his life as sure as the MacKenna who'd died.

Nathan's entire world narrowed to Starr. The red hair that fell around his face and teased his neck, the honey taste of her tongue, the fleshy mounds of her ass that molded in his palms like she was made for his hands, was *everything.*

She broke their kiss and his vision filled with the splash of freckles across her nose, this close even more pronounced, more beautiful, if that was possible.

"Nathan." He'd never heard his name spoken so softly

before. His breathing slowed, and his heart agreed to stay in his chest. First, his hands came alive, then the different parts of his body joined in. A fog was lifting from his brain.

His sight drifted up to her blue eyes. Flecks of gold swam in all that sea blue and so much compassion … Her hands tugged at his shirt. Smooth, soft flesh touched his chest. Her breasts billowed over a white lace bra and brushed against him. His heartbeat ratcheted up for an entirely different reason. She'd reached for his jeans. Awkwardly, and with some effort, she freed him from his pants. God, her fingers wrapped his cock. He pushed her back to make space and caught her hand before he came right there.

"I'm too close."

A wicked smile grew on her face, and she reached behind her to the floorboard. She had condoms and rolled one onto him so fast he was momentarily stunned.

It'd been so … fucking … long since anyone had wanted him with such honesty. If he were stronger at the moment, he'd have rolled her off him, pressed her back into the vinyl of the seat, and told her she didn't need to rescue him. He didn't need that at all. What he needed was her.

More red hair brushed his face as she leaned over him. Fabric rustled, and bare flesh touched him. Jesus, she'd taken off her panties. The second she positioned herself at his tip, he hardened completely. She sank down on him and … God, he'd forgotten the mind-blanking power of a woman's inner warmth. His consciousness clutched at the sensation, not wanting to forget ever again.

Rising up and sinking down, she rode him off a frenzied ledge until his heartbeat stopped punching at his ribs and leveled out to a dull thud.

He paused her moving hips, swiped the hair from her face.

A new hunger took over, one that dissolved his anxiety

like sugar in water. His hands rose up her back to the clasp of her bra. He freed her breasts, and after one second to take in all her milky white skin and the pale peach of her nipples, his mouth latched on to taste. Her soft sighs as he licked and sucked fed his courage. His hips began to match hers, pitching himself further and deeper inside her until he was nothing but raw lust and need.

He didn't last long, and when she gave a soft cry, he was cognizant enough for his ego to swell at the sound.

She draped herself over his chest and shoulders, and he held onto her thighs to keep her from sliding off. Her breathy pants were his new favorite sound, one he'd remember for the rest of his life—as well as the feel of her silky skin under his fingers, and the wet warmth that connected them.

She leaned up and put both her hands on his cheeks. "I'll take us back."

"No. I'll drive." His body might be a little wrung out, but he wasn't letting her go, not yet. "Come home with me."

She nodded slowly.

No more of this falling apart. Maybe she was too good for him, but he was going to man the hell up. Let the angels envy all they wanted. This woman was his angel, and the MacKennas could go fuck themselves.

20

———

Nathan woke with a start when a soft hand came down on his chest. A quick glance at the clock, and he rose to his elbows: 10:00 a.m.? His head hit the pillow again. He'd slept hard and for more hours than he could recently recall. He turned his head, and the slide of fabric under his ear sounded too loud.

"Morning." Starr's sleepy eyes scrunched up as she smiled at him.

What day was it? Sunday? No, it was Monday. He twisted his neck to stare at the long crack that ran the length of his ceiling. Yesterday came back in a set of fuzzy mental post-cards. The salt air, watching boats, and then driving. Starr on his lap, his cock buried inside her. Traffic and the familiar scent of his apartment. The streak of a cat running across his living room, and hot, hot water bathing his body.

He had been in the shower with Starr. The palest, smoothest skin he'd ever seen had been under his hands, and then in his bed. In the dark, his mouth had run over every centimeter of her pliant and willing body. They hadn't talked. They hadn't needed to. Making love to her the second time—

this time in a proper bed—was better than he could have imagined.

"Hungry?" The bed jostled as she sat up and pulled fistfuls of bedsheet to her. He ached to reach out and touch the pale swell of her breast peeking from the side of the bedsheet. She took it with her, and the sharp hit of air conditioning pebbled his skin. Okay, now he was awake.

Starr dragged all the fabric through the bathroom door and yanked it inside just before she shut him out with a soft click of the door. Did he mind? How could he? Midnight Starr had spent the night with him. Fuck, under him.

The bed jolted as a ball of fur pounced on his legs. With delicate prances, the cat made its way up to the pillow vacated by Starr. After circling twice, it stretched out and claimed its spot. Jesus, his world had grown surreal.

The bathroom door opened, and Starr stood in the doorframe in one of his t-shirts that skimmed her mid-thigh. "I'm thinking pancakes. You have mix?"

He'd be lucky to have coffee. "Uh, don't know." He swung his legs to sit up and the room tilted. Oh, yeah, post panic attack headaches were the worst, but it'd clear once he downed half a bottle of Ibuprofen.

She wound her hair up into a ponytail, and the edge of the faded cotton t-shirt rose up and threatened to give him a glimpse of what he still could not believe he'd had last night. "I'll find something."

Just like that, she was out of the bedroom and headed toward the kitchen. The cat jumped off the bed and followed her out.

After brushing his teeth, downing four Ibuprofen, swiping his hands over his unruly hair, and throwing on jeans, he found Starr in the kitchen in front of his stove. Something sizzled, its yeasty scents close to heaven.

He eased himself down on the stool at the counter.

"Guess I had pancake mix. Who knew? Those first few weeks after my release were a blur." He'd never opened the cabinets. Who knew what was in them.

The beep of his microwave sounded. She pointed toward it with her spatula. "And syrup, which is a good thing because pancakes without it are not worth the calories." She opened the microwave and pulled out a bottle of syrup he didn't realize he had. "Luna taught me this trick. Keeps the pancakes warm if you make the syrup hot." She ran her finger over the open bottle top and brought it to her lips. The small slurping sound she made as she sucked the sticky syrup off her finger made him harden. The cat made plaintive sounds as it circled her bare legs, competing for her attention. *Get in line, cat.*

"You hungry, precious?" She'd adopted an adorable little girl voice.

He rose, got out a can of cat food, and after opening it, set it before the cat, who attacked it with its usual gusto.

She reached down and ran her hand over the cat's back. "What's her name?"

He shrugged. "Don't know. Haven't gotten around to naming it. Honestly didn't know it was a girl."

"How about Moonlight?" She leaned down more, got close to its ear. "Would you like that, little girl?"

The cat's tail twitched, but it kept at the little tin like a starving beast, the bottom of the can scraping along the kitchen floor until it got stuck under the counter. Starr kept running her hand down its spine.

The scene made his insides wobble. For one second, he imagined this was his life now. One of them would cook breakfast. One of them would feed the cat. Normal people stuff had been so far off his radar for so long, they might as well be in a *Twilight Zone* episode.

Moonlight looked up at Starr, licked her mouth, and Starr returned to petting her, which amazingly, the cat let happen.

"You're a cat whisperer," he said.

"Nah, animals are just like people. You be nice to them, they'll be nice to you."

If only that were entirely true. Perhaps to Starr it was. "I'd say you're special. That cat's never gotten near anyone."

"She goes near you."

He chuckled, and didn't that loosen more inside him? "I was the closest thing to food."

"I had a cat growing up. I wonder whatever happened to Snow White?" Starr's eyes grew distant but then cleared, and she went back to the sizzling pancakes on the stove. Nathan never had grand life goals, but this morning, the way she jutted out her hip in his t-shirt, in his kitchen, making breakfast, a cat rubbing against her perfect legs, his world became clear. He wanted this morning every day.

She scooped four pancakes onto a plate and set it before him.

"Smells great." After dousing them in the warm syrup, he picked up a fork and attacked them. They were probably the best things he'd eaten in weeks. "Do you need to call your sisters? I mean, I think you all live together, right?"

She leaned against the counter. "Yep, three-bedroom apartment with three baths. We're never giving it up for that reason alone." She pushed the syrup bottle toward him. "Eat up. There's more."

"You're not having any?"

"I never eat in the morning. Feeling better?" She put a glass of milk in front of him.

The concern in her eyes rubbed at him. "I'm fine. You?"

"Fine."

Shit. They'd reverted to polite talk.

She ran her finger along the syrup bottle cap. "So, about last night."

Here it comes. The moment where she says "tell me more ... "

She came around and settled on the stool next to him. "So, I'm just going to ask. Um, you don't think I'm easy, do you?"

He nearly choked on a forkful of pancakes. He took a swallow of the milk. "I would never think that."

She relaxed, and her palpable relief irked him. This woman should never have to worry about being *easy*.

"A man should have to work hard to be with you. If anything, I'm going to have to up my game." He took her hand. He needed to feel her skin, to connect.

She curled her fingers into his. "Good. And, thanks for sharing everything with me yesterday. You don't have to talk about it again if you don't want to. The past can be hard. I should know. So." She stood and wrapped her arms around him. "Since you told me yours, I thought I'd fill you in a little bit on mine."

Did he want to know? A buzzing in the bedroom grabbed his attention. He half welcomed the interruption since they were about to veer into conversational territory he wasn't sure he was equipped to deal with. Talking had not worked out too well yesterday, despite Starr's compassion. In an odd turn, what she'd done was a salve on his ego—like maybe *he* was worth fighting for. Wasn't that a kicker?

He turned to pull her between his knees. "Okay. I'm listening."

"It's not pretty."

"But you are." He tucked hair behind her ear and let his finger trail down the side of her neck.

She blushed a little, which made him harden even more.

His stupid phone buzzed again. Someone wanted him —badly.

"You need to get that?" she asked.

"One sec." He rose to answer the damn thing.

"Hey man, sorry to bug you on your day off." Trick's voice was the last he'd expected to hear.

"S'okay, what's up?" He headed over to the large window in the living room.

"Have a bit of a problem. Someone rammed their Crown Vic into the club's front entrance."

"No shit." He scrubbed his hair.

"The cops are arresting the guy as we speak."

"Drunk?"

"Worse. Sober as a nun."

21

Starr pulled out her phone. She needed to check in with Phee and Luna, though from the way Nathan paced, his fingers raking through his hair, she'd have to make it quick.

"You still with Nathan?" Phee did not sound happy.

Starr huffed. "Well, good morning to you, too."

Phee had answered her text last night, announcing she was spending the night at Nathan's with "you sure you want to do that?" followed up with "sleep with the light on." Starr hadn't answered. Phee's suspicious nature was justified given her past, but she'd crossed the line with her last message.

"Coming home?"

Starr eyed Nathan, whose pacing hadn't abated. She'd overheard something about truffles? Joyeux la Monde? Wasn't that the restaurant Ruark MacKenna had suggested?

"Hello," Phee sang.

"I'm here."

"Well, you need to come back. Guess who's been calling? Our sperm donor. Luna gave him her phone number. Want to take a wild guess what he's been calling about?"

Starr turned away from Nathan and walked deeper into

the kitchen area. "Did he outright ask for money?" That's all he'd ever reached out to them for, those first early years when they were still kids—at least until he'd fully disappeared, thanks to her final deal with him. "Why is Luna even answering?"

"Why has Luna, or for that matter you, done any of this?"

Things were getting worse between them. Nathan's voice also rose, but he soon killed his call.

"Okay, look, I'll be home soon, but I have to do some things—"

"Like what? You and Nathan playing house now?"

What was up Phee's butt? "Oh, better. We're going house shopping today. Jesus, Phee. Lay off. Just ... things. We're taking care of a cat." By the look of the fur on her belly, or rather the lack of fur on her belly, she needed to get Moonlight to a vet, stat.

"A cat? We've got bigger things to worry about."

"Later, Phee. Around" —she waved her hands in the air to no one— "four. We'll talk then."

She ended the call.

So their father had started up again. Shocker.

Nathan's head swiveled her way. "Someone ran a car into Shakedown's front entrance."

"You're kidding me, right?"

"Nope. But it'll be fixed. Declan will call everyone later. Let us know what it means."

"We might close?" That would suck money-wise, but having more time off could be nice, especially now.

"No, nothing like that." He shrugged himself into a t-shirt, stretching it across his pecs.

Yeah, time off with Nathan would be very nice indeed. She wanted to kiss every scar on his magnificent body. He hadn't been kidding about the damage done to him, and it maddened her to the core he'd suffered such obvious violence. She knew first-hand how it changed a person.

"Hey, you ever have a truffle? I gotta pick some up from some French restaurant," he said.

"Ick. They're Phee's favorite. Declan's put them on the menu for her, hasn't he?"

"He's got a thing for her."

"He does." She rolled her bottom lip between her teeth.

His fingers dug into his scalp, then his arm dropped by his side. "Men do crazy shit when they're into a woman."

"So do women." She stepped forward until her body was flush against his. "They heat up syrup for pancakes."

His Adam's apple bobbed, and his jaw loosened a bit. The tension around his eyes softened, and he *almost* smiled. He did that only around her, and it felt so good to know she mattered to him.

Fur rubbed against her ankles. "Hey, if I can get an appointment, will you drop me and Moonlight off at the vet's while you go and get the truffles? She's got a skin problem. Then pick me up later?"

"Later."

"Yeah. Unless you have stuff to do."

"I can do that." He pulled her closer into him. The feel of his hard body soothed her jagged nerves. Nothing bad could happen to her when she was with this man. He'd fight for her.

"How do you know what the cat's problem is?"

"Some things are just obvious." Like how his heartbeat thumped through the thin cotton and made her own heart ratchet up.

"Well, I was convinced she was a he, so it's probably not a good idea to rely on what's obvious to me." He shrugged.

God, he was cute, in a scruffy, gruff way. She held out her

hand. "Come on, cat lover, you're going to get some truffles and Moonlight some cortisone cream."

His hand engulfed hers, the warmth and rough calluses comforting in an odd way. This was the type of guy who'd barricade the door for you if anyone tried to do you harm—unlike the man who'd fathered her and her sisters.

Nathan wouldn't abandon his kids, that was for sure. He'd laid his past out for her yesterday and, if anything, it showed how much he stuck up for people. But he had burdens on his shoulders like an ox yoke. Maybe it wasn't such a good idea to pile on more with her crappy past. It made her think of Phee, suddenly. So many past hurts, so much to wade through, but Phee could handle them. Nathan could handle more than he knew, too. She just knew it, but today maybe wasn't the day to test that theory.

He pulled her down the hallway, which was fine by her. They'd shower and get dressed and have a *day* together just like a real couple. "So, what happened at the club?"

His face sobered, and he didn't answer her.

22

After dropping Starr off at Bayside Animal Hospital and Spa, Nathan headed out to pick up the truffles.

He still couldn't get over the cheery girl behind the counter taking one look at Moonlight and declaring they could definitely "fit in a visit for a rescue." Maybe he'd go back to school and become a vet so he could work in a bright yellow room dotted with aquariums in every corner while well-dressed men and women sat patiently in padded chairs either holding a fur ball on their lap or had a dog lying by their feet.

He'd left Starr to handle the paperwork. The forms rivaled a human emergency room visit, including instructions to download their app and the freaking wireless Internet code for the "guest's use" when visiting. He'd turned that nonsense over in his brain on the way to the French restaurant, and got out of the car, still shaking his head.

"You Nathan?" A guy stood outside La Monde Joyeux, which was really a small white house with red gingerbread trim along the wrap-around porch. Restaurants had changed, too, since he got out.

Nathan took the paper bag from the man's hand.

The guy glanced around nervously. "Tell Declan, we're even. That's $200 worth."

Two hundred fucking dollars? For mushrooms? He peeked inside. A decaying earth smell immediately assaulted him.

The guy scrunched his hand around the bag. "Watch it. My boss doesn't know how many I snagged."

He just shook his head and took the bag of smelly things to his car. He eased back into traffic and cracked his window. He scanned his dash to see if he needed gas. Traffic was tough today. Damn, it was already two o'clock, but Starr and Moonlight were going to have to wait a bit longer because he was not driving around with these smelly things a minute more than he needed to. He'd drop off the mushrooms and go to get them after. It still took a good forty minutes to get to Shakedown's parking lot. Just in time, too, because his gut roiled with the smell of truffles.

Eight workmen in hard hats gathered around the debris, two of them holding beams that supported the roofed portico, while another barked orders at a guy holding a drill as he stood on a ladder. Hammering, sawing, and drilling sounds filled the air. Shit, who knew a Crown Vic could do so much damage to a building.

Declan stood to the side, stone-faced, with arms crossed, his face only breaking its trance upon seeing him. "Nathan. Sorry to put you to work on your day off." He marched to him and held out his hand.

Nathan handed him the bag of mushrooms with an unspoken "good riddance." "No problem. Looks like a lot of damage."

"You should have seen it four hours ago. Glass everywhere."

Oh, man. "He got the new front door, too." Declan was

proud of his custom door with an etched glass rendering of a burlesque dancer holding a feather fan.

"I've got another coming, but we're going to have to make do with *that* monstrosity." He pointed his cane toward a red wooden door.

Nathan couldn't help but laugh at how a door meant so much to the man.

"Having a few good days off?" Declan arched an eyebrow. "Hey, hey, easy on that," he called up to a workman. "Nathan, you mind taking these inside to Trick? And wait in my office for me. Got to talk to you." Declan shoved the bag of mushrooms back at him.

He'd leave with pleasure, as a cop car had just pulled up, and he could probably sneak out the back. Just the sight of a uniform set him on edge.

As soon as he stepped inside, a hint of cinnamon hit him. He really needed to get back to Starr. He stepped onto the main floor, and Trick looked up from a spreadsheet spread out over the bar. "You look happy. Finally get laid?"

Yep, everyone here saw too damn much. Though, how would they really know?

Nathan dropped the paper bag on the bar with a rustled plop. "Your expensive-ass mushrooms."

Trick straightened and took the bag. He opened it and took a long inhale. "Mmm. Pretty fresh, too."

Nathan blocked the bag from coming closer in a protest at the scent wafting closer to him.

The man laughed. "Not a fan?"

"You try driving around with those for an hour. Hey, listen, mind telling Declan that we'll talk later?" He jerked a thumb toward the door. "I gotta go."

Declan angrily pushed through the vestibule's black curtain, a cloud of dust from the construction following him inside. "Nathan, my office."

Nathan sighed. Didn't sound like good news.

Declan sat at his desk and sighed. "We've got some information about who did this. It's not good."

His brain clicked the pieces together because "not good" mixed with "a talk" only meant one thing. The pit of his stomach knotted. "MacKenna."

"No. Someone else. But I have friends on the force. My contact here tells me the guy who ruined my custom-made portico got into a bit of trouble with the MacKennas. The guy owed them money, but he got scared and told the police about their threats. It didn't go anywhere—"

"But they found out." Nathan scrubbed his scalp. "If he went after you, he'd be off the hook for his snitching." He was well aware of the drill.

"Someday, they'll slip up."

"Slip up? That means someone has to get hurt—"

Declan's nostrils flared. "I won't let that happen."

"You're damn straight. I'll—"

"No." Declan's eyes slanted. "*You* won't do anything. We'll just keep each other informed. You got that?"

He needed to do something more proactive. He'd love to go after Ruark himself. That was off the table, thanks to his parole status. No, he'd start asking around to see what they'd been doing for the last decade just in case he needed a bargaining chip. And, do what with it? Tattletale to his parole officer? Jesus, he needed better options, and swear to God if his heart didn't stop this yammering he'd yank it out of his chest himself.

"Nathan."

At Declan's sharp tone, he snapped his attention back to the man in front of him.

"You got that?" Declan injected seriousness in every word.

He had great respect for the man, but he was entirely too optimistic about the options before any of them right now.

"Yeah," he said anyway. He rubbed his sternum until he was sure bruises had formed.

"You're one of us, and we take care of our own."

"That's exactly what the MacKennas think they're doing."

The man's eyes sparked. "But we're on the right side, Nathan. Always the right side."

He wasn't sure if he knew what the right side was anymore because the truth was, he had something to lose now, and he wouldn't let them drag Declan, Starr, or anyone else down with him. He'd kill again before he'd let that happen.

23

———

"Okay then, Mr. Baldwin, that'll be $276.00 for the visit and $85.00 for the topical ointment."

Jesus, for a cat. He swallowed. His own medical visit, post-prison, hadn't cost that much—just a $75 check-up at the clinic down the street to appease his parole officer. Never mind his medical records read like a trauma manual.

He pulled out his wallet and handed over his debit card to the cheery girl behind the counter.

Starr held Moonlight lightly and cooed into her ear. The cat's eyes were half-lidded, its bandaged leg hanging over her arm. The vet had described Moonlight's "issues," as she'd called them, and then explained each and every one with startling complex medical terms and a seriousness that'd nearly made him laugh. When did pet care become such a ... thing?

The receptionist then handed him a stack of papers and a small rectangular box with an official-looking prescription label. Big bald spots had been shaved all over Moonlight's back and belly, where the $85.00 goop was supposed to go three times a day. Were they kidding him? He had a job to go to.

"Is that a tattoo?"

He glanced down at a little girl whose arms were so full of a fat orange tabby cat, Nathan was afraid she'd drop it any second, or squeeze the life out of it, given the look of her grip.

"Yep." He turned back to the cheery girl behind the counter.

The little girl tugged on his leg. "Why?"

"Julia, let the nice man get his kitty in peace." The mother grabbed her arm and pulled her to the other side of her as if he were about to abduct the girl. At least he'd been saved from the "why" game.

In the car, Moonlight curled on Starr's lap like the Queen of England. Thankfully, she didn't do her mournful howling thing like she had on the ride over. Instead, the cat dozed as Starr launched into talking about the new show she and her sisters were about to put on. It was better than having to tell her the latest MacKenna development.

"So, what do you think?"

He'd only been half-listening, as the damage to Shakedown's club kept intruding into his thoughts. How would he tell her without worrying her?

"Sounds amazing. You girls plan all that in one afternoon?"

"While I was waiting for the vet. Three-way call." She scratched Moonlight's head. "Get the truffles okay? And how's the car thing?"

"Yeah, and for the record, truffles are disgusting. Declan's got the other stuff handled, but we're not opening tonight. Tomorrow, we'll be back."

Her mouth stretched into a half-smile. "Well, that's good. I'd love to have another night off. Maybe we can get some more dance practice in." She sucked her bottom lip into her mouth.

He had some ideas about what they could do to pass the time, too, and none of it involved dancing upright.

"Man, I should call Phee and Luna. I know they haven't heard." She reached over to get her phone, earning a disgruntled groan from Moonlight. She suddenly leaned back. "Unless Declan wants the excuse to call. Then again … he wouldn't want to upset Phee. Nah, I'll wait, see what he does."

His little Starr was a thinker, that was for sure. He set his elbow on the window edge and ran his finger over his bottom lip. "The furball needs a lot of care. I was thinking. The cat—"

"Moonlight." Starr scratched her head, and the purring grew louder.

"Yeah, well, she seems to need a lot."

"That's okay. It'll be easy. I can show you how to put the cream on so she won't object."

She would object? He laughed. "Yeah, well, ASPCA is up the street and … "

Starr's whole body swiveled to face him, and the cat meowed loudly in protest at being moved. "Nathan Baldwin, do not finish that sentence. We are not taking this cat to a shelter. Dropping her off like … "

She faced the windshield. The temperature in the car had dropped forty degrees.

Shit.

He tentatively reached out to touch one of the cat's paws, and wouldn't you know, it pulled back like he was the devil. He dropped his hand back to the console. "Sorry." He wasn't exactly sure for what, but he'd say it.

"No shelter." Her whisper was hoarse, fierce even, "Just don't even think it."

God, her voice cracked. He took her hand and braced for

her to pull back, too. By the grace of God, she didn't. He let a little silence sit between them, something he probably should have done from the get go, and prayed she wouldn't start crying for real.

Another sniff. He saw in his periphery that she'd turned to glare out the side window. Oh, shit, she *was* going to cry, for real. His shoulders tensed, and his knuckles whitened on the steering wheel. He struggled to feed himself, let alone an animal. That $276.00 plus $85.00 for some medicated ointment was his food budget for a month. What was the big problem?

The light he hadn't even realized he'd stopped at turned green. He eased into the intersection and struggled to say something to fill the heavy silence between them.

Her leg squeaked a little on the seat as she finally turned to him. "I need to tell you."

"Tell me what?" He glanced her way.

Her face had reddened. Tears rimmed her eyes.

He ripped his attention back to the street.

She adjusted a protesting Moonlight in her lap. "You told me your past. So, here's mine. And, no feeling sorry for us, okay?"

His hands gripped the steering wheel, and he slowed down to ten miles under the speed limit.

"When we were nine, our mom died." She raised her hand to keep him from reaching out to her, an automatic reaction he might have for the rest of his life. His hands itched to touch her, hold her.

"My dad tried. He really did. But he lost his job as a welder. We lived in Huntsville then. We went to school in dirty clothes, never had lunch money, and always seemed to be getting hurt. Well, we were. Dad had a short fuse and … anyway. Someone reported us to Child Protective Services. Social Services came, but it wasn't until Phee landed in the hospital that they did anything about it. By the time we were eleven, we were in foster care."

Oh, fuck him. "I'm—"

She held up her hand, shook her head. "Don't say I'm sorry."

He shouldn't have said anything. Hell, he should cut out his tongue. He was rarely on his game, but Jesus, could he have been any denser? If he could swallow back his suggestion to drop off Moonlight at the equivalent of foster care, he'd do it. He hadn't known the extent of her past. And, fuck, he'd gone on and on about his own when they should have just been on a date …

She huffed. "My dad was a full-blown alcoholic, and he wasn't equipped to take care of three girls even if he had been sober. He had these rages, and eventually, the booze became more important to him than us."

Her voice hitched, but her words didn't trail off. Maybe there was more to say. Of course there was. An alcoholic, single father with three girls? He managed to release one hand from the steering wheel to scrub his chin. "That should have never happened to you."

Damn. Where was the guy now? He wasn't dead and buried, so Nathan could get to him. If he was within driving distance, he could easily go find him, which wouldn't help either him or Starr. But, man he wanted to.

She shrugged. "We lost touch with him—at least until recently. What was rough was that we weren't always placed together. Phee took it the hardest. After Luna and I were placed together for the second time without Phee … well, that's when the cycle began. The family that had her was really bad. She ran away a lot. It wasn't until right before our seventeenth birthday that we finally got into a family together. By then it was too late."

"Too late?"

"Phee was … well, anyway … You know L found him in Rockville, and our one and only visit didn't go well. Anyway, that's the story." She nuzzled Moonlight's neck. The cat's eyes remained glazed, and her purrs mixed with growls.

Fuck him, the man was within reach, and he had an unexpected day off. He could … do what? Jet over to Rockville, punch the guy a few times, and land back in jail? *Smarten your ass up, Baldwin.*

He lifted her hand up to his lips and pressed a kiss onto the back of her hand. She had the softest skin he'd ever felt on a human being, and something eased inside him, which was good given his fight instincts were on fire.

"Now you know all my secrets." Her eyes settled on his face.

Trust—that's what he saw there.

His chest ached from holding in his secrets—other ones he hadn't let out. Like he was once married and the MacKennas wanted him dead. Now wasn't the time. Making her feel better trumped clearing his conscience.

The cat yawned, actually yawned. Starr pulled her hand out of his and rubbed Moonlight's head.

She seemed attached to the cat. He could do something for the critter. That might work to raise her spirits. "Hey, I have an idea. Let's go to one of those pet stores. Get her some toys." He'd passed a whole store somewhere dedicated to pet supplies. How expensive could cat toys be?

"Pet Land?" Worried lines around her eyes smoothed a bit.

"Yeah. Pet Land. Do that phone thing and ask Siri."

She moved to square herself more to him and laughed, swiping under her eyes. "Nathan, you take me to all the best places." She grasped his wrist and brought it down from where he was rubbing his chin raw. "You'd make a great boyfriend."

His brain took a few seconds to catch on. He squeezed her fingers as he drove one-handed. *Boyfriend. With a cat.* He could do that. This girl also deserved a protector, and he named himself for the job.

For a full minute, he forgot all about Ruark MacKenna. A full sixty seconds passed—the best time of his life.

24

Nathan pushed open the door of his apartment building, and a wave of heat smacked him in the face. Hades had nothing on August in Baltimore. He was running late, having unexpectedly slept in until Moonlight's plaintive cries jerked him awake. The thing was tearing at its bandaged leg like an alien was trying to invade her body. He figured if she got the stuff off, she deserved the win, so he'd left her to it.

Starr had gone and had left him a cryptic note about needing to run home, a request to meet her there, and her cell phone number. The best part of the note? She'd signed off with an "XO." He'd texted her immediately with an, "I'm on my way," and deleted the part about how she should have woken him so they could have gone together. He wasn't her warden.

He rounded the corner that led to the parking lot.

Ruark *Fucking* MacKenna leaned against Nathan's beat-up Toyota. He shouldn't have been surprised. MacKenna was bound to cross the line and invade his personal space. With any luck, rust from his beater would stain the guy's cheap-ass suit.

"Why are you here?" He was so damn sick of taking his bullshit.

"Visiting old friends."

"Sure you are." He strode to the man, half hoping he'd get clocked so he could at least go to his parole officer with evidence he'd been mauled. Nathan crossed his arms as he stood four feet from him. "Still playing this game."

Ruark pushed off his car and closed the distance between them. "A game? Not a game, and I'm not playing."

"You sure you want to be caught harassing me?"

Ruark dramatically swiveled his head from left to right at the empty parking lot, then turned his mug back to Nathan. "Caught by who?"

"What the fuck, MacKenna? Want me back in prison? Not happening." He had something to live on the outside for, a certain red-headed dancer. This guy wasn't goading him into shit.

"Oh, no." He chuckled. "That would be too easy. I want something far more than that."

"Pound of flesh?"

"More than a pound, my friend. Way more than a pound," Ruark called as he sauntered toward his Porsche, illegally parked in the handicapped spot across the lot.

He'd had enough. He had things to do, like placate Erin and go see Starr. Fuck, Starr. Had MacKenna seen her exit his building? Alone? "Keep threatening—"

"I don't make idle threats." The guy spun to face him, spittle flying from his lips. "You took something away from me. Get ready to lose everything, inmate number 167842FLN."

Nathan charged the man and stopped just inches away from Ruark. The guy scoffed, and he almost snapped-- almost. Fuck this guy. Fuck his family. Fuck the consequences. Showing up here, acting like he knew everything about him?

Ruark grasped his arm before he could land the punch sitting in his fist like an unlaunched rocket. Nathan jerked away from Ruark's hold so violently, he nearly dislocated his arm, and stepped backward, his muscles twitching from head to toe.

One fucking punch, that's all he wanted. He couldn't have it, though, not if he wanted Starr or any life at all.

MacKenna's face didn't lose his smirk, but he released his grip and sauntered to the driver's side of his car. That's when Stu, his building manager, a short, squat guy with a shiny bald head, stepped out of the maintenance truck parked next to MacKenna's Porsche. Before lowering his sissy-suited ass into the front seat, starting his car and pulling out of the lot, Ruark gave the building manager a nod.

"Hey, man. You got a minute?" Stu called to Nathan.

"Sure." Why not? He needed to calm down before seeing Starr anyway, and the worst was over for the time being.

"I hate to do this to you ... " Stu dropped his eyes to the ground.

Yeah, it could be worse. The man didn't need to say another word because he knew what was coming. "What's MacKenna got on you?"

Stu scrubbed down his face. "I've tried to keep it straight and narrow since I got out. Can't go back in, man, but they threatened to have the place searched and ... " He shrugged.

"They'd find something. Yeah, I get it." Man, did he ever.

"Sorry, guy, it's just. Fuck. You got messed up with the MacKennas, and I don't want any trouble."

There was a time and place to fight, he reminded himself. This wasn't it. "How much time do I have?"

"You're gonna have to find a new place at the end of this month. So, I'll ask around for you, okay?"

He shook his head and crossed the lot to his car, lowered himself into the front seat, and slammed the door. He wasn't taking charity from Stu or anyone. But, with any luck, the cat he wasn't supposed to have in his apartment had pissed all over the place.

He'd been fortunate to find even this place to rent. He'd gotten a line from a guy he'd met in prison. *"Go see Stu,"* he'd said. *"He's the manager of an apartment complex and has done time. He'll understand what it's like, and he'll treat you fair."* Yeah, until the MacKenna family showed up.

He waited for anxiety to rear her ugly head. She didn't, so he supposed that was one win for the day.

Nathan started the engine. For now, he needed to check in with his parole officer, didn't he? "Welcome to the fine line of post-prison life," he grumbled to his windshield.

"Jesus, Nathan, you didn't think to tell me all this before?" The tapping of Erin's pen came through the phone.

He sighed and scrubbed the back of his neck. He should have told her before now that the MacKennas were hanging around. He cranked the A/C higher as his car idled in his soon-to-be-ex parking lot.

"We've got a real problem here." The creak of her chair sounded. "Ruark MacKenna is not on parole. He can go wherever he wants. You can't. Stay away from him."

"It'd help if he stopped showing up where I work and where I live." Or his now temporary address.

"You giving me attitude?"

His blood pressure rose. Of course he had an attitude and no ability to swallow any more injustice. How could she not see the obvious? "They're threatening me."

"You got proof?"

"Verbal threats, nothing in writing. He gets others to do the messy stuff. That's how the MacKennas operate."

"Until you have proof, this is going nowhere." Of course she didn't believe him. He was the guy who killed a man. The guy who couldn't fucking defend himself and stay on the outside.

An odd chill broke out over his skin. "One more thing. I need to find a new place to live."

"What's wrong with your old place?"

"I got notice." His head fell back onto his headrest.

"What did you do?"

His whole body numbed, but thankfully his mouth still worked. "MacKenna threatened the building manager."

"He willing to go on record about that?"

He scoffed. "Doubtful." The drugs Stu was likely dealing would be revealed. Again, he didn't have proof, but Stu fit the profile. Nathan understood "profile" now, which disturbed every nerve in his body.

"Then we're finding you a new place to live." A keyboard tapping as fast as a snare drum came through the phone. "Best thing you can do is lie low and ride this thing out."

Ride it out? That's all he'd been doing. The problem was, Ruark MacKenna wasn't about to cooperate with that plan. The guy wanted Nathan to slip up. He just had to figure out how to keep everyone around him out of it when it happened. He killed the call.

He dialed Starr. Her voice would snap him out of the shit cloud that lived over his head.

"Hello."

"Starr." Thank God. "Headed your way." He tried to stay calm. He really did. "And, about Moonlight, she's ours to keep." *Ours.* "I'm going to find a new place—a better place—that allows cats." Man, that rolled right out of his mouth despite the fact he wouldn't have a home in less than two weeks, let alone a place for a cat. "Of course, he can be just yours if you want him," he added.

"Her."

"Yeah, her. Your note said you needed me."

"I was hoping you'd come with me somewhere." She sounded too hesitant, which was not like her at all.

"Of course. Where?"

She drew in a breath and let it whoosh through the phone line. "To see my father."

Shit.

She then explained how she and her sisters had had a huge fight that morning and that she'd "handle the guy once and for all."

This was not a good idea, but something was wrong. Then again, "wrong" was everywhere today. No matter, as he was going with her and would put his body between this "father" and her if it was the last thing he got to do as a free man.

25

Starr stared at the Sunset Home sign that boasted the Lao Tzu quote, *The journey of a thousand miles begins with one step.* What a crock. She turned and waved at Nathan. He'd agreed to stay in the car—with some convincing. She loved how he wanted to fight her battles, but this was one she needed to do alone. He only agreed after she said she'd never be alone with the man, which might have been a lie, but no way would deadbeat dad try something here.

Mimi had met her at the receptionist's desk. "Why, Miss O'Malley, we weren't expecting you."

"He called for me," she lied. "Okay to see him?"

Mimi rocked back on her heels and eyed Starr. "You okay, honey?"

"I'm fine."

Mimi's mouth screwed into a frown, but with puffy cheeks and red-rimmed eyes, she had to look terrible. Her throat ached from choking back emotion, which did not go unnoticed by Nathan. He kept glancing over at her.

Then there was the message from Ruark MacKenna asking her out. First, how did he get her number, and second, like she'd ever speak to that guy again? She should have told Nathan right away. It's just when she woke that morning, his sleeping face had held such beautiful vulnerability. His dark lashes fanned across his cheeks, and for one brief minute she glimpsed what he might have been like back in college—full of youthful hope and trust. Then the scar on his cheek twitched, as if he reacted to a dream, and she'd nearly cried at the evidence of the cruelty he'd endured.

One thing at a time, she'd told herself. First, she'd handle her father. Then, she'd move on to making peace with her sisters. Then she'd fill Nathan in, and together they'd handle whatever was next.

Mimi led her down to the "common room" as she called it. Starr paused in the doorway.

The man who'd fathered them stood stooped over, his hand on the windowsill, gazing out on the lawn in the back.

"Dad? It's me. Starr."

He turned slowly, cocked his head. "I know which one you are." He faced out the window. "You came to tell me to stop calling Luna."

"Yes."

He finally pushed off the window and turned to her. He was shorter than she recalled, and his shoulders curled forward.

"Luna made a mistake." Starr was going to fix this. She had once. She could again. "How much?"

He chuffed. "My straight shooter. You come all this way just for that? To pay me off to go away again?"

Ah, so he did remember their not-so-little deal nine years ago. Her chest tightened over the one and only secret she'd kept from her sisters—until very recently. *I wanted to see him first. See if he was safe to see. Then I was going to tell you. But he wasn't okay. Not by a long shot. Then, we were done with him, which was good, remember?*

She dropped her purse in a nearby chair. "So, you do remember it."

He'd been stone-cold drunk. Kept calling her Cara, her mother's name. Then when he rose from his chair and lurched for her? She'd nearly split his head open with a lamp. He'd ended up sprawled on the hotel's filthy bedspread, spitting mad, yelling he'd call the cops. So she'd paid him off with all the money she had in the world—three thousand dollars. He clutched it to his chest, not a single ounce of remorse evident in his cold eyes.

His head bobbed up and down in understanding. "You never told them, did you? About coming to see me when you were eighteen?"

"Seventeen."

He grasped his chin. "Yeah, seventeen. Luna keeps referencing how you all were still kids, so I reckoned … "

He reckoned? "Yes, kids. Taken away. Split up. You remember, old man. We had a deal to keep the details of our meeting secret." She strode forward so there was only a foot between them. "Luna knows, but you break Phee's heart again, I swear—"

"Furthest thing from my mind." He looked down on his gnarled hands then back up at her. "I hurt you all. A lot. I know that. But I miss my girls."

She managed to swallow back the sharp tingles that threatened to cut up her insides. "You miss the past. Vast difference."

"Don't you? I mean the early days?"

Her skin pebbled as he leered at her. "No. There is no point missing something you can't have."

"I know you want to tell me to go to hell, but don't bother. I'm already there."

She almost said "good," but stopped herself. Hell was too good for him.

He eased himself down to a chair and gestured for her to take the one near him. Fat chance. "Luna tells me you have a boyfriend?"

God, she hated that Luna had told him that. Every detail of her life that this man knew felt like a violation, and she'd be damned if anything about Nathan—even just knowing he existed—got shared with her father. She didn't respond, just glared down at him.

"What's his name? He good to you?" The wrinkles in his forehead deepened.

Just thinking about Nathan, the way he touched her—possessive but protective, tentative yet sure in his desire—loosened the invisible fist clutching at her heart. He was her new benchmark for what constituted a good man. "Very."

"Good. You make sure he is. Don't take any crap." He wagged a finger at her.

God, a thousand invisible snakes crawled over her skin. "You mean like Mom did? The way we did as children?"

His eyes grew watery. "I deserve that. I just … " He studied his hands, then leaned back in his chair. "Men, when they get overwhelmed? They don't always make the best choices. They take things out on the people they love."

"He would never do that. He'd never hit a woman. He'd cut off his right arm before he'd hurt me."

"That's good." He sucked his bottom lip into his teeth, released it. "That's real good. Men who hit women—"

"Or little girls." Her eyes ached from glowering at his lined face.

"Yeah, well, they're the worst. Scum."

"They are."

When he leaned forward, put his elbows on his knees, she jerked backward. Her heart stammered, and a distant memory pounded against her forehead as if it wanted out.

He'd once lurched at her from that stance, hadn't he? More than once.

"I know I have no right to ask this, but I'm going to anyway. I'd like to know … " He cleared his throat. "Well, what it'd take for a chance to make everything up to you. To all three of you. Whatever you want. Whatever you need. I'll do it."

"It's too late." Oh, how she wished Luna hadn't pressed to find him. She wished for so much more than … this. She stepped backward more. "Leave us in peace."

His lids raised, red-rimmed eyes took her in. "Will that do it?"

Stupid tears rose up at his question. She'd seen enough Dr. Phil episodes to know that sweeping him under the proverbial carpet wouldn't erase what he'd done—or its effects. But this? Seeing him again? She stood on the edge of two minds. One part of her wanted to clutch at the opportunity to move on, to hear his apologies, to let her and her sisters finally let go of the past. They didn't deserve to carry around his sins. They deserved to *freely* love—not just love in spite of what had happened to them.

Her other mind wanted to hate him forever because he did not deserve to *ever* be off the hook. He deserved their hate.

Her chest ached from the sheer exertion of holding both of those minds at bay.

One thing was clear. Luna reached for the love. Phoenix reached for the hate. She didn't know what she was capable of reaching for.

She longed for Nathan to be here, his big hand around hers, offering support and comfort, but burdening him with this wasn't right. He had enough of his own nightmares. He didn't need to deal with hers. It was enough he was nearby.

Her father's seat squeaked as he shifted. "I was just hoping we might talk now and again. Give me a chance to apologize a thousand times." He gave her an empty laugh.

She sucked air inside, willed herself to stay in a mental limbo for a bit longer. Truth was, this decision wasn't just hers to make, and she had to stop trying to fix everything by herself. "We three have a pact. We don't make decisions without each other. We stick together."

His hands shook as he raised his hand to his hair to scrub his scalp. "That's right. You three always did."

"I need to go." She turned, but his hand brushed her arm. She nearly jumped out of her skin at the contact.

"Sorry." He wisely dropped his arm to his side. "Can you give El … I mean, Phoenix, a message for me? I want to apologize to her. Luna thought it might help. She said your sister wasn't doing well."

The image of Phee, her body nearly lost in layers of white sheets as machine beeps, and hospital noises played a sick symphony, crowded her mind. It had been that last beating that had launched the final Child Protective Services investigation. Hadn't it? Who could remember the details anymore?

"You beat her until she was almost dead. I doubt there are any words that will matter at this point."

He swallowed hard, and he nodded, short little bobs of his head angled down to the floor.

"Stop calling. Stay out of our lives. That's what you can do for her."

His gaze lifted from examining his hands, and a rush of words spilled from his mouth. "Okay, just tell Phoenix something for me. Tell her, none of it was her fault. It was all me. Tell her she didn't deserve a single second of my sins. If there is a God, I'll make sure he knows, right before I'm sent to hell, that you three kids deserve everything that is good for the rest of your lives."

She refused to shed the rising tears. It maddened her to

the core she might soften on the inside at his little speech, at his obvious remorse. In truth, his words should have given her some relief, as if, perhaps, he understood the depth of pain he'd caused. They didn't.

She turned. There was nothing more to say.

"I'll wait for you all to reach out to me." He chuffed, raised his hands, and let them fall back to his lap. "I'm not going anywhere."

Just as she was passing through the doorway to go back out in the hall, his voice rose a notch. "And, I'm going to pay you back that three thousand."

She paused but didn't look back. She didn't believe him, but she was glad he'd at least said it. "Thank you."

"And for what it's worth, Starr. I never stopped loving you or your sisters."

Her blood simmered. She glanced back at him. "If you believe that, you don't know what love is. My boyfriend. He's the best man I've ever met, and he knows what love really means." She and Nathan hadn't declared anything like love to one another, but she was certain of one thing—should she ever fall in love and have children, it would be with someone like Nathan, a man who'd never put her in danger, not ever.

She scooted out, knowing she would never return. Their father may want forgiveness like people in hell want ice water, but wanting wasn't getting. Her stomach churned like a volcano. She would *not* get sick—not here. From now on, Luna could do what she wanted, and so could Phee. She was done being the self-declared messenger and referee for the three of them.

26

———

Nathan bolted out of the car as soon as he saw Starr falter through those sliding glass doors. As soon as her eyes caught his, she ran to him, which was the only thing he needed to know. Big Daddy inside wasn't so big if he left a woman in tears like those she now shed.

"I hate to cry." Her muffled words into his shirt tore him up as much as the wet staining his shirt. If anyone deserved to unload grief, it was this woman. Between sobs, she described the conversation she'd had with her father. The guy'd had the gall to ask for forgiveness. He'd offered her nothing but words—goddamn *words*. His fists ached from clenching, needing to land a few cracks where they were deserved.

Instead, he cupped her face between his palms. "I'm taking you home. You don't ever have to come back here, but if the urge strikes, I'm coming in with you. Non-negotiable."

She gave him a weak smile and sniffed. "You can't afford to hit him."

"I'll make sure there are no witnesses."

She laughed a little at that, and a sliver of tension eased

inside him. She got in the car, pulled out a tissue from her purse, and blew her nose. She pulled on her seatbelt and focused straight ahead. "I'm ready now. I know you need to get to work, and I do, too." She lifted her cell phone to check the time and let it fall to her lap. "Soon."

He started the car. "Guess what? We're taking the night off."

She rolled her head to the side to look at him. "It will be better if I dance. Otherwise, he wins a little then."

Oddly, he understood that. Anytime their lives were interrupted because of another—like her father, like Ruark MacKenna—the nemesis won an inch. Screw that.

"Okay, but we're making a pit-stop at my place first."

"Oh, right, Moonlight."

"No, babe. You."

He managed to get home fast without getting a speeding ticket. They had an hour before needing to be at Shakedown, so there wasn't much time, but he was spending every second of it making this woman forget everything but him. He lifted her up, pressed her into the shower tiles, and buried his cock so deep inside her warmth that he couldn't imagine heaven being better than this. Thanks to her, he'd discovered sex was a spectacular way of burning off a shitstorm.

Her nails dug into his back, and she moaned loudly into his mouth. God, her sounds could make him come on the spot. He pulled himself out, and she murmured a protest.

"Shhh." He pushed wet hair off her face. He knelt down in front of her, lifted one leg and hooked it over his shoulder. God, she was beautiful everywhere. Her peach-colored lips shone with arousal. He had to taste her. As soon as his lips met her flesh, he couldn't stop himself from devouring her.

She cried out as he sucked and licked her for long minutes. She came on his lips, and he still didn't stop. Darting his tongue inside, he fucked her anew until her moans grew desperate. Until he grew desperate. He rose to his feet and wasted no time seating himself inside her again.

"What do you want?" he growled.

"I want you to fuck me. Hard."

She'd called him a gentleman, but there was nothing gentle about what he was going to do to this woman. With his hands protecting her ass, he battered her against the tiles, grinding against her clit until his knuckles ached at the friction. Stopping wasn't happening though, not until she came again.

When she did, she called out his name—so full of emotion, his eyes pricked. Only then did he allow himself to spill inside her.

Leaving this apartment was going to be damn hard—if he was able to do it at all.

27

Nathan took a swig of ice water and quickly scanned the full crowd. The lights were dimmer than usual, or his eyesight was failing him. Losing the front door hadn't deterred business one iota. He overheard some guy whisper to a girl, "They have gangsters here," as if it were a selling point. By the way she beamed up at him, it was.

Jackie held her hair off her neck and waved her hand toward her skin. "Man, when will this humidity break?"

The heat wasn't so bad. He liked that the large doors on the side had been opened up. It allowed some summer air in the usually stuffy place.

Gabrielle set her tray down on the waitress stand. "If Declan doesn't let me change into flats soon, my toes are gonna start bleeding."

"He said when everyone's good and drunk." Jackie set an entire bottle of Lagavulin 16 on the girl's tray. "Take these to the group of guys in booth twenty."

"Big spenders. Let's hope they're good tippers. Tell Declan I'm totally up for a drink with him later." She winked.

Jackie smirked. "I've run their card. It's good."

Man, the women in this place had some spirit. Nathan shifted his position so he could get a beeline view of the "big spenders." *Of course.* Ruark MacKenna and friends. Nathan moved to the handicap ramp leading to one of the exits. Better to see the entire crowd—and watch the man who just needed to fuck off already.

"Ladies and gentlemen," Miss Cherry Noir slung open the curtain.

"Eyes on me." She prowled the stage. "That means you, too, sweetheart." She pointed to a balding man who nearly spat out his drink. "Oh, yes, especially you." She took careful steps to the edge of the stage and winked at him. Raising both arms, she gave the opening spiel Nathan had heard a hundred times.

"Tonight, you will immerse yourself in a veritable wonderland where the conventional is challenged by the extraordinary. Where wonder and magic are not only real, they're required."

Her voice faded a little as his glare drilled straight into the back of MacKenna's head. The music changed, and the slow roll of drums resonated in his chest. Starr, Luna, and Phoenix stepped on to the stage, one after the other. For their patriotic rumba act, Phoenix blazed in red sparkles, Luna shone in white, and Starr sparkled in a dark blue. They sashayed, all rolling hips and long legs, to the edge of the stage and paused in a pose.

Whistles pierced the air, forks clinked against glasses, and a growing rumble of voices rolled through the room. Ruark cupped his mouth and hooted like a teenager in Starr's direction. Her smile was forced and tight. She might have seen him. The fact the fucker had any influence on her mood, after the day she had? He had half a mind to ask Jackie to replace his drink with gasoline.

"We're watching him." Trick had sidled up to him.

"MacKenna came to see me today." He trained his eyes on Starr. "Got me kicked out of my apartment. I'd say that calls for a change in tactics, don't you think?" The guy had waltzed into Shakedown and was acting like he hadn't just fucked with Nathan's life again, and probably worried Starr.

"Paying customer. Causing no trouble."

"Are you shitting me?" He turned to stare at Trick's profile.

Trick faced him. "Yeah, I am. Max is outside having his Porsche towed. He parked over the line into the handicapped area."

His lips twitched upward at that bit of good news.

His attention followed Gabrielle as she delivered a tray of giant coconuts with umbrellas and fruit sticking out of them to a group of girls who sat at the table nearest to where they stood.

"Bachelorette party," whispered Trick. "They thought tonight was a male strip show. Man, were they pissed when they discovered their $50-a-head didn't include some guys ripping off their Velcro pants. So we're giving them some free drinks."

A bark of laughter escaped his throat.

"Good to hear you can still do that." Trick placed both hands on the brass railing and stared up at him. "Ya' know, forgiveness is a powerful thing."

"The MacKennas don't do forgiveness."

"Talking about forgiveness of self. None of this is your fault."

"Shrink talk."

Trick laughed, but at least he stopped staring at him. "Keep watch on the floor, okay?" Trick patted him on the shoulder and sauntered onto the crowded main floor, periodically stopping to "glad hand" customers.

Over the next hour, Nathan swiveled his head left to right

over the massive floor space and caught the dance acts in his periphery. Phoenix danced her twenty-minute matador act, and Trick, always seeking a way to market the place, sent a round of flaming beachcomber drinks to the front table so everyone could see.

For a few minutes, Gabrielle stopped at a table that blocked his view of MacKenna and his gang of men, and when she moved, he nearly lost his shit. When their acts were done, the dancers often drifted into the crowd to say hello to some of the bigger spenders, but the last thing he needed to see tonight was Starr, standing by MacKenna's table.

Ruark had his mitt wrapped around her wrist.

He was going to burst a blood vessel in his brain.

Starr was in profile, her back ramrod straight. Was she smiling at Ruark? Did it matter? Hell, no.

He darted around a few people, and within seconds, his legs ate up the distance between him and Starr. He caught her under the elbow to lead her away. "Got a minute?" He began to steer her.

"Nathan, what are you doing?" she hissed—an actual hiss. It made him think of the cat he was keeping because of this woman.

By the time they got to the exit, she'd yanked her arm free. Her eyes fired like blue flames. If MacKenna did something, said something ... "Did he threaten you?"

She didn't answer. Just turned on her heel and headed for the backrooms. He followed.

He'd never understand women, not ever, but he'd be damned if he'd let Ruark continue his cat and mouse game with either of them.

28

———————

Starr gaped at him with arms crossed. "Ruark grabbed me when I walked by. I couldn't create a scene on the floor." The cool storeroom did little to tamp down the heat rolling off her body.

Well, so the fuck what. "What did he want?"

"He suggested, again, that I go to dinner with him. He also asked me if I was dating you."

"Tell me you said no."

She cocked her head. "I *said* it was none of his business. He said he could fill me in on some things about you. That if I stayed away from you, there would be rewards for me. Like he wouldn't have to tie me up and throw me in the trunk."

He would kill the man. "What the—"

"Nathan. Stop. I shouldn't have told you."

"More threats. Just great." He scrubbed fingers through his hair. If MacKenna succeeded with his intimidation tactics, he was going to snap the man's neck in two.

She uncrossed her arms. "You don't trust me, do you?"

Well, if that didn't come out of left, right, and center field.

She waited for an answer, one he didn't want to give.

That was the problem wasn't it? He didn't trust anybody. He should have more confidence in her, but she was on Ruark's radar. She was naïve as hell if she couldn't see the danger posed by just standing here with him.

She stepped up to him. She moved all her glorious red hair and adorable freckles so close he was enveloped in an intoxicating cloud of cinnamon and rosemary. "I trust *you*. There's nothing Ruark MacKenna can do to me."

"Starr." He shook his head. While her loyalty moved him to his core, it could get her hurt. "He got me kicked out of my apartment this morning." Yeah, he hadn't told her that yet. "What he could do to you … "

"You can stay with me until you find a better place." Blue eyes blinked up at him.

This was going to hurt like a bitch. He stepped back because he had to break her spell on him. "We need some time apart so the target can be removed from your back, and I can figure something out."

She huffed, crossed her arms. "Sure we should because it's convenient for you."

"Convenient?" He needed to get control of his voice. "Nothing about this is convenient for me, babe."

"Well, then, no. You don't get to dump me using that guy" —she pointed to the storeroom entrance— "as an excuse."

"Excuse me?" He pushed forward, driving her against the wall. "I'm trying to protect you."

She lifted her chin, uncowed. "You think Declan, or Max, or anyone else out there, would let anything happen to me? Screw Ruark MacKenna."

"You don't know him." His teeth ached from biting down so hard.

"Not. Caving." She leaned her breasts into his chest.

He backed off—an inch. "Starr. It's to *protect* you." He clenched his fists to keep from embracing her. One touch and he'd give in to her magic, for that's what she was to him. She was fairyland, paradise, and heaven, all rolled into one. Someone had to defend all her goodness.

Her hands settled on his pecs, and his heart threatened to leap out of his chest at the contact. He knew what she felt like under him now, what she tasted like, how she moaned when he first entered her. Her hands traveled upward until they hooked behind his neck.

"I call bullshit," she whispered. Her eyebrows twitched upward. "Afraid of me?"

"I'm afraid for you. Vast difference." His hands found their way to her waist.

"I don't let the bad guys win, Nathan. Too often, they do."

He yanked her closer to him because he just couldn't help himself. "But next time—"

"There won't be a next time." She curled her fingers into the hair at his temple. "My gentleman, always worried about everyone else." She stiffened her spine. "So. It's time we take a stand. Do you like me?"

This woman was going to give him mental whiplash. "What do you mean?" He knew exactly what she meant. Despite the fact he'd worshipped her body, it wasn't enough. Women liked to hear things, flowering stuff—that much he understood.

"Do. You. Like. Me."

Now her whole body pressed against him. The beads of her corset dug into his chest, sharpening his sense of her form. This woman did not play fair. "Of course I do. I told you that, but I've got so much shit and—"

"I know men, and you're one of the good ones. I won't let them get to you."

He half-smiled at her concern but sobered. She couldn't go up against the MacKennas, but God love her for wanting to. He'd never had anyone go to bat for him. It felt fucking great. And just like that, she'd gotten inside him.

"Thank you for growing your beard back. I like the way it feels against my skin. Especially here." She circled her leg and captured his.

His little vixen had no concept of fair play. "Distracting me with sex?"

"Yes."

Resisting her wasn't possible. His lips came down on hers. He'd had enough talk anyway. His palms couldn't move well over such an elaborate corset, but his hands found a zipper that ran down the back. He used it, releasing the restriction, freeing her perfect breasts.

Her flesh had fabric stripes across them. "What's that?"

"Fashion tape. Keeps the girls in. Don't worry about it."

When Starr unhooked her stockings from the garter belt, dropped her thong, and pressed against him wearing only her high heels, nothing but her mattered. She fumbled with his jeans button. Within seconds, her hands wrapped his cock. He grasped her ass, lifted her, and glided inside.

A slice of light cut into the storeroom. They were half concealed behind the wall of shelves holding cleaning supplies, but not hidden enough. He pulled out and jumped in front of Starr to shield her.

"Christ." Trick had the decency to turn away. "Declan needs you, Nathan."

"Was just taking a break."

He raised one hand, silhouetted in the hallway light. "Yeah, well, you may have a permanent one. We just lost our liquor license."

29

Starr pressed the side of her face harder into Declan's closed office door.

"They were seventeen."

Who was seventeen? Nathan and Declan had been talking behind closed doors for a while. Ruark's name was spoken a few times, so her spying was justified. She did not appreciate being shut out of this meeting by sexist, overprotective males.

A curse accompanied Nathan's low growl.

"Yeah, well ... field agents ... watching ... waiting."

Agents? What kind of agents?

Declan's voice grew louder. *"Comptroller's office. How did those girls get inside in the first place?"*

"Sorry, man. I ... I.D.-ed them at the door." The edge in Max's voice was new, and at least he was speaking louder.

A long string of curses—but from which man?—was followed by a thunk.

"My, my," a deep voice purred.

Starr shot up, and a quiet exclamation burst from her throat. She slapped her hand over her mouth and turned.

Cherry stood with her hands on her hips, looking every inch the queen towering over Starr in her platform shoes.

"You scared the crap out of me, Cherry."

"Mmhhmm. Hear anything good?"

"Not much. Something about a bunch of seventeen year-olds, I.D.'s, and I think Nathan is pissed, and Declan, well, he doesn't share much. Men. They never give enough information."

"Move over and let me listen. I've got hearing like a bat."

Before Cherry could position herself closer, the door opened. Declan's face registered surprise but then he smirked at her and Cherry. "Ladies." He strolled by, his cane punching at the floor. Max and Trick followed their boss.

Nathan paused in the doorway. A wash of red colored his cheeks and forehead as if he'd been running a marathon. To call him pissed off was an understatement.

"Girl, I'll leave you to it." Cherry backed away, and with a dismissive wave of her hand, sauntered down the hallway.

Starr swallowed and grasped Nathan's forearm. "What's going on?"

"Nothing."

Well, didn't that take the cake? "Don't tell me nothing, Nathan Baldwin. Tell me," she prodded.

He ran his knuckles over his beard. "There was a bache-lorette party here tonight. Only they were seventeen and not legal. Field agents from the comptroller's office picked this night to check on things. Too much of a coincidence for me, but Declan's got a plan."

Oh, wow. "What?"

"Starr." He grasped her waist as if to pull her into a hug.

She slipped free. "Don't Starr me. Just tell me."

"It was a MacKenna setup. Had to be. Declan has some hefty fines to pay, but he got an attorney. That's all he needs."

Little lines circled his eyes and his words dripped with fatigue.

"If Ruark has a line into teenagers, that makes him both evil and a pervert."

Nathan burst out laughing, instantly cooling her irritation and worry. She liked hearing him laugh. He had a good one.

"The good news is that the suit filed by the kid who grabbed you on stage has been settled."

"See?" She mock-punched his arm. "Declan always handles it."

Nathan's face grew too serious. "The problems have just begun, believe me."

"Well, that settles it. You're coming home with me." She held up a finger to silence any protest he might dare to utter. "I'll be safer that way."

He cocked his head, a long pause settling between them. "Well played, Midnight Starr."

"Oh, we're going to play all right. You started something in the storeroom, and I'm not a quitter."

"Just so you know, I was coming home with you no matter what." He moved closer and slid his hands around her waist and across the small of her back. His fingers massaged either side of her spine there. Lordy, that felt amazing.

"I'm better with my hands than words anyway," he growled.

Need hit her between her thighs, and suddenly, she didn't care what Ruark MacKenna had up his sleeve, just so long as Nathan kept doing that. "So you do like me."

"Yeah, I like you. More than ... I'm hooked." His lips twitched.

"Bewitched?"

"Yeah, that, too. You're ... my North star."

Oh. She didn't need much more of a reason than that to

be attracted to this man when so many others had failed to even earn her phone number. She liked who she was with him: desired, normal but special, not an object but an artist. He respected her.

She leaned in so her cheek could rest against his rough beard. "You sure you want to wait until later when you're off?"

"I'm not sure of anything. Except maybe this." He brought his mouth down just as a loud crackle from around the corner sounded. Joshua, one of the handymen, cursed as he walked by.

"Let's go somewhere more private."

She moved her face to his ear. "Lead the way." She nipped his earlobe, which she'd have to remember he liked because she found herself back in the storeroom, Nathan deliciously grabbing her ass and pounding her against huge wooden crates. He filled every part of her body with an aliveness she'd forgotten she'd lost. This man was good, decent, and oh, so wicked when it came to sex.

She didn't care what the hell was going on in the world swirling around them. Too many people left when there was trouble and then tried to come back into your life when things were back on track. She wouldn't be like that. As she'd told him, she was not a quitter, be it hard times or good.

30

———

Starr yawned and followed Luna into the dressing room. She was not used to being at Shakedown so early on a weekday morning. "I still can't believe we were set up. By a bunch of seventeen year-olds?" Of course, look what she'd done at that age. "At least Declan's still paying us."

Declan had called an all-staff meeting, and it was short and to the point. The club was closed for a bit, but they would be paid, regardless.

Luna blew out a breath. "Thank God."

Despite having a few days off last week, Starr had to admit, being told to take some vacation time wasn't unwelcome news. Maybe she'd surprise Nathan and take him somewhere. They allowed camping in national forests, and it'd be so good to get outside and get some fresh air.

"It was nice of him." Phoenix scooted by them and plopped herself on the stool before her makeup station. "Now maybe we can work on those new dances. I'm so bored with everything we've been doing."

Starr crossed her arms before her sister. "Wait. Did you just say something nice about Declan?"

Phee lifted one shoulder in a delicate shrug.

"Maybe we can go visit Dad." Luna worked her bottom lip with her teeth. "Stop ignoring the fact that he's just hours away."

Phoenix gave an unladylike snort. "He ignored us first. Besides, Starr just did that."

That morning she'd filled them in on her conversation with their father. To her amazement, Phee was happy she'd gone to tell him to stop calling, and Luna was happy she'd gone at all. She'd also delivered her father's message to Phee. Her sister stared blank-faced at her, answered "message received," and then went back to scrubbing the pot she'd been working on at the kitchen sink.

"Phee, it may be time to let go of the anger, ya know." Luna never quit.

"I have let go. The guy said he was sorry, so let's just get on with our lives."

Starr rolled her eyes. "Now who's lying?" She didn't have to be happy about her father's too-late apology, but it would do Phee good to release some of her hatred toward the man.

"Look, just because you're all googly-eyed over Nathan, doesn't mean the rest of us have lost our senses." Phee spread her arms wide in a circle. Costumes hung haphazardly on hangers, and make-up stains decorated her stand. "Look at this place. It could use some cleaning."

Starr groaned. "I'd rather get that show together we've been talking about."

Luna's face brightened. "I agree."

Starr and Phee glanced at one another. Something was up with L. She didn't give up that easily.

Luna's eyes darted from Starr to Phee and back again. "In fact, I have an idea. Promise me, you'll hear me out."

"Of course." Starr nodded.

"No, I need you to promise."

She sighed dramatically. "I promise."

"Good. Let's develop a new show and then debut it in three weeks for all those people who want to come to a place like this but are in recovery. We won't serve alcohol." Her words came out in a big rush. "We could do it for charity. Give Shakedown some good PR. I mean, right after the renovations are finished. It might buy Declan more time in case the license gets delayed."

Starr shook her head slowly, utterly amazed at her sister. The idea was good.

"I know exactly who we can raise the money for. Sunset Home. They are part of a larger network of alcohol and drug rehabilitation centers. We could do it for them."

Phee's lips thinned to one disapproving line, and she plopped down on her stool. "You have got to be kidding."

"You promised to listen."

"Listen, not agree," Starr corrected.

"Why not?"

Phee swiveled her stool and started organizing her makeup. Here Starr went again—playing referee between a justifiably-ticked off sister and a genius-albeit-manipulative sister.

"Starr?" Luna pleaded.

"Is this your way of doing something for our father?" She had to be kidding if she believed her plan wasn't transparent as glass.

"No. It's a way to best him."

Huh. Starr paused and chewed on her fingernail. She had to admit, despite her own fury at the guy, the idea had merit, and it would appease Luna without pushing Phoenix toward her father, or causing Starr to have to deal with him again. It was a compromise in an odd way.

Hold her horses. "Why would a rehab center get involved with a burlesque show?"

Luna crossed her arms. "You know the burlesque world has raised tons of money for causes—many of them medically related."

Starr tapped her lips with her index finger. "True, it would help out Shakedown and Declan, someone being quite generous with us," she emphasized those last few words, staring at Phee. "We won't be dancing every night, so we would have time to choreograph a few new dances. It's actually brilliant."

Luna's face lit up. "I'm glad you think so, because this morning, I got Sunset Home to agree to cut Dad's rehab bill in half if we do it."

Luna, she screamed in her head. Why did she always act first, think later?

Phee swung her stool back around so she faced her two sisters. "I'm not dancing for that piece of shit."

Luna stared straight at Phee and didn't back down. "It makes us look good to Declan and the rest of Shakedown. It's for a good cause, and it might help some families who've been hurt by alcoholism. Like us. It shows we're better."

Never again would Starr underestimate Luna Belle. She sure had balls. "You little Machiavellian strategist."

Luna flounced to the door. "Good. Then I'll go and run the idea by Declan. If he agrees, we're in, right?" She paused in the doorjamb. "Phee? Show him. Show them all."

A long silence stretched out between them. "It will help out Shakedown." Phee stated the words as if attempting to convince herself.

"Yes." Luna chewed on her lip, her voice softened to butter.

Phee surprised them both. "Okay. I'll do it. But only if he does *not* come." She swung away but not before Starr caught a tear rolling down her sister's cheek.

She hadn't seen Phee cry in years. When was the last

time? It had to be that day in the hospital room when she and L. had to say goodbye to Phee. Shivering in the cold air conditioning, they were given five minutes before they were taken to a government office and separated.

Luna reached her hand out, which Starr grasped. Starr's throat closed, but she managed to squeeze Luna's fingers before she traipsed out. Starr didn't have to forgive and forget to do this show. She could rise above it all and do something nice for people who deserved it, like her Shakedown family. But only if it ultimately served Phee.

As soon as Luna was down the hallway, she stepped over to Phee and placed her hands on her sister's shoulders. "Are you sure?"

Phee picked up a brush and yanked it through her hair. "No, I'm not sure, but it seems important to L." Her lashes lifted in the mirror, and she locked eyes with Starr. "I'll do it for her. And you."

That was the best she could hope for.

She kissed the top of her sister's head. "For the record, we are already better than him, we don't need a show to prove it."

Forgiveness started with doing something nice for someone else with similar hurts, or so the stupid Sunset Home brochure had said. Okay, then. Since they were victims of an alcoholic father, it made sense for them to help those like them by supporting rehab centers. Luna really might be the smartest of them all.

31

Declan tapped the top of his desk with his index finger and pushed the notice from the comptroller's office around like he was playing with it. "So, this latest development is not the biggest surprise. I've got legal working on it."

Nathan didn't know what to say so he kept his lips zipped. Trick leaned against the wall, also silent.

Declan, however, was in quite a chatty mood. "You report to your parole officer about Ruark MacKenna?"

"Yeah." He cracked his knuckles.

"And?"

"She didn't tell me to quit Shakedown. Just said to watch it." Nathan eased down into the chair before Declan's desk and scrubbed his hand through his hair. She'd texted him three potential apartments to check out, too—all of them rat holes. "It's going to get worse with them, ya know."

"Of course it is. You give men like MacKenna an inch, they take the whole fucking mile. I'm not having it. Not at my club."

Trick pushed off the wall and stuffed his hands in his pockets. "Anything he does to us makes it easier to put him away." His gaze locked on Nathan. The man's utter calm in this shit storm was oddly unnerving.

Nathan stared down at the Oriental carpet—a piece like that was worth thousands. Declan could lose everything—again—if he wasn't careful. "Nothing sticks to them. They're Teflon. Declan, you know this more than anyone."

"And they underestimate my ability. I've put word out on the street. They have enemies, too, you know."

"Gang war. That what you want to get into?" he huffed.

"No. Let's just say I have friends on the force who'd like nothing more than to nail a MacKenna."

"He's fixated on Starr." Nathan would be damned if his fixation turned into anything.

"We're watching the girls, and honestly, if Ruark's identified Starr is important to you, then she's already in this mess."

Exactly what he wouldn't stand for. "I won't let them near her." He'd ensure even distant relatives of that revenge-thirsty family couldn't get within a mile of her.

"Neither will I. Now, what else do they have on you that I don't know about?" Declan leaned back in his chair. "And don't bullshit me."

Nathan rubbed his hand through his beard. He'd stay and see this out. "You know I have an ex-wife in Florida?"

Declan nodded once.

"Well, I've got a kid, too." He took a second to exhale. "When I got served divorce papers, I released full custody. Signing them was the least I could do. I knew the MacKennas would come for me. Had to leave them out of it." Fuck, he didn't know how to talk about this. Yet, here he was, spouting out words.

"Anything else?" The man's tone was bored, flat.

"My ex doesn't know where I am, and I'm going to keep it that way." At least that way, they'd have a chance to be off the

MacKenna family's radar. Ruark couldn't be in two places at once.

Trick stared down at him. "Given the circumstances, understandable, smart and kind."

Yeah, he was saint material.

Declan's chair righted with a thunk. "I'm sure Ruark would rather go after someone closer."

Like Starr. Was that supposed to make him feel better?

"Here." Trick held out his palm.

"What's this?" Nathan took a key from the man's hand.

"The key to my old apartment. Rach and I just bought a house."

"I can't afford—"

"It's paid up until the end of the year. Rachel hates my taste, so it's fully furnished. Just take it, Nathan, and don't let my plants die."

"Why are you doing this?"

"Because sometimes the good guys have to win." The man's good natured smile wasn't an act.

He scrubbed his chin and blinked back some emotion that threatened his eyes. His fist curled around the key. "Thanks, man."

They heard a rap, and then Max cracked open the door. He stepped in, grinning from ear to ear. "Just heard from my buddy on the liquor license board. Eighteen-day suspension but nothing more."

Declan stood. "Good. Now let's discuss an idea our formidable Luna Belle brought me thirty minutes ago."

32

Starr fingered a canary-yellow jacket adorned in real ostrich feathers. God, she'd missed their costumes. Unfortunately, their tiny closets at home gave them no choice but to move them to Shakedown's warehouse. She pushed its hanger to the side to inspect the military jacket next on the garment rack and caressed it like an old friend.

"Don't even think about it." Phee's voice echoed in the warehouse space, the sound bouncing off the corrugated steel walls. "We need fringe."

"I know. And don't forget crystals, not sequins, or it'll look cheap."

"Agreed."

Phee was less careful than her with their babies, quickly scraping hangers over the metal rod, rejecting dresses, and jumpsuits, and corsets, with a speed that made Starr's inner diva wince. Phee wasn't normally rough with things. Something was up, and Starr's hands itched with the need to intervene, but picking battles you could win was the key to dealing with Phee.

"Please tell me we won't spend all of our time off, working," she said.

"God, I hope not."

They weren't the only ones who thought three weeks allowed major projects to be undertaken. She had hoped she and Nathan could go somewhere for at least a day, but he ended up helping Declan get the club "spruced up." Nathan was putting in sixteen hours days at this point, but then again, so were she and her sisters as they cobbled together as many new dances as they could in the short three weeks.

"I heard Declan is spinning this forced shut down as 'renovations'. The man is smart, covering up the liquor issue with that little message." She eyed Phoenix, who ignored the comment obviously meant for her.

Phee massaged the small of her back. "I'm going to be too tired to dance when we finally do open." She plopped to the concrete floor, stretched out her legs, and brought her forehead down to her knees. Starr would kill for her flexibility.

From her purse, Starr pulled out the list Luna had put together of acts they'd lined up—old dancing friends who'd offered to come in as guest artists—from aerial acts to tango routines. "L lined up a flamenco act. That's always a crowd-pleaser. That brings our total to seventeen dancers. Oh, and we need to add my 'Hey Big Spender' act to the lineup." Starr popped the top off her pen and scribbled on the list. "It's nostalgic, and people love it. Now I need to find that blue corset for it."

She turned back to the garment rack. "Hey, did Aspen Snow ever get back to us? We need those silks acts to break things up. Make it slightly more circus-y."

"If we don't shake some serious ass, the audience won't believe they're at a burlesque show." Phee's jeans-clad knees muffled her voice.

She was right, of course. People would pay $250 a head to

see a show they believed they'd get nowhere else. Look at Cirque Du Soleil.

Phee rose and yawned. "I still don't understand how all this is going to work. I mean, why would Sunset Home agree to have this charity thing pay for any of our sperm donor's bills?" Ever the cynic, Phoenix questioned the need to pay their father's rehab bill.

"Remember that nurse, Mimi? She says they'll make more in the long run. It's good publicity for them, doing something different." Starr snapped her fingers. "Declan said some well-known senator is locked in to come. You know Declan will do anything to ensure our success."

Phee had her usual reaction whenever Declan's name was mentioned. She pretended not to hear her. She stretched her back. "The good senator isn't going to drink for a whole evening? I will believe it when I see it." Phee chortled. "I just hope after all this work, people come. A non-alcoholic show? Who wants to come to that?"

"Hey, what do you say we open the dress rehearsal up to staff? Nathan would love to see us dance when he can actually sit down and watch."

Phee snorted. "Rescuing an alley cat doesn't make up for—"

"Pot, meet kettle, Phee."

Raising Phoenix's juvenile record was low, but her sister's attitude needed to change. Nathan was a decent guy who'd been served a plate of bad circumstances that finally might be turning around. He didn't need Phee's disrespect added onto an already unfair burden, and Phee might show just a little appreciation for Nathan's concern about all their safety.

Since Ruark's last visit to the club, Nathan and Max had alternated nights sleeping at their apartment. On Max's bodyguard watch, she and Nathan hung out at his new place, gifted by Trick. Ruark had disappeared—no sightings, no more messages on her phone for dates. And, dear old Dad had gone silent. Thankfully, on the subject of him, so had Luna.

Tight-lipped, Phee glared at her before she returned to swiping at hangers. She pulled out a black mini-dress, dripping with ropes of gold beads in a waterfall pattern, and held it out to Starr. "This. This is perfect." The beads tinkled against one another as she shook it.

"Pretty." Her mind sifted through past performances and came up blank. "Nathan likes me in gold." She fingered one of the strands—for about two seconds until Phee pulled it back.

"So, this is how it's going to be." Phee's lips pursed, and she smashed the dress to her chest.

Her skin prickled under her sister's cold scowl. "How's what going to be?"

"Everything we do from now on is going to be in relation to pleasing a man."

Was she serious? "That's a leap."

Phee raised her voice and batted her eyelashes. *"I'll be at Nathan's tonight. Would you like to go to dinner with Nathan and me? Nathan likes me in gold."*

Phee's little-girl tone really irritated. She wasn't getting away with crapping all over Starr's happiness. "What is up your butt, Phee?"

"What is up yours? Not everything can be about men."

"Actually, with you, everything is about men, isn't it?" Starr willed her voice to be soft, sympathetic.

Phee's right eyelid twitched.

"I mean … " Her words died in her throat because once that twitch went off, it was gird-your-loins time.

Phee thrust the dress at her and tromped toward the exit.

Blood thumped loudly in her ears, and every nerve in her

spinal cord tingled. She sucked in the dusty air and shouted, "Sisters forever. Friends always."

Phoenix stopped and turned, her back as rigid as the concrete floor. "You're kidding, right? First, Dad, this show, and then … "

Then, what? "No. We were trying to help you." Starr stepped toward her. She would not be cowed, not on this topic. "You think Luna or I would abandon you … us? If you only knew… " If Phee only knew the lengths she'd gone to already for both her sisters.

"Knew what?" Phee's eyes fired.

Starr cleared her throat. "Don't get mad, but … When we were seventeen, I paid him off to stay away from us."

"You did *what?*" Her question echoed in the space.

"Luna had the same reaction."

Phee huffed and sat on a crate, dropping the dress between her knees. "That takes the cake."

She was shocked Phee didn't have stronger words. Instead, she'd stilled, like she'd turned to stone. This wasn't good. She'd seen that frozen face before. It scared her a little bit. Phee's toughness was something she'd counted on. If she'd started giving up …

"You're in love with Nathan." Phee's words were tight, as if it hurt to say them.

Starr swallowed. "Yes, and Declan is in love with you."

"I know. It doesn't matter."

God, her throat had constricted so it hurt to suck in air. "Why not?" She'd never asked before, first out of respect for her sister's privacy—they had so little—and then because she knew she'd never get a real answer.

In a millisecond, Phee's eyes glassed over. She blinked. The tears filling her eyes overflowed and ran down her cheeks. Had she ever seen Phoenix cry as much as she had lately? Was any of what they'd been doing helping her?

"You want to know why I won't go out with Declan? I'd only hurt him in the end. I'm … damaged."

Oh, God. Just like Nathan …

She really believed she was so damaged she didn't deserve a good man. Their father didn't deserve the second chance Luna was pushing for, but Phee did, and more. She didn't know what else to do, so she let instinct take over. She jogged to her sister, threw her arms around her, and held on. One little shake from Phoenix's shoulders and Starr's own eyes too filled with tears.

"No, you won't hurt him. You're better than that. Phee, you have so much love to give." Starr breathed in the familiar scent of her cinnamon-scented shampoo. They all used it. "Yes, I'm in love with Nathan. I don't know how far things will go, but there's one thing I know for certain." She pulled back and held her sister's gaze, her hands cupping her shoulders. "No one—and I mean no one—will ever separate me from you or Luna again. Not Nathan, not Dad, not Declan. I won't let it."

Phee didn't say anything.

"Believe me." Why would she, though? Of the three of them, Phee'd had it the worst. "This Dad thing? You don't have to spend any time with him. Okay? You don't even have to dance in this show." She meant it.

Her sister just nodded.

The fragility of the delicate frame under her hands scared her. Her sister's attitude had made Phee seem larger, more physically imposing than she really was.

Phee swiped under her eyes. "Just hormonal, that's all." Her eyes cleared, and she swallowed hard, but at least her features were no longer frozen. "I won't let *him* take dancing from me. He won't take anything from me ever again."

She wouldn't let Robert O'Malley take from her again, either. "Hey, how about we find those blue salsa dresses? The ones with the angled fringe and the mass of crystals here." Starr ran her hand over her left shoulder and over her heart.

Phee's mouth twisted upward. "Much better. The salsa dresses would work for all of us."

"We're triplets. We pretty much look good in the same things." She bumped her shoulder against Phee's.

"Some things look better on you." Phee walked back to the garment rack and began swiping dresses left and right.

"Like gold?" she teased.

Phee's hands stilled, but she didn't turn. "Like love."

Starr got it. In fact, maybe she'd ask Nathan to marry her. Her life wasn't going to be about men, but it might have room for one man.

33

Of all the MacKenna-forced changes in his life, moving into Trick's apartment was the easiest. He'd woken up that morning plastered to Starr's back, which was all the incentive he needed to start something. He'd flipped her over to find sleepy eyes glazed with hunger, just as they'd been every morning that week. Where they'd lived or slept didn't matter anymore. What mattered was she was with him.

"Please, Nathan."

He circled his finger between her legs. "Please, what?"

"Fuck me."

He pushed a finger into her, and she groaned.

"But more."

"You want more?" He curled his finger inside her.

"Yes, like that, like you love me."

He grinned. *Oh, hell yes.*

He withdrew his finger, captured her wrist, and pulled her arm up over her head. Her delighted gasp made him harden to steel. When he pitched deeply into her, she blew a puff of air in his ear and whispered, "Oh, God." Fuck, he hoped he'd never get used to her tight clamp around his cock, his body instantly filling with warmth everywhere as if he'd been lit up from the inside.

He nipped her neck just under her ear, which earned him another satisfying cry. He picked up the pace. Her hips met every thrust. It was her signal to go harder and faster, and God, he loved that he knew she had signals.

Her lips locked on his. She keened into his mouth as he took her over the sweet edge of oblivion and then followed.

During sex, she was loud, and he liked it. She held nothing back, not her love of sex, not her stubbornness to keep seeing him even though she shouldn't. They'd had some rip-roaring fights about separating, one out on a public street. A woman walking by had offered to call the police on him. He hadn't noticed before, but, women, strangers, came to each other's rescue as if sisters in arms. He'd never paid attention, but then he'd never been in love before. There'd been no love in his marriage.

Both of them panting, he eased himself off her and took a moment to let his skin cool. It would have been the perfect time to say those three little words: "I love you." He really needed to just spill. He drank in her profile as she stared up at the ceiling.

"Starr, I ..."

"Shhh." She raised a finger. After a minute, her eyes cleared, and she smiled at him. "I was running choreography in my head."

He chuckled. She was never far from the stage, even one minute after sex.

She turned to her side, head on arm. "I keep forgetting this one part, so I'm running it a lot up here." She pointed to her forehead.

"That help?"

"Absolutely. Hey." She leaned up on her elbows, her

nudity on full, uninhibited display—a trait he adored in her. "What time is it?"

"Ten."

"Shit." She'd kicked at the sheets to climb out of the bed. "I'm going to be late."

His hand fell to the pillow. "You need to wait for me so I can go with you."

"What for? Declan has every bouncer on overtime guarding the place."

"That's only when you get there. I'm driving you."

"Overprotective male." She leaned down and pecked him on the nose. "I kinda like it. Now that Declan is reopening, we're going to be busy tonight."

Thank God. The eighteen-day suspension Declan endured had Nathan's shoulders and back aching every night from rearranging furniture. While the girls practiced for their show, he and every other muscle guy employed by Declan helped workers with every job conceivable. They switched out a broken railing, put up new mirrors in the bathroom, and moved the newly reupholstered chairs and booths around. The place looked the same to him when it was done, but Jackie had squealed about the new "nouveau beaux arts" look or some shit.

Starr stretched her arms to the ceiling. "I am so sore."

"Too much practice?"

"No such thing." She leaned backward.

"It looks like your show's going to sell out."

She grunted at the tingling in her shoulder. "It was the *Baltimore Sun* piece. Thank God for Declan's contacts and the Fitzroy Hotel." She dropped her arms.

The number of tickets sold had required a larger venue, so the show had moved to the old hotel next door, which would only add to the ambiance. The ballroom had been witness to a mob murder back in the prohibition era. Declan wasn't happy about Shakedown not getting the gig, but he capitulated when he learned he got top billing. He brought in special rigging to the Fitzroy for the aerial acts, half of which were paid for by the hotel, grateful for the renewed exposure they were getting. They donated hotel rooms to the out-of-town acts, which helped Starr and her sisters sell out-of-town performers on appearing. With no liquor to buy, most of the tickets sales could easily cover the ballroom rental and produce a tidy profit —stuff Trick went on and on about that was all Greek to him.

She nudged Nathan. "You getting up?"

"Hey." He grasped her around the waist before she darted away. "How about a shower together first?"

"Only if we make it fast."

"I like it fast."

She giggled, pushed him off her, and headed to the bathroom. She paused in the doorway, her hand resting on the frame. The light silhouetted her curves. "Well?" She laughed. "What are you waiting for?"

"I love you." Maybe the words leaped out because they'd sat on his tongue for too long. "I mean—"

"You do?"

His heart did that hitching thing whenever near her, not anxious just ... alive. "Yeah. I do."

Her eyes twinkled with a happiness he couldn't have dreamed of. "Good. It sucks to be in love alone." She slipped into the bathroom.

He sat on the edge of the bed for a minute, half imagining her response. When he heard the rush of water, that was all he needed to rise and go to her. *She loved him.* Holy shit. It would take a miracle for them to ever leave this apartment again.

The shower proved to be a fine time to demonstrate how much he loved every single damn inch of her. By the time he was able to turn off the water and let her go, the air was thick with steam, condensation trailed lines down the mirror, and even the tile floor was slick with moisture. He'd gotten lost in her hair, her warmth, and her scent. If this was all he'd ever get in his lifetime, it was enough.

34

———

Nathan could no longer watch the woman swinging on the trapeze. She had a death wish. How she sat on that little bar with a huge bubble of material in pink, green, and white hanging off her backside, he'd never know. But between the delighted gasps and sudden bursts of applause, Nathan's pride in the girls grew. The show's crowd was twice what they'd expected.

Along with huge swaths of parachute silk and gauze to add ambiance, large screen TVs had been set up in four corners so no one missed any of the acts. The incessant horns, drums, and flapping of fabric lost all musicality and dissolved into noise. He should be used to this by now. The club was noisy as hell, but perhaps this crowd's size was getting to him. It was five times the size of Shakedown, and the press of warm bodies made him gulp air as if there was a limit to the oxygen in the room. Or perhaps it was because Ruark MacKenna hadn't made an appearance anywhere in over twenty days, something he should be glad about, but instead, served to increase his unease. The man was planning something.

Nathan wiped his forehead with a napkin and continued to scan the floor. So far, the crowd was fairly tame despite the delighted applause and shouts of appreciation for the acts. Guess the no-alcohol rule helped keep things to a civilized level.

Moving deeper into the vast ballroom, he glanced around as much as he could and marked the exits to either side out of habit. Max roamed the place like a panther stalking prey, his back as rigid as Nathan's felt. Cocktail waitresses hurried between the table rounds. A greasy bacon scent wafted up from a tray Gabrielle held as she scooted by.

He eyed the broad back of a man with unruly black hair, lifting a drink to his lips. A stab of anger pierced his gut. The man turned. He was not MacKenna, so his body stood down —a bit.

With dry ice smoke snorting through its nostrils, Phoenix Rising took to the stage on a mechanical bull. He had to admit it was an impressive act. The next act was the hunter-prey bit Starr had told him about. The stagehands erected the forest of mannequins dressed in safari gear. Nathan had a momentary jolt of fear only seeing Phoenix and Luna take the stage for the act. Starr's idea should include her, but yet she didn't dance.

Instead, Luna and a girl he didn't recognize stalked the stage in undulating movements like sensual birds on a mission. At the end, the mannequins broke apart into individual limbs when the heavy netting dropped from the ceiling to ensnare the predators. Luna placed one foot on the head of one of the captured mannequins and struck a victory pose. The act had the audience on its feet.

Cherry Noir stepped out on stage again as stagehands dressed in black began to pull the captured mannequins off the stage.

"Ladies and gentlemen, especially, you gentlemen. Protect

your loins because our next act is not for the faint of heart. I give you our guiding light ... A woman of vast power and prestige ... Our protector of the valiant ... She will only take you if you are worthy ..."

Cherry really needed to just get to the point.

"I give you ... Midnight Starr." Cherry bowed and stepped backward just as the curtains jerked to the sides.

The stagehands cleared the stage just as Starr stepped into the center light accompanied by the strings and brass opening of *Ride of the Valkyries*. Placing her hands on her hips, she cocked her head and let the crowd take her in.

Fuck him—she was a sight.

Her hair cascaded down her shoulders, half in braids laced with gold and silver threads, and the other half in loose waves. Breastplates covered in crystals, along with armbands, leg guards, and a cape with yards of fabric trailing behind her completed the outfit. Two men stepped out on either side of her wearing black lycra bodysuits and horse head masks. As Starr glided forward, drenched in so much light it made his eyes hurt, the horse people waved the hooves on their hands and clomped their hoof-like shoes alongside her.

"That's my girl." A guy had sidled up to him, way too close for comfort.

"Huh?" Nathan stared at the guy.

Watery blue eyes peered up at him. "My daughter."

His belly curled tight. So, this was Robert O'Malley, Starr's deadbeat dad. With lines across his face, sallow skin, and shaky hands, the ravages of alcohol abuse were evident. Knowing what he'd done to those girls, Nathan wanted to pummel the shit out of him.

Instead, he held out his hand. "Nathan Baldwin." He represented Shakedown, so he'd at least feign manners.

The skin on the man's hand was thin as paper. "Starr's boyfriend."

Someone had filled him in—and it wasn't Starr. That meant one of the other girls might have, like Luna. Shit, this man didn't deserve any of the sisters.

He held on to the man's hand longer than he should have and stared without blinking. "Yes. I'm a lucky man. I get to look after her."

Robert huffed a bit. "Guess she filled you in."

"She did." Only then did Nathan let go of the man's hand. "I'm always watching over her." The message had been sent—and by the look of the guy's face, he understood "watching over" meant protecting her from him.

Nathan returned to watching Starr prance through thin clouds of dry-ice smoke snaking across the stage, giving her the illusion of walking on clouds. She struck a strong, centered, and inhumanly beautiful figure. She always did when on stage, but tonight she was in rare form. His girl really did love the spotlight, and it loved her back.

Robert clapped his hands together and lowered himself to his seat. A sick chill climbed up the back of Nathan's neck at the clear admiration emanating from Starr's father's face. Supporting her, sure, but this guy's eyes roamed Starr a little too intently.

Starr raised her arm, and a lightning bolt shot straight from her arm—a trick of the lights, one he'd seen at Shakedown, but it was still damn impressive. She'd been stressing about this new dance she'd put together for tonight, but hadn't told him a damn thing about it.

As she sashayed with both power and grace across the stage, more lightning bolts emanated from her fingers. He grew so enamored at the special effect, he almost lost track of her costume. Her movements, liquid and fluid, made the glitter move across her ass cheeks and appear to be water sheeting on her skin. *Holy shit. No panties.* Sparkles dusted those glorious cheeks—*naked* cheeks.

His brain inventoried her costume, or rather the glitter and body paint that replaced a costume. The armbands and the guard on her thighs looked like fabric. The rest? Sparkles and crystals stuck to bare fucking skin. He grew dizzy yet strangely stiff, and if those men in the front row didn't stop jeering … *Fuck.* A guy standing a few feet over adjusted his pants, and he nearly lost his shit. It wouldn't be his finest moment to clock a patron during Starr's show.

When Starr finally drifted back behind the curtain, Cherry urged the crowd to acknowledge the act even more, as if they required any more encouragement.

He tamped down his Neanderthal desire to run backstage and throw a blanket over her. She was a burlesque dancer, for Christ's sake. She stripped down to pasties and a G-string sometimes. Since they'd been together, she hadn't done that, and he'd like to think he had something to do with that. So, he stayed put.

He crossed his arms and focused on the stage and other acts—a dragon-slaying number, a mild striptease to an old-time Burlesque song, and a bizarre piece where the woman came out dressed like a burrito. Only when the finale was announced, when all the performers took the stage, did Starr emerge once more. She still wore her nothing-costume, earning a resounding roar from the crowd.

Robert slumped in his seat, but his gaze was trained on Starr. A sick feeling settled in Nathan's stomach. He debated whether he should look for Starr or stay and watch the man. Starr won.

He ambled over to Trick, who stood in the back, arms folded across his chest. "I'm taking a break."

"Yeah, go and see your woman. You've been chomping at the bit ever since she stepped out in all her Valkyrie glory."

Yeah, he owned it. He was being the jealous boyfriend. "She looked good."

Trick eyed him. "She did. Just make sure you're not wearing that face when you go back to see her, okay? She probably worked hard on this thing, and your jaw looks like it might shatter any minute."

He scraped his hand through his hair. "I'm proud of her."

"Make sure she knows it."

He was proud of Starr. It's just ... fuck, he didn't like the way all those men watched her. He didn't like the way her own father looked at her. Of course, he didn't get three feet toward his destination when Max signaled him. He raised a flask. Great. Somebody had snuck in alcohol. At least he got to help throw someone out.

35

Starr's whole body buzzed with the adrenaline rush of a good performance. Her muscles sang. She hummed the Ride of the Valkyries. Maybe that'd be her new theme song. She hopped a little on her standing leg as she yanked off her boot. A dusting of gold glitter drifted to the carpeting. Oh, well. For once, she wouldn't need to sweep it up since any minute, the hotel staff would be hustling them out.

Next to her, two dancers hugged with promises to keep in touch. Others stuffed costumes into duffel bags and chattered away. She'd really missed working with other dancers. Her mind began to spin about how she could convince Declan to hire more acts to give her and her sisters some breaks.

Slow clapping sounded to her right. She straightened and turned. *Not now.* She'd been in such a good mood, too.

Her father's hands, clasped together, shook. Nerves or nerve damage? "Well done. You girls certainly are pros. Beautiful. I mean, really—"

"What are you doing here?" She turned back to folding up

her boots, stuffing them into a fabric bag. "You promised to give us some space."

He cleared his throat. "I know. It's just … I thought I'd come to support you." His hands trembled even more, and a sliver of something like pity managed to sneak inside her.

Starr glanced up, searching for Phoenix, hoping she wasn't in the room. She saw her idly chatting away with the flamenco dancers, and thankfully, had her back to them.

She turned to her father, using her body to shield him from Phee's view. "You need to leave, now. Please."

He simply nodded and backed away.

She angrily finished stuffing her things into her bags—her high vanished, which pissed her off—it was because of *him*. She yanked on a skirt and threw on a T-shirt.

"Did you see Dad?" Luna's voice startled her.

"I did. Did you know he was coming?" She fluffed out her hair.

"No, he didn't mention it. Don't worry. He's headed back to Sunset Home. I just saw him in the hallway."

Smart man. "That's for the best. Remember our deal." She'd finally convinced Luna to just lay off this Dad thing already.

Luna nodded slowly and glanced across the room at Phoenix. "Thanks for doing this. I know it was awkward."

Labeling it *awkward* was weighing his sudden appearance far too lightly. They'd found him. They'd helped pay part of his rehab. Forgiveness and reconciliation could wait—for an eternity if needed.

"Uh, I don't know if you caught it, but I noticed Nathan talking to Dad."

What? Where was Nathan anyway? She couldn't see him in the room. She turned to go search for him in the ballroom and plowed straight into a hotel employee.

"Miss Starr?" A man held out a bouquet of red roses

arranged into a bucket that obscured half of the man's upper torso and all of his head. "These came for you."

"Bet they're from Nathan." Luna waggled her eyebrows.

Starr grasped the bucket, and the man scurried away. She lowered her nose into one of the multitudes of rosebuds. A sweet scent wafted upward—strong, oddly tangy, too.

"I don't see a note." She turned them around, and her fingers grew sticky. A prick lanced her finger. "Ow." She laid the bouquet down on a nearby table, sucked on her scratched fingertip, and blinked. A gummy, red substance colored her hand, and a metallic rust and salt scent, mixed with something rotten threatened to choke her.

"Oh, my God, you're bleeding." Luna scanned Starr's hands, up her torso, and to her face.

Starr's mind blanked as a long, wet, red drip trailed from her knee to her bare foot. A smear of crimson marred the body paint across her arms. "Bleeding? No. I'm ..."

"It came from the flowers." Luna moved some of the stems in the large bouquet. She gasped and stepped backward.

"What is that?" Luna pointed to the hunk of meat inside the bouquet.

A glob of flesh shone under the harsh light. Bile rose up in Starr's throat. She swallowed, afraid to move, or she might get sick.

One of the other dancers swept over in a rush of swishing crystal beading. "Oh, my God. Starr? Are you all right?"

Starr shook her head, and air passed her lips but didn't reach her lungs fast enough. Wrong, this was all wrong. She patted her belly, which only smeared more of the icky substance into the glitter and gold paint.

"A pig's heart." Amber's voice—that was the woman's name—sounded so far away.

"A-a what?" The metallic scent sickened her stomach and

dried her mouth. She couldn't stop looking at the mass of rotting flesh, striped blue in places.

"I worked in a lab once." Amber moved a stem of greenery over with a fingertip. "It's got something in it."

Steely gray spikes peppered the disgusting thing. *Nails.* Her blood-soaked hand flew up to her mouth, the stickiness meeting her lips. She couldn't swallow anymore. She doubled over, and her stomach contracted, as hands—so many hands—grabbed her arms, her back. The floor spun as she hit the rough carpet. Someone had to make the whirling stop.

36

Nathan had enough of this do-nothing talk. "You're saying this isn't a crime?"

"I understand this is upsetting." The cop scratched the side of his cheek with a finger. "No laws have been broken. You can get a pig's heart from any butcher—"

"But not put them in fucking flowers." Jesus, he was pushing it, but the dirty stench of the city with its mix of asphalt, dumpster, and car fumes, only exacerbated his irritation.

The officer's eyes narrowed. "And who are you again?"

Cherry appeared, her height blocking the parking lot light, putting the cop into shadow. "Oh, he's the boyfriend. You have to understand." The uniform looked up at her, given she dwarfed him by a good ten inches. "He's protective," she whispered.

Protective, his ass. Someone got to Starr in a crowded hotel room, and Nathan had spent the last thirty minutes trying to unclench his jaw. Now the place crawled with cops, enough to raise Nathan's blood pressure to artery busting. He wanted them here, and gone, at the same time, and Jesus, his heart began to punch at his ribcage in double time. He had no idea why Cherry still hung around, except she hovered like a mother lion over her cubs.

The cop eyed Nathan, his eyebrows furrowing. "So, who do you think did this ... uh, Mr. Baldwin, right?"

"Ruark MacKenna."

"Why do you think it's him?" The guy at least wrote the name down.

"He's been harassing my employees, Mr. Baldwin and one of our dancers, Miss O'Malley," Declan's voice rumbled between them. "Thanks for coming out, Jake. Appreciate it."

The cop shook Declan's hand.

So, turns out, Declan did have friends on the force, though that wasn't going to matter in this mess. The MacKennas likely had more friends—cops, attorneys, and judges.

"Evidence, Declan?"

"Sightings. Threats. Showing up at my club, which I have on camera."

The cop's face showed real interest for the first time. "Threats on video?"

Nathan ground his teeth. "No. Of course not."

"Ruark couched his words well enough." Declan glared at Nathan—the stand-down message transmitted loud and clear. "Bit of a mouth, but nothing incriminating to my knowledge."

The cop jiggled the baggie holding the small card, smudged with pig's blood, they'd found tucked inside the bouquet. Nathan had snapped a picture of the card for evidence, a gift for his parole officer who he now had to call. *Fuck me, very much.* "Well, whoever it is, we've got a hand-writing sample. We'll run it through, and we'll go see this MacKenna." The cop looked down at his notebook.

"He won't be hard to find." Declan reached into his suit

jacket and drew out his cell phone.

The cop rocked back on his heels a bit. "You know this guy well, Declan?"

"Unfortunately, yes. The MacKennas are well known. Here's a number."

It made no sense that Declan would keep Ruark's number.

A long minute of silence filled the space between the two men as they held each other's stare. The cop finally wrote down the number displayed on Declan's phone. He slapped his notebook closed. "Got to tell you, this is a hard one. I'll let you know if we find anything."

They wouldn't find squat. Ruark was too smart to leave evidence. The handwriting probably wasn't even his.

Jake, the cop, stared directly at Nathan. "Oh, and don't take matters into your own hands. Let us handle it. If the MacKennas have got it out for you and Miss O'Malley, it's trouble. This shows psychotic stalkerish tendencies."

Nathan swallowed the "ya think" and just nodded.

Nathan helped fill the back of Cherry's car with props, plastic bins of costumes, and a suitcase containing makeup, then slammed the hatchback shut. Doing something, while waiting for Starr and Luna to get cleaned up, helped burn off some of the adrenaline.

The girls finally came out to the parking lot, their faces lax and white as if shell shocked. Starr wore a skirt and a simple green t-shirt, and her hands were scrubbed clean. Despite the lines across her forehead and her fingers twisting around each other at her belly, she still looked like a goddess.

She lowered herself to the front seat of Luna's car. Declan leaned down. Murmurs came from their direction. Nathan should be over there, comforting Starr, saying things that mattered, making things better. Instead, the full weight of the unjust situation sat like an anvil in his gut. She didn't deserve this crap he'd brought into her life.

He could get in his car, hit I-95, and head south. Perhaps disappear somewhere out West. Of course that meant he'd be a fugitive. He'd miss his goddamn 9:00 a.m. meeting with his parole officer, scheduled thanks to the text he'd sent Erin tonight at Declan's urging. Nathan was shocked she'd answered. He'd thought she'd see the message tomorrow, he'd go in, and they'd figure it out together. Instead, her message was typical Erin.

<<Tuesday. Nine sharp.>>

In just under ten hours, he'd sit in that metal chair before her desk and listen to all the things he should not be doing, like finding Ruark MacKenna and beating the truth out of him. Yeah, fugitive life was looking real good.

Starr's eyes met his, and the pain living there could have sliced his heart out of his chest. It was pain Ruark had put there. She'd had a fantastic night until he had to ruin it all. He was so fucking tired of that family's hold on him and the people in his life.

His feet finally moved him to where she sat in the passenger seat, her sneakers on the pavement. Her blue eyes focused on him like a laser beam. All those light-filled flecks he'd memorized had stilled, her eyes now red-rimmed and quiet.

He scrubbed his chin. "Starr, I—"

"You don't need to say anything, Nathan. I'm fine."

She wasn't fine. God, he wanted to grab her, crush her to him, but she sat so rigid she might shatter under his hands.

Luna touched his arm, cocked her head a little. "I'll be

over there. Let me know when you want to leave."

The lie he needed to tell rose up quickly. "Max is going to go home with you all. Declan and I need to talk." He just needed a little time to process, maybe talk himself out of doing something royally stupid, like hit I-95 headed south.

Starr dropped her gaze to her hands. Her knuckles turning white from twisting her fingers as if trying to wring out her hands. "I'll wait for you."

He crouched down to her, placed his hand on hers, stilling them. "You need to go home. Rest. You killed it on stage. You've gotta be tired."

Her eyebrows rose in hope. "You'll come to our place when you're done here?"

"I don't think that's a good idea. Max will."

Those little lines around her eyes deepened as her eyes sparked. Her head cocked. "I need you."

Yeah, that indignation in her voice? He knew she wouldn't understand. She didn't realize how evil and fucked up the world could be, how someone might use her to get to him. No matter what Declan had said the other day, he was a fucking liability. It was time to turn his status around, starting with a new plan—one he'd yet to form. Every time he thought about it, he came up with only one solution. Ruark needed to forget Starr existed.

"It won't be forever," he lied. "but some distance—"

"Distance?" Starr's mouth pursed into a hard line, and the betrayal in her eyes gutted him. "That's your answer?" She rose and pushed at his chest with her hands, a shot of warmth arrowing through his spine. This wasn't going to be good.

He fought to keep his spine erect, his breathing steady. "Look, Starr, if you didn't know me—"

"This again? You going to tell me I'd be better off?" A fire that could have melted the pavement darkened her blue eyes.

"Yeah, I've heard that before, remember? Don't you dare. Don't you fucking dare."

Luna sidled up to him. "Max is driving us home and staying." A vision of mountainous Max sprawled out on their couch normally made him laugh, but humor was so far away at this point.

"Good. Nathan is going to join us, too." She reached down to the floorboard and brought her purse to her lap. She fished around in it, pulled out her keys, and pressed them into his hand. "Let yourself in." A sheen of moisture dampened the fire in her eyes, then without warning, she threw her whole body against his chest. "Promise me, you will. *Promise*."

His arms banded around her warmth and all her cinnamon scent. He needed this woman, needed her so much it made his bones ache. Her breath wet the front of his shirt, and her thin arms clutched at him. He could have stood out in the parking lot with her forever, despite her whole body shaking from rage, or fear, or whatever hell was whirling around inside her.

"Not your fault, Nathan." She dropped her head back, her eyes locking onto his. "And if you don't show up, I'm going to break out my inner Valkyrie. We whisk worthy men off to Valhalla, ya know." She curled her hands into his t-shirt.

How did she do that? Turn everything around in five seconds? His hope rose like a tide, and he palmed Starr's cheeks. "You win. Come on. I'll drive the two of us to your place."

Her responding smile lit up his insides. He pressed his lips to her forehead, earning a delicate sigh. Yeah, he was powerless in her orbit. He was a selfish bastard, but a selfish bastard who was going to make this threat of Ruark MacKenna disappear one way or the other. He got her into the maw of the beast. He would get her out—tomorrow.

37

Nathan cracked open the passenger door and helped Starr out of the car. Her sisters had gone with Max. The man had driven like a bat out of hell and had lost him miles ago. Nathan had let them speed away. He'd wanted some alone time with Starr, which amounted to him holding her hand the whole way and not talking. Her eyes were lined with worry, and she kept chewing on a fingernail, which made him worry more. She wasn't one to fret.

The elevator to their second-floor apartment was out of commission, so they'd had to climb the steps. He carried her, and she let him.

With each step up to the second floor, all the possible scenarios to reverse this situation sifted like a dealer shuffling cards. First step up, he imagined confronting MacKenna and trying to strike a deal. Second step up, his mind switched to the bloody image of Starr and her sisters with MacKenna standing over them, knife in hand. Third step, his mind's eye showed him getting back in his car and not stopping until he reached Kansas City. By the time he got to the seventh step, Ruark continued to stalk Starr, and the

MacKennas were following him everywhere he went anyway. His imagination was a dangerous place.

He pushed the apartment door open and stepped into the scent of perfume and burnt toast. Max's legs were sprawled on the glass coffee table, and an old *CSI* television show illuminated his face. Max had put the volume on mute, but the light cast a dull blue and gray over his face. Nathan lifted his chin in acknowledgment and set Starr on her feet.

"I'm going to take a shower, get into bed." She glanced at Max and then back to him. "Come whenever you're ready."

He could use a few minutes anyway.

Nathan lowered himself to the chair just to the right of Max. "*CSI?*"

"Getting things wrong as usual."

Nathan huffed and leaned back in the chair, wide-awake and jittery. They spent long minutes staring at the screen, his eyes stinging from the contrast of the dark room and the bright TV. He soon lost track of time.

"He's not going to stop, ya know." Max turned to face him.

"I know." There was no need to say a name aloud. Ruark may not be physically present, but he was always, some-fucking-how, still in the room.

Max brought his legs down and set the remote on the coffee table. He stared at the carpeting, elbows on knees. "The cops aren't going to find anything on him."

"I know."

"You got a plan?"

"Nope."

Max turned his head to him. "Want one?"

"Like … "

"You've heard about me, right? Used to be a full-fledged member of the Flaming Tides."

One mention of the West-coast gang and Nathan's face

heated. He didn't need more trouble, and why would Max want to revisit any of that anyway? If the man survived an exit from the Tides, he sure as hell wouldn't survive re-entry. Nathan swallowed hard. "I've heard."

"There are always things that can be done. People to handle things for you."

Hell, no. "No, man, I'm not getting involved in any of that."

"You sure?"

"Yeah, I'm sure."

Max sucked on his front teeth for a second, eyed him up and down. "Good answer."

Well, score one for him. "Was this a test?"

Max didn't reply, instead, leaned back, and put his feet back up on the table.

Nathan rose, ready to end this strange interaction.

Max's voice stopped him. "Nathan? Stick with Starr. She's worth it."

She was worth everything, but the universe might not play fair. It certainly hadn't in the past.

38

A slash of hallway light cut over Starr's sleeping form to reveal her wet, red hair spilled out over the pillow and her pink, pale skin bearing no trace of the previous sparkles and glitter. She sucked in air and released a long, wet purr. So the woman snored sometimes. It was cute.

He moved to the window overlooking the well-lit parking lot. His gaze swept the area, the shadows shifting as if alive, his gut on high alert. It turned out his gut was pretty good at identifying threats because in the long swath of trees at the far end stood a silhouette of a person against the branches. A pinprick of light from a lit cigarette floated in the air next to him. "Nathan."

He turned away. Starr's face, half shadow, half streetlight, glowed like the finest porcelain.

He went to her, sat on the bed, and put his hand on her shoulder. "Go back to sleep."

She scooched closer on her side and folded her hands under the side of her cheek. "Are you and Max planning something?"

His Starr always did get to the point quickly—and little

got by her. He tucked some hair behind her ear and caressed the delicate outer shell with a fingertip. Everything about her was impossibly soft.

She nestled her cheek further into her folded hands. "I get you may feel you need to take matters into your own hands."

"No, we have no plans."

"Good." She let out a sigh. "You're sure?"

His girl was smart. "Don't worry, Starr. Nothing's going on, but I'm not going to lie to you. It's damn hard not to retaliate."

"I know it's going to work out." She pulled one of her hands free and laid her arm across his thigh. "Nothing bad is going to happen."

Oh, how he wished he could believe that.

"I've been thinking." She rubbed up and down his leg, which sent all his brain power south. "I've known men like Ruark. They just want to win. What would it take for him to feel like he's won?"

Nathan dropped his head back and stared hard at the ceiling. "My death." He looked back down at her. There. He'd said it aloud even if it did cause a shudder in Starr.

"That can't be all of it. I don't know, Nathan. I feel like something is missing here."

"It's pretty clear. Revenge is a powerful motivator. He wants to make my life, and that of everyone around me, hell."

"I've lived in hell. This ain't it. If that's his endgame, he's being a pussy about it."

Nathan chuckled but instantly cooled. "I can't stand the thought you were ever unhappy, ever in danger, ever afraid. It's so goddamn unfair." He eased down to the bed, sat against the headboard. "You didn't deserve it. You should have grown up like those campground ads. I can see you in a Sunshine Campground T-shirt, sitting around a fire and roasting marshmallows." He grinned. "Or better, in a bikini

—a blue bikini to match your eyes—jumping off a rope swing into a lake, with lots of kids splashing around you, and everyone smiling because it'd never occur to them not to."

"Oh, yeah, me rocking the khaki shorts. Not my best look." She rolled to her back. "Phee had it worse being the super-sensitive one."

She had to be kidding. "Sensitive? Phee?"

"You don't know her. Everyone thinks Luna is the emotional one but, no ... Phee hides a lot." Her blue eyes glowed a little in the dim light. "If you tell her that, I'll kill you."

He laughed. "Your secret's safe with me. She terrifies me. I think Declan's the only one who isn't afraid of her ... next to you and your sister."

"That's because he loves her. And she needs it."

"What do you need? Want?"

"Many things."

"Like what?" He would get them for her.

She moved up to snuggle into the crook of his arm. "I want to be able to dance without men thinking I'm asking for sex. I want my own house where I can grow my own flowers and not wait for some guy to give them to me. And, turns out, like Luna, I want answers. I want to know how my father could do what he did. I want to know how to forget it. I want ... " She let her words die.

"Wow. I didn't expect that answer." He grasped her hand. "I'm sure it was complicated."

"How could it be? He beat one daughter nearly to death and then waved goodbye down a government hallway to the other two? I finally remembered the details—just tonight. After visiting Phee in the hospital, L. and I were taken to this office building. He was at the end of the hall and he just ... *waved*." Her voice was strung tight with tension.

He drew her tighter into his chest. Her face fit perfectly into his neck.

"Being ripped apart from someone you love is terrible." Her muffled words blew heat against his skin. "Feeling like you aren't loved is worse. I don't understand people who give up kids."

His stomach turned over. "Yeah." The timing wasn't right to tell her about his daughter, Madeline. Jesus, he had tried so hard not to even think her name, but there it was.

She pushed back a little, raised her face. "Can I tell you another secret?"

"You can tell me anything."

She rose up on one elbow, the sheet slipping down to reveal those creamy mounds of flesh. "Well, actually, it's more of the same secret I told you in Annapolis, about going to see my father when I was seventeen. You have to promise not to tell anyone. My sisters, especially. I'm going to give them all the details someday, but it's just not the right time."

A chill ran through him at the mention of more secrets. Was there no end to them? He pulled the sheet up higher to her shoulders.

"So, you know I went to see him. He was drunk in an airport hotel in Huntsville. I went to ask him why he'd left us. He just shrugged. Can you believe it? Shrugged." She mirrored the movement.

"I'm sorry, baby."

"That wasn't the worst." She pushed herself up so her back was against the headboard. "He kept calling me by my mother's name. Then he asked about Luna and Phee. Asked if they were still as pretty as me. If we were single." She gave off a visible shudder. "Then ... it was the look in his eye. He ... moved for me."

Her memories were worse than he'd anticipated. He grasped her hand, and she pulled it back. Her irritation had nothing to do with him, of that he was certain. It had everything to do with her past. "God, Starr, tell me, he didn't … " Now he was going to have to deal with the man—soon.

She shook her head. "That's when I said I had three thousand dollars. He could have it if he promised one thing."

"Never look for you."

"Yes. Never find us. Leave us the hell alone." The grit in her voice told him everything he needed to know. There was a good reason she and her sisters landed in foster care. It might have been God's way of preventing something unthinkable from happening.

"And you know what?" She half-laughed. "He took it with no remorse. It was all the money I'd saved since I was fourteen, doing odd jobs and babysitting, and whatever else I could do, so I could at least start college. I left him sitting there, *counting* it."

She turned to him, eyes dry, face still as a stone, just like the long-timers in prison, the ones who'd been on the inside so long they'd forgotten what it was like on the outside.

She grasped his hand, her eyes wide and shimmery in the dark. "I want you to know so you'll understand why I'll never forgive Robert O'Malley. Phee and Luna don't need to know he took everything from me and might have taken more like … " She stopped, as if unable to say the words—words he didn't even want to think like *beaten* or *raped*.

Jesus, if that man had touched a hair on her head, he'd have ended the man's life.

"Nathan, I *never* want them to know what I've given up so we could be safe. They'd wallow in guilt and try to make it up to me, and I don't want that. Promise me you won't tell them. They deserve peace."

He engulfed her hand with his. "I promise, and you deserve peace, too."

"Thank you, and I have it now. With you."

Safe with him? Jesus, he'd hoped so. Fuck, hope. She *would* be if he had to die for it.

She eased herself down. "There, now you know the worst of me."

"You protected yourself and your sisters. That's not 'worst,' baby, and none of that is on you."

"I'm glad you think so. I honestly had put it out of my mind until ... recently." She turned to face him. "Hey, you going to get out of those clothes? I mean, you're not leaving again, are you?"

Never. "Not leaving. Can't leave my North star."

He eased himself up, shed his clothes, and climbed back in, his skin meeting her warmth, his muscles relaxing in a long sigh, the perpetual knot in his stomach uncoiling. In the dark, with touch taking precedence over all other senses, he tuned into her fresh, clean skin, scented with cinnamon.

He nuzzled her hair. "I want you to know something. I do regret killing Daniel."

"Of course you do."

"No, I mean . . . I am really sorry about it, even if he was an asshole." With his arms full of this good woman, he couldn't conjure up any memory of hating anyone that much.

"I know, Nathan."

"And, there are other things from my past. Things that might upset you."

"I'm a lot stronger than I look."

God, he hoped so. He wasn't sure how long he could keep his own secrets from her. "Hey, how about we get out of here tomorrow? Go back to Annapolis?"

She lifted her chin to peer up at him. "I'd love that ... but, hey, you ever been to Gravelly Point?"

Yeah, he had. "Yeah, I've been there. It's fun. Whatever you want."

"Good. Then that's where we'll go." She pulled herself back suddenly. "Where's Moonlight? Where is she?"

It took a second for his brain to catch her sudden change, something she did a lot. "Home. Remember she has a food dispenser."

"But water—"

"Relax. I got this water fountain thing that holds a gallon of water at a time. It's like a little waterfall ... thing." Or whatever you called it.

"Where did you get that?"

"Amazon. Amazing place, I gotta tell you."

"Why, Nathan, you do like your cat."

"She's okay."

"You're good at taking care of things."

He caressed her hip. "Actually, I'm not, but how about I take care of you? Right now?"

Sex wasn't always the answer, but it seemed as good as any right now. She fell to her back, the simple movement the sexiest thing he'd ever seen. She widened her legs, an invitation he'd always accept from her. They weren't going to get any sleep, but who cared.

39

Nathan had to get Starr out of the apartment. She'd had nightmares later in the night. In the morning, her leg bounced as she stared out the window, coffee cup in hand, as if pining for fresh air. Yeah, they had to go. Max grunted his disapproval at them leaving the apartment, but he agreed to stay with the other two sisters while they headed out.

As soon as he pulled out of the parking lot, she brought up Gravelly Point again, the spit of land at the end of the Reagan International Airport in Virginia. Further away than he intended, but he couldn't deny her a thing.

The first hour on the road, he kept watch for anyone tailing him—old habits die hard— but Starr soon distracted him by belting out every Beatles song she could recall. His left ear might never recover from her off-key singing, but it was worth seeing her bounce in her seat, dimples set deep in her cheeks.

Two hours later, he turned into a crowded Gravelly Point park and killed the engine. Blessed silence filled the car—or as silent as one could get at the end of an airport runway.

Starr unbuckled her seat belt. "I can sing the rest of the songs on the way home."

"Oh, good." Nathan opened the door and set a foot onto the pavement, blood reallocating itself in his legs. A flat stretch of grass along the Potomac River, the place looked exactly the same as it had the one time he'd visited years ago. He retrieved a blanket from the trunk. Thanks to the summer air, sweat prickled on the back of his neck.

Starr wasted no time commandeering a spot, snapping the blanket over the crisp, yellowed grass.

The air rumbled. He pointed to the barely-visible end of the runway. "Watch."

Three seconds later, waves of air, thick as ocean water, rolled over him. All sounds were swallowed by the whine of a jet engine as a silver 727 glided over their heads.

"Whoa." Starr hugged herself and crouched a little. He laughed and pulled her closer, his body mass dwarfing the woman. "Closest you'll get to a runway in the country."

Her head fell back, and her glasses slipped to the top of her head as her face traced the path of the jet overhead. "They're so big!"

She dropped her sunglasses back to her nose and grinned toward the sky as the belly of a second plane, a big mother, soared overhead, far slower than Nathan anticipated. A delayed, new wall of hot air, tinged with scents of jet fuel and fetid river brine, swamped them.

They spent a good thirty minutes lying on their backs, watching planes, some larger, some smaller, careen overhead. Some, shockingly close, settled to land on the tarmac about 500 feet away.

She turned her head, her hair catching on the blanket fabric. "I wonder where they're coming from." Her eyes held that wistful, dreamy cast he'd seen in Annapolis.

"Chicago, probably from some endless, boring business trip." God, Nathan sounded cynical even to himself.

"Or back from vacation. In the Caribbean."

"Maybe." She deserved tropical cruises, swanky resorts where they put those umbrellas in giant coconuts. She deserved all that and more. He didn't have money to travel, let alone the permission. *Fuck. Permission.*

He sprang up to sitting.

"What's wrong?" Starr laid her hand on his thigh.

He was in Virginia. He'd left Maryland. Leaving the state without telling Erin was a parole violation. He should have thought of that before promising her a day out. He'd like one day, one frickin' day, where he didn't have to worry about anything—not who he was, what had gone down, and how close he could be at any moment to going back to hell.

His heartbeat clanged inside his chest. The air out here was too hot. The thick, fuel-tinged air could drown a man's lungs.

Yet, how would Erin know? It's not like he wore an ankle bracelet. Maybe he'd tell her when he got back. Wise? Probably not.

Nathan rubbed his sternum. Declan knew they were going out because Max, like an effing babysitter, had insisted he call in before leaving. It was enough his boss knew he was on the loose. He was with a coworker, albeit one he was in love with. He wasn't running.

His clammy shirt pulled across his shoulders.

"Nathan? You okay?" She sat up on her elbows. Great, she was worried about him when it should be the other way around. And, you know what? He was tired of it. God, he was tired of not knowing when the train might come off the tracks. Tired of panic attacks and worrying about what he couldn't control. It made the MacKennas win a little. *Fuck that.* This was going to be okay. Hightailing it back would only create more angst, and he'd be damned if he'd erase that light from Starr's face.

He pulled the fabric clinging to his chest and wafted a little air over his skin. "Fine."

The roar of an approaching plane threatened to drown out any further conversation. Starr's hair fluttered in the breeze, the sunlight lighting up all her red hair.

He stood. "Got to make a quick phone call."

She shielded her eyes from the sun. "Okay."

"Perfect. Be right back." He jogged back to his car, got in, and started it up so at least he had some A/C.

Declan picked up on the first ring. Before the man could get two words out, Nathan confessed his location. Declan didn't miss a beat.

"I'll check in and tell her I asked you to go down there for me," the man said.

He'd lie for him? "You sure?" Not like Declan, but he'd take it.

"I'll handle it." He hung up but called back a minute later. "Nathan, text Erin where you are and say when you'll be back."

"But—"

"Don't argue with me about this little instruction. Just do it."

"Not so little."

Declan's chuckle didn't ease shit inside him.

"Okay, doing it."

The line went dead.

Nathan stared at the phone in his hand for a few seconds, but finally, ever the good ex-con, he did what Declan said to do, and waited for the other shoe to drop and break his foot. When her return text came back with a simple "don't do it again," he had to read it three times to be sure he wasn't hallucinating. Was it possible Erin was letting him off the hook? His fingers dug into the top of his head with his hand. What did Declan say to her?

Her second text followed shortly after. "Strike two."

Okay, he wasn't exactly off the hook, but she didn't tell him to hightail it home, either.

The passenger door cracked open. Starr dropped herself into the passenger seat and threw the blanket in the back. "Too hot. Hey, you hungry? There's food at the marina down the way."

Her hand snaked across his shoulder, and he shuddered. The contradiction of the softness of Starr and the harshness of his life collided so hard, a laugh burst from his throat. "I'm starving." He yanked the car into drive and pulled out.

He didn't trust life could be this easy. Yet, here he was with Starr's hand trailing down to his thigh and his phone sitting in the console with a good message for once. Maybe he was finally getting a break.

The parking lot of the Washington Sailing Marina was full of cars, though he managed to get a spot. A few people strolled along the pier as if shopping for a boat or something. Must be nice to just leave the pier open and trust people would be content with looking at your boat and not trying to steal it. He couldn't remember if he'd ever been that trusting.

"Hey, boats first." Starr tugged his hand. "Then food?" She jogged lightly to the gate that led to the docks.

"My woman has spoken." He ambled after her, easily catching up and steering her toward a historic schooner at the far end. Starr had a different idea, however, and yanked him toward the more expensive yachts. His girl certainly had an eye for the finer things in life.

She stopped, cocked her head, and gazed down at the side of a massive two-story yacht. "*Beauty's Secret*." She glanced up at him. "What do you think? His wife or mistress?"

"Who says it's a man's boat?"

She drew closer to him and laid her palms on his pecs. "Someday, I'll have one of these, and I'll name it *Nathan's Star*." Her head fell back, and he caught her around the waist before she tipped backward.

"Hey! Be careful. You could have fallen in."

She raised her head. "I knew you'd catch me."

Trusting and limp against his palms, he swung her. Her red hair shimmered like molten copper in the sun. His hands, full of her warm, toned body, itched to grab a fistful of all that red while he worked her rosebud mouth with his own and thrust inside her until she couldn't walk straight—until he couldn't walk straight. His desire to claim every bit of her luscious body grew with every second she let him hold her. She pulled herself up, her palms curling around his biceps. "I just love being outside. I'm indoors so much."

"Sunshine and fresh air are highly underrated." He should know.

"Hey, let's go sit on the end." She broke free from his hold, and he followed closely, unwilling to be more than a foot apart from her, her familiar cinnamon scent mixing with the briny air.

They sat at the end of the slip and let their feet dangle over the edge. Airplanes still powered overhead, but they were a distant second to the slap-slap-slap of the water against the pier mountings and the occasional squawking of a bird.

"It must be fun to be the captain of a ship." Starr leaned back on her palms. "I wonder, if things had been different, if my father hadn't been a drunk or my mother hadn't died, or if I'd gone to school—where I would be? Maybe I'd be on one of these boats" —she swung one arm in the air— "or one of those super deluxe yachts in Annapolis."

"I'd like to give you your dreams. I wish I could buy you a boat."

"You would?"

"I would."

She bumped his shoulder with hers "What could I get you?"

"To see a smile on your face would be enough."

A peach stain grew on her cheeks. "My smiles for you are free, and you'll always have them." She held his gaze, just as she had so many times. An overwhelming sense of being trusted filled him, as if this woman would stick with him no matter what.

"Tell you what. I promise someday you'll have an entire fleet." It wasn't a promise he should make, but why the hell not? With her by his side, maybe he could turn his life around, and in turn, hers. She'd had too much unkindness in her life.

Her smile returned. "And my first boat will be named *Nathan's Star*."

If goodness were tangible, it'd be the energy rolling off her right now. He inched closer, as if whatever she had could be absorbed into his own skin.

"Generous of you to name your first boat after me. I mean, talk about pulling a Johnny Depp." He laughed at the puzzled look she gave him. "You know. The actor who tattooed Winona Ryder's name on his skin before ..."

Her face stilled as if he'd shocked her.

Yeah, going down that particular trail was too soon. He got it.

"Oh, don't you worry, Nathan Baldwin. I'd put a ring on it before I'd get the tattoo."

Okay, she shocked him more. A ring. He'd done that once—a hurried affair, picking out the cheapest gold band he could afford. His love for this woman, however, demanded a diamond someone could see from space.

She unfolded her legs and let them dangle once more over the side of the pier.

He could do it. Hell, he'd propose right this second if he had anything to offer except complications. This woman, however, deserved to feel wanted. "No, *I'd* put a ring on it."

She turned to face him and flashed him a wide smile.

Suddenly, he could see himself bending on one knee before her, holding out a little black box. It had to happen someday because for once, he had someone he wanted who wanted him back.

"Tell ya what." He got to his feet and held out his hand. "Next weekend, you and I are going out for a real date." No more of this picnic stuff. Maybe he'd take her to that fancy French restaurant where he'd picked up those truffles. "Now, how about some lobster?"

She took his hand and let him pull her up. She must have liked his date offer because her lips found his with such ferocity he couldn't mistake her earlier meaning. If he asked her to marry him, she would say "yes."

For once, his heartbeat ratcheted up for something other than panic. Happiness—that's what this had to be.

Light streamed in from Starr's bedroom window, which should have woken him up. Instead, it was Starr's hand curling around his hip and gripping his ever-present erection —the one that rose like a flagpole every time she was around. Her hand traced a greedy message into his flesh, and this was a message he could answer.

He turned, twisting the thin sheet around his middle. It slipped down to her waist, exposing her breasts. Starr's body was a gift from God. He trailed fingertips from her rib cage to her waist and hip and indulged the movement a few more times just to feel the satin skin under his calloused index finger. "This might be my favorite part."

"What about here?" She took his hand and pushed it down her belly to between her thighs where his fingers met petal-soft folds shaved smooth. His finger traced the seam, lightly, reverently. Air ran ragged over his lips, and his face found its way into her neck. He had to scent her, breathe her in.

His cock pressed painfully against his belly as it made contact with hers. Yesterday had been amazingly perfect. On their way back from the marina, somewhere between Virginia and Maryland, he'd even figured out a way to get MacKenna off their backs. He just had to get a voice recording of Ruark threatening him. That couldn't be too hard. Where and when and how eluded him, but he'd do it even if it meant he had to hire his own P.I. to follow Ruark around. He wanted an infinite number of days to feel her skin like this.

He pulled back enough for his Starr-seeking organ to find its place. He glided into her, and heard her soft moan rumble through her chest. Hell if his ego didn't take a rocket ride along with his lust.

"Jesus, Starr," he said into her neck. Not even air could circulate between his front and her back as he moved inside her, crushing her to the mattress.

How'd he live before—without her? His love for her smothered all other emotions. The words, "I love you," weren't nearly sufficient to express all she'd awoken in him.

His hand found her breast, and he rolled her nipple between thumb and forefinger until her soft pants grew into louder moans and little begging sounds. He began to thrust so hard she cried out.

"Okay?" His word was nothing but a long, drawn-out pant

"Mmmhmm. Good."

Her legs wound around his. Her hands grasped his ass and pulled and kneaded, and her mouth … Jesus, her mouth was so open and pliable. His mind split, half desperate for his cock to stay buried right where it was, half wanting to pull out and give her mouth a test.

As if he'd said something aloud to that effect—hell, he might have because God knows what was coming out of his mouth—she inched backward. He got the signal. He was being too rough.

"You sure you're—"

"Shhh." In some balletic move, she swung her legs free and pushed him back down to the mattress. When her lips met his cock, the raw, dirty, uninhibited way in which she just threw herself at him made his head explode—both of them. By the grace of God, he didn't come right away.

She sucked him off for an eternity. She teased, pausing, and then starting, controlling his pleasure. He let her have that control because he got it. Prison had fooled him into believing he was barely a man, that nothing was in his control anymore. It was wrong.

He may have been a walking shell when he exited prison, but this woman reminded him of himself, or what he could have been. Sure, he could end a life with his bare hands now, but this woman between his legs? She made him want to *start* a life. He'd care for her, shield her, give her everything, That's what his strength was designed for.

Even as he was coming, she didn't stop with those devil-blessed lips and tongue of hers until he was spent.

She laughed a little, probably at his throaty groans. "Glad to be of service."

He captured her chin in his hand. "You don't think we're done, do you? That's the last time I come before you, ever again." He crawled down to her legs, split her thighs, and showed his someday future wife—for all doubts on that score had been erased—exactly how much he meant what he promised.

41

"I can't believe it's Tuesday already." Starr yawned into her reflection in the makeup mirror.

Luna popped open a lipstick. "Thank God we have a repertoire to rely on. I have no creativity left."

They both could have used more time off, given they'd just put on a show for charity and dealt with a sociopath's insane gesture of a pig's heart, but allowing what happened to interrupt their lives anymore was not happening. She wouldn't let whoever sent that disgusting bouquet to dictate her life. She chalked up her resolve to Nathan and his insulating attention.

The last few days had been a bizarre mix of rest and relaxation and waiting for the other shoe—or pig's heart—to drop. Nathan had been stellar at distracting her with a day trip out of town. He was also a willing participant when she did what "experts" said never to do. They tumbled into bed and went for each other's bodies. Whoever said sex wasn't the answer wasn't getting any, at least not getting anything good, and Nathan was very, very good.

He knew exactly how to settle her nerves. He let her set

the pace but always left her desperate for a little. It was a delicious combination of respect and lust, which until him, she hadn't realized had been missing in her life. Hell, it'd been missing for her sisters, too. They got one or the other, but she was never living without this magical combo again.

In fact, God, please, let them be heading somewhere more permanent. She was not letting this man go, and if she had to drop to one knee and propose to him, she'd do it. Nathan still glanced around like someone was about to jump out at them, but they were surrounded by friends who wouldn't let anything bad happen to them. She wished he could see that. Then again, he'd not had anyone watching his back for far too long.

"Hey, let's go and check out the setup." She grasped Luna's hand. Their hunter act had been such a hit at the charity show, they'd decided to lead with that tonight.

As soon as they entered the hallway, they ran into a familiar friend, a bouncer from the old days of one-night gigs in the clubs up and down the East Coast.

"Amos!" Luna leaped at the heavy-set man who sported more tattoos than Max. "How have you been? How are you here?"

"Right as rain, Miss Luna." Amos gave her a head nod. "Dec called. Said he needed some temporary extra muscle, and when I heard you three were here, well … " He shrugged.

See? Declan had things under control.

They headed to the stage, which was a good thing because the male mannequins were all in the wrong order, and the camo pants were even on backward on one of them. The stagehands must have been messing with them.

Phee plunked her bag down dramatically on the stage, startling her. "Jeez, Phee. You're awfully late today."

"Yeah, well, Moonlight had a follow-up visit."

Starr suppressed a smile. Phee and Moonlight had

bonded the second they'd brought her home. All of Phee's protests about cat hair and cat litter smells vanished as soon as the cat curled up on her lap.

"How's she doing?" Starr asked.

"Fine, and Nathan owes me $85 for more of her cortisone cream."

Luna's forehead wrinkled. "We had a cat once, didn't we?"

"Snow White, but Dad got rid of her." Phee lifted a pair of red, satin pumps. "I picked these up to celebrate our new show. What? I needed them."

"Uh, huh." Starr aimed a smile at her sister. It was okay by her—anything to make her happy. "Oh, I love this." Phee swung her legs up on the stage and stood. She stepped slowly along the row of standing mirrors positioned behind the mannequins, a red shoe in each hand. "Makes the army look larger."

Luna waggled her eyebrows. "More men to capture?" Her phone rang. "Be back. This has to be Max. He's supposed to bring us more dry ice."

When her sister headed off stage, Starr studied Phee. She looked good, lighter somehow. Perhaps now was a good time to bring up an idea she'd been mulling over. "So, what do you think of Moonlight living with us forever?"

Phee glanced at her. "Like move in with us?"

"Yeah. You like her. Or, rather, she really likes you."

She crossed her arms. The two shoes poked out of the side like malformed wings. Her sister was no dummy. She knew what Starr was getting at.

"Why don't you just come out with it and ask me. You want to move in with Nathan permanently, and his apartment can't take cats."

No, let's all get a house together. Something larger where we all can have a floor. That's what she wanted to say but couldn't. There was one chink in her fantasies of marrying

Nathan. Being with Nathan forever meant not living with her sisters.

Luna's stricken face appeared in the mirror between them. Phee and Starr turned her way.

Her skin was too pale, her lips drawn too thin.

"Hey, what's wrong?"

Luna's dazed eyes lifted from her phone. She took in a shuddering breath. "That was Mimi. Dad checked himself out."

For a long minute, Starr wasn't quite sure she'd heard Luna right. Starr stepped closer as if that would sharpen her hearing. "What?"

"They found him face down in an alley. Alcohol poisoning."

He didn't. He couldn't have. A twinge went off in her heart. She'd dismissed him so thoroughly at the show. No, she wouldn't allow guilt to get a hold of her. He chose this. He did this. Her giving him the cold shoulder had nothing to do with his choices.

"Phee?" Their sister stood too still. Her hands clutched around the red satin pumps, mashing the sides together. She turned, stopped at the mirror, and stared hard at her reflection.

Jesus, was she having a breakdown or something?

Luna stared at Phee's back. She took one step forward, placed her hand on her sister's shoulder. "Phee are you ..."

Phee lifted a red satin pump and smashed the pointed heel into the mirror, a million tiny spider cracks bursting on impact.

L. turned to Starr, and she didn't need to say the words for her to get what she was thinking. He'd gotten drunk—and he'd known how to find them. He hadn't come to them—but he *could* have.

42

Words from doctors and nurses floated into Starr's ears and back out again. *Critical condition. Blood alcohol content of .42. No corneal reflex. Breathing tube.* Doctors, nurses, and technicians had thrown an encyclopedia of new words at them every twenty minutes for the last few hours as she and her sisters, along with Nathan and Declan, sat in a waiting room down the hall from an ICU Unit at Baltimore's St. Joseph Hospital.

They'd seen their father twice. His shriveled body lay in a hospital bed, intubated, on a ventilator, with IV lines stuck in his arms. He looked like a science experiment.

She had to stuff down a continuously rising and, quite frankly, *irritating* guilt for her cold responses to him these last few weeks. The flip side of that emotion—sympathy—wouldn't work either. The man didn't deserve her compassion.

The worst part was she couldn't figure out why they hung around and listened to the rush of the respirator, and the constant beeps of the machines: all familiar, terrifying sounds. She couldn't shake those noises from her head even when sitting in the waiting room. The last time the three of them had stood in a hospital room like that was to say goodbye to their mother. No doctors had thrown big words at them then. In fact, no one had talked to them at all.

Of course, there was the last time with Phee, who had refused to enter his hospital room and only agreed to come and sit in the waiting room with her and Luna.

"Here." Nathan handed her yet another cup of coffee. He didn't know what else to do. Hell, none of them knew what to do but sit and wait.

"Thanks." She sipped the bitter coffee and glanced at Phee, who studied her manicure.

L stood by the window, staring off into the parking lot. Declan hovered around her. He knew if anyone broke down, it would be her. After all, Luna had found their dad and then agreed to cut him off—all because Starr had asked her to.

A man in a white lab coat, swinging an iPad in one hand, strode in. "Miss O'Malley?"

She and Luna looked up to face him. He gave them a practiced smile at their identical movements. "I'm Dr. Broadstreet, the emergency psychiatrist on call." He hugged the iPad to his chest. "Any reason to believe your father was trying to harm himself?"

"Probably." Starr's tired whisper caused the man's brow to knit.

"Well, it's just five times over the legal limit has us wondering if this was a—"

"Call for help?" Phee rose to standing. "Trust me. He's just a drunk."

"Stop. Please. Just stop." Luna's face grayed.

Starr pulled her top lip through her teeth and then sighed.

"I see. Well, I'll send a counselor by." The doctor backed away, seemingly nonplussed by their reaction. He'd likely seen it all before.

Luna hugged the back of her arms. "You think he did it on purpose?"

No one answered because no one could, just like they couldn't give the hospital any insurance or billing information, or answer any health-related questions—except he'd been in rehab. It then occurred to her that the people who knew their father best were complete strangers to them, people paid to watch over him drying out. And they'd failed even at that.

Phee picked up her bag and slung the strap over her shoulder. "This is pointless. I'm going home before they come looking for someone to pay the bill."

"I'll take you." Declan pushed up and grasped his cane.

Phee didn't object, which only meant one thing. She had no fight left. Starr bristled a little on the inside. Her sister wasn't one to melt into sentimentality, and it wasn't until that second Starr recognized how much she counted on that, as if Phee's hard edge kept her and Luna from dissolving under pressure over the years. It was oddly a gift.

The maddening injustice of the whole situation hit Starr in a mad rush. He'd been rejected. Now, he was lying in a hospital bed on the brink of death? Vegetative state? Did it matter anymore what state he was in? It was like he was holding them hostage all over again.

Phee cocked her head. "L, you should come with me."

Luna nodded. "I'll come back tomorrow."

"Nathan, Starr, you coming?"

That was the first time Phee had even remotely acknowledged Nathan was part of the group. Starr should have been comforted by that fact, but an unsettled nest of bees droned in her belly.

"Give me fifteen minutes? See you in the parking lot. I'll go and tell the nurses we're leaving."

"Okay." Phee sighed in an obvious why-bother tone.

Starr turned to Nathan as soon as they were alone. "I need to go do something. Mind waiting for me here?"

"I'll go with you." Nathan's hand engulfed hers.

"No, please. I need to do this alone."

He nodded once. "Only because you won't be alone in there with him."

She squeezed his fingers.

She didn't need to tell anyone they were leaving. Visiting hours for the ICU were over, but there was something she needed to do. Declan had pulled her aside earlier, told her not to worry about hospital bills or insurance, that he'd help. His generosity only maddened her more because Declan didn't deserve to be saddled with their father's fuck-ups, but then again, neither did they.

She paused at the nurse's station. A nice man covered in head to toe blue scrubs with a cap on his head smiled up at her. "Miss O'Malley, what can I do for you?"

"I was wondering if I could just pop in for a second? We're all leaving, and, well, I wanted to give my father a message before I left."

He squinched his eyes. "Okay, but just for a second."

He escorted her down the hall, darkened for the evening hours but still with too much light for anyone to get any real rest. An anxious quiet mixed with the incessant beeps and rhythmic wooshes and thumps of ventilators.

They paused in the doorway. "Hey, Jean, Miss O'Malley here wants to tell her father goodnight."

Oh, if he only knew.

"Just for a second." The woman's face was mostly covered by a facemask, but Starr caught the stern and admonishing message in the woman's eyes.

Whatever, lady. I don't want to be here any more than you do.

Starr moved to her father's bedside, and stared down at the shriveled figure, limp and lifeless. She didn't care if Jean, who hovered by the side of the bed, heard what she'd come to say. She didn't care if the world heard.

"Well, Dad, you did it again," she spluttered and made her eyes stay on his face. In her periphery, she saw Jean's hands curl over the bed railing.

"We're going home now. Jean, here—" she glanced up at those stern dark eyes— "is going to take care of you tonight. You probably don't deserve her."

She was getting off track.

"So, you broke our deal. How fucking dare you?" Her throat burned as if scalded by her own words. "You landing in this place means we are forced to deal with you. But that may be what you planned all along. A big grand gesture to get our attention? Or maybe you were trying to kill yourself."

Would his death have been better? She couldn't say.

"Well I'm here to tell you, you're not doing either. You're not going to hold us hostage." God, her voice cracked. It was such a weak sound that could be taken as a sign she wasn't sure. But she was—as sure as the sun rose and set—about what was going to happen next.

She leaned down, close to his face, and inhaled the stale scent of an old man's skin mixed with bleached cotton. "This time, old man, you're going to make good on your promises. You're not going to die because that would kill Luna, who seems hell-bent on finding peace." She nearly spat her final words. "And you're not going to revert to your old ways because that will kill Phee. Just knowing you're out there, that you could continue to hurt people like you hurt her would cause her worry." Heat seared her throat, and maddening tears spilled over her lashes.

His sallow face sickened her, and she drew away a few inches. "Because you know what? She's a good person. She doesn't think she is, and that's all because of you." Starr swatted at her wet cheeks, and she cleared her throat to unstick all the stupid emotion rising up. "So listen up. You're going to get better. You're going to make things up to us. I don't know how, but you will."

She drew in a long breath and puffed it out—hard. Then she drew close to him again, teeth clenched so hard they ached. "I'll see you atone for what you've done to Phee if it's the last thing I do on this earth, and you have no idea how far I'll go."

He didn't know because he didn't know her. He didn't know any of them. But she coughed up those words anyway, slowly and deliberately, so the Universe or God or whatever the hell existed that allowed this man to get away with so much shit couldn't mistake her resolve.

She straightened. There was nothing left to say. She looked up at the nurse whose eyes had widened. "Thanks, Jean. See you tomorrow." She then turned on her heel.

"Miss O'Malley." The words were muffled from behind her mask.

She turned back to her. Jean had pulled her mask down so Starr could see her face. The woman was younger than she'd expected. "I'm breaking protocol in telling you this, but he might not ever wake up."

"I know."

"I've been working in this unit for a long time. Even when they are unconscious, you'd be amazed at how much patients remember about what is said to them." She then pulled her mask back over her mouth.

Starr nodded once and marched back to Nathan. She didn't care whether Jean was trying to make her feel better, as if her father might remember her words, or make her feel worse. It didn't matter. That man would not get to die—a free pass in her mind—*or* continue to cause trouble.

This cycle of them ignoring the fact they'd been abused, abandoned, and neglected couldn't stand. It was like invisible chains had wrapped around them, and it was time to break free. It would start with everyone, including their father, admitting exactly what had happened, and what needed to happen next. Her father was not going to mess up their future. No one would ever do that to them again.

Things were going to change starting now.

43

Nathan grasped Starr's hand as soon as they stepped through the sliding glass doors into the thick August air. It was like walking into a wall of cotton. She snatched her hand back.

She shook her red hair out of her face. "It's hot."

This situation was hard. He knew that, but her reaction to being touched didn't sit well with him. He searched her tone of voice to assess her frame of mind. Two words weren't much to go on. Should he let her be? Press her? Ask her what's up? What did she need?

He lifted a hand toward Declan, who leaned against his car door, engine running. Phee and Luna sat inside, their hair lifting in the air from the air conditioner vents. Declan blew out a long thin line of smoke.

Nathan held out his keys to Starr. "I need to talk to Declan, Starr. Give me a sec?"

"Sure." Her fingernails scraped over his skin as she snatched them from his open palm.

His hands rose up automatically to frame her face. "And you? You okay?"

"I'm going to be." She cocked her head to slide free from his hold. "I should call Cherry. She's worrying. I can feel it from here."

He nodded, though couldn't stomach not knowing what was swirling in his girl's mind. He still left her to her call.

He strode over to Declan. "Thought you were trying to quit."

"Some things are hard to give up on."

"Some things should never be given up on." Nathan glanced at Phee sitting in the front seat and back to Declan.

Declan eyed him. "Need more time off?"

"No." That was definitely something he did *not* need. "Just wanted to thank you. For the Erin thing."

Starr stood by his car, her cell phone held up to her ear. Her other hand ran through her hair, fingers running through the strands as if detangling them.

"Can't afford to lose you." Declan tossed his cigarette to the ground, twisted it into ash under his shoe. "How's Starr?"

"Hard to say." He stretched his neck as if that would ease some of the growing tension there.

"Well, the father-daughter thing is a tough one."

Declan wasn't aiming arrows at him, but his words landed that way just the same.

"How much do you know about Starr and her sisters' past? With their father, I mean?"

"A lot." Declan looked over at her "It's why Phee's so pissy with me all the time."

"Women like their secrets."

"And hate ours."

And didn't that truth sting? Yesterday would have been the perfect time to tell Starr about his daughter, Madeline, but he hadn't found the words. Today would be the worst time.

Declan cracked open his door and lowered himself into the driver's side. He'd never understand why the man loved his old Jag so much. It broke down every other day, along with all his other antique cars.

After Declan pulled away and disappeared around the corner, he studied Starr pacing back and forth two rows over. Her phone was still pressed to her ear. She swiped at something in the air—a mosquito, perhaps. A trickle of sweat ran down his back. Man, it was hot, even at 9:30 at night.

He moved to the trees that stood in the parking lot median to give her some privacy and him a break from the heat. He'd rather go inside and take advantage of the air conditioning, but leaving Starr out here by herself wasn't happening.

He pulled his shirt from his clammy chest and tuned into the distant car engine rumblings of the highway close by. A train was moving fast on railway tracks somewhere nearby, too. It wasn't silent, but rather quiet for a Saturday evening, as if something was about to happen, like the moments before racehorses are let out of a gate.

On the side street, a plain white workman's van approached the lot, turned in, but instead of slowing down, it sped up.

The van door slung open. Two men—brown skin, tattoos, jeans, it was all such a blur—reached for Starr. Arms banded around her chest, her neck, and a meaty palm covered her mouth. Her blue eyes, large and shocked, caught his, and his legs moved fast. His feet beat the pavement, but they weren't fast enough. If only his lungs could take in more air. His hands smacked the hot metal side of the van door just as it clanked shut. He pounded the side and tried to follow it as it hurtled away from him.

Thick exhaust seared the inside of his nostrils and his

brain blanked. The disbelief didn't last long. They had her. They'd *taken* Starr.

A black BMW swerved around from behind the van to stop so closely to him that the front tire narrowly missed his foot. A tinted window lowered, and Ruark smirked at him from the driver's side. "If I were you, I'd get in."

44

Black, scratchy fabric covered Starr's face. Smothering, it was smothering. Big, rough hands tossed her forward, and her ankle twisted against an uneven metal surface. A cry broke from her throat. Still, too little air came when she inhaled.

"Shut up, bitch."

Just as little pricks of light danced before her eyes, the sandpaper fabric was dragged off her head. Light washed her face as her head was freed. Her body seized the opportunity and filled her lungs with blessed cool air. She tried to raise her hand to rub the grit that had landed in her eye, but a grip from behind stopped her.

"W-wha—"

Pain exploded across her forehead, cheek, and chin. The hard metal floor smacked the side of her face, and the vibration of the road thrummed underneath her.

"I said, shut up."

The tang of rust and salt settled on her tongue. *Blood.* She'd bitten the inside of her cheek. Bile rose in her throat, and her throat muscles threatened to contract. She took a second to collect her thoughts, blink back the hot tears stinging her eyes.

Phee. Luna. Nathan. Where were they? Sucking in air, she took a second to determine her surroundings. Oil mixed with sweat. She was in a van. And there were men—strange men. Ice filled her veins followed by a rush of adrenaline drowning her ability to think beyond that fact.

A man crouched before her. He cocked his head as if he observed a wounded animal on the side of the road. His lips curled in a twisted snarl, and his dark eyes filled with feral glee. A fury punched through her fear. His scalp was marked in colored tattoos, but it was the angry, pink scar across his neck that captured her attention. She only hoped the cause had been a murder attempt. Her head throbbed from his punch.

"Get there already, will ya?" A voice behind her roughed out the words in some accent she couldn't place.

"You want me to attract the cops?" Another male voice came from where the driver would sit. She swayed at a sharp turn and reached out with her arm to steady herself. Her fingers rested on a nest of ropes.

"Fuck, Remy, learn to drive." Tattoo-head looked back at her. "So … " He pushed her hair over her shoulder, and she shuddered. "You be a good girl, and maybe we'll be extra nice to you."

Icy spangles of fear snaked up her legs and spine. She had to get a grip. She lowered her gaze as if that would help. Like maybe if she wasn't looking at him, he might not notice her?

He rose up, spreading his legs wide to steady himself. "Tie her up."

Calloused hands forced her to sit upright. A shot of pain went through her right shoulder as her arms were yanked behind her back. Her wrists and forearms were roughly bound with scratchy rope. Her hands would be numb from the constriction in seconds. When done, he stepped back, and she toppled back to her side. The dress she wore rode up to expose her panties.

"I always did like pink." It was the accented voice. A cold grip of fear seized her. They were going to rape her.

Over my fucking dead body.

She tested the ropes a little. Her legs were strong. She'd get a good kick to at least one set of balls before they did whatever they planned.

"Leave it." Tattoo-head guy must be the leader.

Think, think, think. She demanded her brain to come up with something. What was she supposed to do when in danger? Make noise? Adrenaline pushed her heartbeat into her throat, her ears, her chest, blocking out any brain power. *Think, girl.* Something about a second location. Her brain fought to latch on to something, anything, she could do to help herself. *Yes, never let them take you to a second location. That's where the rape-murder happens.*

She willed herself to look—really look—at the inside of the van. Was there anything sharp she might get a hold of? The door had two handles that needed to be pushed down to open them. Car sounds outside grew closer. If she could just kick the door handle, let someone behind them see who was in this van … Her fingers sought for purchase on the knots binding her hands. Damn it, where were they?

The vehicle slowed, turned, and her body jostled against the grooves in the van as it clanked over something hard and metal. The light dimmed.

When she was yanked upright, she finally got a look at the guy behind her. Twice the size of the head tattoo guy, his baby face did little to counter the menace in his soulless black eyes.

Forced to jump down to the ground, her bare feet hit rough concrete, gritty and cold. Where were her shoes? If she had to run, it'd be easier to be barefoot than in high heels, but already the uneven ground stung the soles of her feet.

They forced her to keep moving forward, and the pain in her shoulder sharpened.

She glanced around the space, trying to take in as much as possible. They were in an industrial warehouse. A row of fluorescent lights beamed a path over the uneven concrete floor. *The second location.* The cavernous space was stacked high with huge metal containers like those she'd seen whizz by on any of the endless trains that roared through Baltimore. So many places to hide a dead body—after they did whatever they were going to do to her.

Nathan saw her get snatched. Someone would come. Someone would surely come before things went too far? But who?

Nathan was on parole. He couldn't risk it. Would he? He'd be outnumbered even if he could have somehow followed them.

That left the police. He'd call them but with no leads, no idea where the van was headed, no one would find her before they used her.

She was left with only one option. Save herself.

The most ordinary guy in the world, dressed in jeans and polo shirt, jumped from the driver's seat just as tattoo-guy kicked an old metal chair toward her. "Sit your ass down."

She didn't have a chance to obey because her other captor roughly sat her in the chair. He pushed her forward, and her shoulder threatened to spasm. She couldn't hold back a yelp. Her captors didn't care, and the rough rope scratched and bit into her wrists and forearms as he yanked them free. When her arms were released, tingles of blood ran through her veins, and her skin burned. She pushed her hands into her lap, hoping to pull her dress down without them noticing.

Yeah, because driving attention away from her sex was going to help—not.

"You're not going to run." The guy with the tattoos pulled up a second chair, turning it so he could straddle the seat. He leaned toward her until he balanced on two chair legs, and his liquor-breath ran over her face. "Are you, sweetheart?"

She shook her head, told her quivering chin to still. She needed time. So long as she acted compliant, she might not get smacked into unconsciousness. She couldn't out-muscle these guys but she'd find a way to out-think them.

"That's a good girl." The rear feet of his chair thunked back to the ground.

They'd left the large doors open, which was good because she could run. But faster than these two? Maybe not, but her screams could shatter a glass factory. It was a start—and something.

The whine of a car engine grew closer. Tattoo-man stood up and twisted the metal chair out of the way. All three of the men stood to attention as a BMW rolled up to them.

She blinked. "Nathan?"

His face stared at her from the passenger side. A deep gratitude warmed her chest and dulled the pains, now moving around her body like pinballs. He'd come for her. A rush of fear followed. They might hurt him.

He dove out of the car and rushed to squat in front of her. "Starr. Are you okay?" He ran his hands down her arms, taking in the scratches and bruises that lit up anew with his fingertips.

An odd paralysis took over her, and she was unable to form words.

Nathan shot to his feet and swung his fist hard toward the man with black eyes, a thick thud followed by bloody spittle splattering to the side. The guy righted himself with a smile and he punched Nathan in the gut so hard, he was knocked off his feet.

She darted up, but Tattoo-guy grabbed her around the waist.

"You leave it," he growled.

Nathan lay sputtering on the ground. She tried to reach for him and failed as iron arms held her fast. He had come for her, and they would kill him for it. An ache started low in her chest and spread like a cancer until she was veiled in sheer bleak truth. They weren't going to be okay—not by a long shot. Only one emotion blazed strong, red-hot wrath because they didn't deserve this torture.

"Now, now, Miss Starr."

She looked up at the familiar voice. Ruark MacKenna had the gall to stand there in his cheap-ass suit, grinning at her like they still sat at that coffee shop. Fire obliterated her thinking, and she struggled against the thickly muscled arms that squeezed her and held her to the hard metal chair. She kicked and sputtered, unable to form words, the pain in her shoulder growing distant and fuzzy. Fury raged on and on inside her, fed by Ruark's smug face grinning down at her.

She stilled when the tattooed man kicked Nathan, hard, in the back, and Nathan grunted, blood bubbling out of his mouth.

"Leave him alone," she managed to snarl.

"Now, Slate," Ruark said. "Is that any way to treat our guests?"

Nathan spit blood and pushed himself to standing. "Fuck you." He spun and punched the guy named Slate, hard, so he stumbled backward.

"Leave it, Slate." Ruark clapped slowly. "Good man, Nathan. I'm sure your parole officer would love to hear of you throwing some punches."

A line of blood spittle hung from Nathan's lips toward the

floor. He swiped at his mouth. "That your plan? Get me back behind bars? You lack imagination."

Ruark sucked air between his teeth. "Well, when they find out you've killed your girlfriend here, there'll be a chair waiting for you."

Nathan groaned as he rose. He had to be hurt, given how he stood slightly hunched. "MacKenna, swear to God—"

Ruark reached behind his back and pulled out a Glock. She couldn't tear her eyes from it, the gunmetal-black against his skin, the way his hand molded the contours with ease, as if he'd used it—often.

Nathan shook his head slowly from side to side, a half-smile on his lips. "You always were dramatic. Sending a pig's heart, and now the big man with a gun on display."

How could Nathan goad him? Forcing their hand to do something wasn't wise. But then, Nathan was a man of action. Her flagging hope kicked up a notch that maybe he had a plan.

"Tsk, tsk, guy." Slate—what a stupid name—leered at Nathan. "Teasing Ruark isn't real smart."

"Shut it." Ruark pointed the gun at Nathan. "Now. Talk is over."

45

———

Acid rumbled in his belly and climbed up his throat, which oddly, dulled the pains shooting through his back. His heart threatened to punch itself out of his rib cage. *Not now.* Fuck him if he was going to go down looking like a pussy. He glanced at Starr, latching on to the sight of her to steady himself. He needed to buy them some time so he could get her out of there. He fingered his phone in his pocket. Too bad his hands didn't have eyes so they could hit the record button.

He spit blood from his mouth. "What do you want? You got any specifics for once?"

Ruark arched his eyebrow. "Want? I want what you stole from me."

"I can't bring your brother back." His throat was raw. "I'm sorry he's dead. Truly, I am." The guy had no idea how sorry he was. He'd spent too many nights lying on a striped camping mattress, nursing bruises and cuts, listening to men cough and moan in the dark corners of cells, not to passionately regret his actions.

A maniacal laugh from Ruark cut through all the heaviness in his chest "You're sorry Daniel's dead? I'm not." Ruark turned away, his lips twitching, his eyes downcast, as he slowly paced like a caged bird shuffling on a perch. "You just don't get it, do you? I hated the fucker." He stopped and raised his gaze toward Nathan. "Wanted to kill him myself. Instead, you made him a God to my father and mother. My brother." He rushed forward until he was inches from Nathan's face.

The gun barrel pressed on Nathan's temple. Cold fingers of dread wrapped around his limbs. He'd be no good to Starr dead.

Ruark sucked air through his teeth. "*I* was the one who was going to take him out, not some pussy college kid." He stepped back and lowered the gun. "How dare you."

The man was a psycho. He might have been speaking in Arabic for all the sense he made. Nathan forced air into his burning lungs, eyed the other men, and took stock of their positions. Ruark's three accomplices stared at him unflinching, their eyes flat with disinterest. The devil's soldiers awaiting orders.

"You asked what I want?" Ruark jutted out his chin. "I want back my opportunity to lay him in the ground myself. Be the one to rise in my family. My father's time is over, and it should be me who takes over. You gonna give that to me?" He snorted. "Naw, I didn't think so."

Nathan swayed a little. His ribs pinched and shifted inside, stealing his breath. "You're insane, man. You can have whatever you want, MacKenna. Take it out on me, but let Starr go."

"No can do, busboy. She's your collateral damage. Just like everyone else in your life." He cocked his head. "Like your wife, your daughter. Oh, yes, I know all about them."

His ribs swore at him as he inhaled sharply. The floor would just not stop tilting. Nathan glanced at Starr, her eyes a mixture of confusion and fear. He didn't believe it was possible to hate Ruark MacKenna any more than he did right now. The fucker stepped around Starr and stood behind her. He brushed her hair from her shoulder with the gun barrel. Trembling, her hands grasped the sides of the chair, and her eyes glazed over in wild alarm. He leaned down and whispered in her ear. "Did you know that, sweet Starr? That your boy abandoned a wife? A kid?"

Nathan fixed his eyes on Starr.

"Nathan?" His name was nothing more than a whisper.

He ached to crush his mouth to hers, to whisper he would fix everything.

MacKenna continued his rant. "You see, when I kill her and you" —he lifted his gun and gazed down the barrel— "I'll be sure the gun ends up with your prints. That should be the end for you. Me, the brother, gets revenge for the death of Daniel, trying, but sadly failing, to save the girl. My parents will love that shit. Plus, taking care of unfinished business is always rewarded in my family." He moved the gun to her temple, and Starr stiffened. Ruark's eyes, two dark beams of hatred, bored into Nathan.

Nathan shuffled a few inches closer. Just two more steps and he'd be close enough to shove her aside, wrap his hands around MacKenna's throat.

"Okay, Ruark. That's enough." A male voice thundered into the room. A silhouette of a large, stocky man framed by sunlight and black shadow stood at the entrance, hands shoved in pants pockets. "Now, you mind lowering that gun?"

When this new guy stepped inside, his features became visible. He had the same cloud of black hair and the same ice blue eyes as Ruark. *Great. Another MacKenna.* Yet this man was taller, wearing an I've-seen-this-all-before expression.

"Hello, brother." Ruark stepped forward, putting some distance between him and Starr.

Nathan stared at the two men, his eyes trained on the gun hanging along Ruark's leg. His heart thumped with adrenaline. He was about to do something stupid.

Ruark pointed the gun toward his brother. "Stay out of this, Carragh."

The guy strutted forward until the gun touched his chest. "Like I said. Lower the gun."

Ruark obeyed, but his chin rose, and one of his legs danced as if this interruption agitated him.

Now was Nathan's chance. With them occupied, he closed the distance between himself and Starr and got behind her. He placed his hands on her shoulders, shook his head a little as her lips parted to speak.

Ruark sputtered. "You wanted out of this, so stay out of it."

"Mind telling me what 'it' is, brother?"

"Don't play dumb."

"Looks like you're ratcheting things up. First you went by Shakedown and got poor Seamus to run his car into the awning. I rather liked the door you smashed to smithereens, by the way. Yeah, we've been listening to the chatter, so I was sent to watch you. Sending a pig's heart? You got us noticed by the police—again."

Watch. All those sightings, at the club, outside his apartment ...

"Got a call from our father. You know how I hate to get those, Ruark. I was put on babysitting duty. He was curious to see how far my fucked-up younger brother was going to go. This is far enough, don't you think?"

"That's not our way," Ruark spat. "No one lays one of ours in the ground and gets away with it."

"I'd say no one got away with shit. Daniel was a fuck-up.

Baldwin here paid for that fuck-up. So, you mind not furthering this *fucked up* situation? You're calling attention to us ... *brother*. Enough is enough." His shoulders hardened. "We're calling it quits."

"Like hell." Ruark spun and raised the gun toward Starr. Sirens went from background noise to close vicinity. They were coming here. Carragh reached for Ruark's arm, and a gunshot blast pierced Nathan's eardrum. His whole body lurched forward, met Starr's body, and pushed her off the chair. His chest collapsed, and air wasn't possible.

On the other side of a fuzzy ring in his ears, shouts sounded. Then blue and red lights danced against the shadowed corrugated steel of the building. His fingers touched silk. *Starr*. When he'd fallen, he'd crushed her underneath him.

46

Nathan cracked open his eyes. Through the emergency room's white curtains, the back of a blue uniform was visible. Nathan shifted on the gurney and grunted in discomfort as something unseen stabbed his shoulder. The pain was sharp in contrast to the dull thud, thud, thud of his ribs. At least the bullet had only grazed his shoulder. No "internal damage," they'd said, so he could go—at least to jail, which was next. They'd run his name, caught the not-so-little bit about him being on parole, and Erin was on her way. Yeah, life turn-arounds were only for the rich and free.

He pushed himself off the gurney only to land on a hard floor that tilted and moved. Damn painkillers. They could lessen pain, but it never was gone fully, and they made him unstable and muddled.

At least Starr was okay, or so said the nurse, the one kind person in the place who'd relayed his "girlfriend" just had some bumps and bruises. He needed to find her, that is, if she'd ever want to see him again after the Ruark bombshell. He should have shared that with her weeks ago.

He took his time putting one foot in front of the other as

if walking slowly would delay the inevitable. As soon as he was through the curtain, one of the cops grasped his bicep. Fuck him, he was getting an escort. The cop jerked him forward. "Your parole officer is here."

Thick block wooden chairs, padded in orange and green fabric, lined the waiting area walls.

Erin stood and crossed her arms. "I've got this," she said to the officer whose grip hadn't lessened one bit during the long, slow trek to her. She held a plastic bag, which probably held his phone and wallet. She handed it to him.

The cop nodded once and left them alone in the quiet waiting room. It was, what? 4:00 a.m. by now?

She jerked her jeans jacket into place. "Tell me."

"MacKenna nabbed Starr. The police—"

"You called them?"

"No. I think it might've been Carragh MacKenna. The brother." At least that was as much as his brain could deliver as an answer. The cops had been just as rough as MacKenna's goons, and between getting beat up, shot, and attempting to save Starr, he was lucky if he could remember his name.

"Plausible deniability." Erin's voice was definitive. "Makes this Carragh look like he's on the straight and narrow, showing up to break up a fight. Hmm. Ruark MacKenna might get off if no one presses charges, and the payoff is high enough."

Her words made sense. For all the cops knew, Ruark was merely there to stop the thugs he'd hired from harming him and Starr. Nathan had seen first-hand how the word of a MacKenna overrode truth, no matter how obvious.

"Nathan."

He stopped contemplating his boots, stained with dried blood, and looked up at her.

"You fight MacKenna?"

"Does harsh language count?" Sure he'd clocked that

scum who'd manhandled Starr, but Ruark had gone untouched.

"Good man." She took in a long breath. "But this is the third strike." She sat in one of the chairs and patted the one next to her. "Okay, start from the beginning, and don't you fucking dare leave out a single detail. I'm recording this." She pulled out her phone. By the end, she'd done him a solid and gave him the truth. He'd go to jail until the investigation was sorted, which could be never. He was sure they would find some rule they could use to revoke his parole despite the fact Ruark was responsible for this whole cluster, and it involved felonious activities. Nathan had been coerced into the car with Ruark, but the law would only see he'd gotten involved. Instant parole violation.

"Well, at least, the cops are fairly convinced you didn't start the fight. Ruark and company still might get charged. Anyone ask you to press charges?" Erin asked.

Why would they? "Starr should do that. Ruark was going to kill her."

"Yeah, well, she may not even have to." Erin rose. "Listen, let me talk to the cops over there. Find out what the fuck is going on. Don't move. I'll be right over there." She pointed to the entrance area where two cops stood clutching coffee cups.

After she strode away, he hung his throbbing head. If he could just close his eyes for a minute …

"Nathan." Starr's distressed voice nearly made him jump out of his skin. He grunted at the resulting agony. The damd painkillers were starting to wear off.

He rose, slowly, as every part of him ached and creaked.

Her face, grayed with fatigue, etched with deep lines in her forehead, was almost too much to bear. Dark circles under her eyes competed with the purpling on her neck and arms. She touched his arm, tentatively, as if one might touch a stranger. "You look terrible."

He didn't know why that made him laugh, but it did. Sharp glass spikes from his bruised ribs drove into his side, and he bent over a little. "Just got grazed. It's nothing." His injuries wouldn't stop him from being chained, hobbled, and taken to a cell until they could transfer him.

Starr shuffled on her feet. "Is what Ruark said true? You're married?"

Shit. Okay, they were starting there. "Divorced."

"And you have a child."

His throat squeezed just enough to make him force down a swallow. "A girl. Madeline." God, he hadn't said her name in so long it razored his throat when it came out. But that might be just his battered ribs that sent a shooting pain through his body every time he moved.

She grasped her bottom lip in her teeth for a second. "How old is she?"

"Nine. I think." He tried not to think about how long it'd been.

That was clearly the wrong thing to say as her face hardened. Those eyes of hers, though, they colored with something entirely new—disappointment.

She elevated her chin a little. "You never mentioned her."

"I've never seen her. Dawn, that's my ex, told me to stay away. She didn't want a convicted felon around her. So out of respect, I did what she asked."

"Don't you want to—"

"See her? Hell, yeah. I mean, I had a family who abandoned me once I got put away. I'd never want Madeline to think I didn't want her." A searing hot poker went through his chest when he sucked in a frustrated breath.

"I'll bet she's a doll. With your kind eyes and smile. The dove tattoo. It's for her, isn't it?"

"Yes." He couldn't look at her.

"Miss O'Malley." Carragh's unwelcomed voice filled the space. He sauntered over and stuffed his hands in his trouser pockets. "I understand we've had a … misunderstanding."

"Is that what you're calling it?" She showed off her arm. "I'm sure the witnesses here would agree these bruises didn't come from harsh language."

So she wasn't so cowed by what had happened.

Carragh widened his stance. "My brother could have been trying to protect you from those two criminals."

Ah, so he was going with the "them versus us" theory. The guys they hired were the scum, and the MacKennas? Golden boys. Nathan shook his head at the guy whose face wore such serenity it had to be a practiced mask.

Starr raised an eyebrow. "Is that why he pointed a gun at Nathan and me? Repeatedly?"

"She could press charges for kidnapping, not just false imprisonment," Nathan stated. "Oh, and threats of sexual assault on top of kidnapping? Felonies everywhere." If he were going to go down, he'd go down fighting, and there was one advantage to incarceration, if you paid attention, you learned a fuck-ton about the law.

"No such thing occurred." The man's cool, smooth tone wasn't helping Nathan tamp down his anger—not one bit.

Starr didn't give an inch. "Says the man who didn't see the half of it. Unlike you alphaholes, I don't lie."

God, Nathan loved this woman.

MacKenna scratched his chin. "How about this? If you don't press charges☐"

"We don't need to press anything." Nathan wasn't going to be cowed anymore by this family. "Facts are facts. This isn't a *CSI* episode."

MacKenna's mask cracked and he glared at him. "If you'll let me finish? We'll pay for everything that was … *inadver-*

tently damaged in this misunderstanding. I understand Mr. Phillips' club had to put in a new door. And, of course, Miss O'Malley, any work you may have to miss due to your encounter with those *other* gentlemen." He ran evaluating eyes over her body. Nathan had never wanted to hit a man so badly as in that moment—and that was saying something.

"We'll cover any lost wages for as long as you need." He straightened a cuff, a move so patronizing Nathan almost risked a move.

His eyes shot over to Nathan. "And as for you. This feud you have with my brother? It's over. We'll chalk it up to some testosterone matches."

"You're kidding me, right?" Nathan couldn't believe the man's bullshit could grow any deeper yet here they were.

"We've lost one brother. I'm sure my father doesn't want to lose another son."

"Guess he should have had better parenting skills."

"What's going on here?" Erin appeared and muscled her way between Carragh and himself.

Carragh didn't flinch. "I was just expressing my dismay to Miss Starr here. Such poor behavior. I don't know where those men came from."

Erin squinted up at the man. "Uh, huh. They're keeping Ruark overnight, as well."

"Why?"

"Bail hearing will be held tomorrow. Thing is, exactly how this goes down depends on Miss O'Malley's final statements." The woman turned toward Nathan and Starr. "If they consider them 'complete.'" She considered Starr, in particular.

Holy shit, his parole officer was giving her an opportunity. Was it to recant or to expand on what she said had occurred?

"I might have more to say." Starr smiled at Erin. "Of

course, it's my understanding at any point in the next seven years I can press charges, right?"

"I'm no lawyer, but I'd say if you remember anything, Miss O'Malley, they'd be happy to hear it."

Starr eyed the man once more. "Well, since Mr. MacKenna here is assuring me his family doesn't have anything else to say, I might not, either. It's interesting how when two people agree, when they are, how should I say, *at peace* over things, life can go on. Wouldn't you agree, Mr. MacKenna?"

"I would indeed, Miss O'Malley."

"Oh, and that goes for Nathan, Declan, and my sisters, too." She stepped closer to Carragh.

Nathan wanted to pitch himself between them, but watching this bizarre exchange, he found his feet frozen.

"We've always been a hardy bunch. It would be unusual for the stress of this situation to impact our health." She laughed lightly. "In fact, I do believe we'll all live to be a hundred."

"Then that is where we are the same." MacKenna's face slowly stretched into a grin. He looked ... amused? "To a long life, Miss Midnight Starr, for you and your sisters." He nodded his head at each of them and turned to walk away.

So his little firecracker tried to broker a peace deal. Even if she could, the MacKennas would never honor such a thing. Besides, Ruark was going to do time. The law didn't take kidnapping lightly.

"Come on." Erin inclined her head. "Car's out front. We've gotta go."

"I'll go with you." Starr hooked her arm in his. He reveled in her warmth, in the softness of her skin against his. It helped with the pain a little, though the good feeling wouldn't last. He was going to have to let her go for real this time.

47

———————

Bus exhaust and summer heat smacked his face as soon as he was through those double glass doors of the emergency room. A pinkish dawn had broken outside. Holding Starr's hand, he took time to drink in the scene, letting the humidity, as thick as being smothered in wet blankets, coat his skin. Two cops kept watch over them; Erin moved twenty feet away to yammer into her cell phone.

They'd been told he had ten more minutes before he'd be taken away.

Lowering heavy eyelids, he concentrated on the sounds all around him just in case he might not get to hear "normal" again. When he popped open his eyes, the sky's light had given way to a bright yellow, morning sun. That's how fast life changed. One minute you're a college student. Then you're a felon. One minute you might get your life back. Then, you don't.

Declan pulled up. Phoenix and Luna rushed out of the car immediately to embrace their sister. He still didn't let go of her hand. He was unable and unwilling to break contact with Starr, even when they hugged, chattered, and fussed over her.

Knowing she had such family backup soothed his worry a bit.

Declan positioned himself in front of him. "My attorney will meet us at the court office."

"Thanks, man." No legal mind was going to change the fact the law considered him a parolee who'd broken his agreement by way more than just crossing a state line. He appreciated the futile attempt anyway.

The glass doors whooshed open, and Carragh sauntered out with two more cops, one of them laughing at something MacKenna had said. Nathan's skin chilled. The level of familiarity, not to mention friendliness between the men, shouldn't have been a surprise.

Then the inexplicable happened. Declan strode over to Carragh.

Before he could puzzle out what was happening, Phoenix spoke to him.

"What was that?" He hadn't really heard her, his eyes not believing that he saw the two men talking in hushed tones.

"Thank you," she whispered. "For saving our sister. When you guys didn't show up at home, well ... we didn't know."

Home. Yeah, he'd almost had one, hadn't he? "I wasn't going to let anything happen to her."

"We know." Luna squeezed his wrist.

A shadow fell over them as Declan and Carragh joined them.

"Declan, take care of her for me. Please." His eyes shot up to Carragh. "You fucking go near her—"

"Back down, Baldwin." His bored tone matched his lids hanging half-mast as if he'd been through this scene a million times.

Declan thumped his cane. "They aren't going to harm her or anyone else. I've made sure of it."

He couldn't promise that.

"See you around, cousin." Carragh slapped Declan across the back and swaggered over to meet a black Mercedes that screeched to a halt in the fire lane. Sunlight gleamed off its perfect exterior.

Nathan stared hard at Declan. "What was that? Cousin?"

"I can explain later."

A man rose from the back seat, adjusted his glasses, and drew a briefcase from the floorboard. Another older man, silver-haired with a face as still as stone, stepped from the front passenger side. The two of them stared at him, and then their gazes drifted lazily over each of the others.

The elderly gentleman's nose appeared as if it had been broken more than a few times, but he wore his expensive suit as if it were made for him. They left the car with its driver sitting in the fire lane as if they owned the place. They might. Carragh met them halfway and shook their hands.

Nathan turned to Declan. "Why do I have a feeling that's Ruark's legal team?"

A muscle in Declan's jaw twitched. "Not exactly." He swung his gaze to him. "It's Papa MacKenna. When in doubt, go to the top."

"You know him?"

Declan didn't answer but squared himself behind his cane when the elderly man nodded at him.

The guy then turned to Carragh. "Button it up, and don't take too long."

Carragh simply ran his finger over his bottom lip but trailed behind the two men as they stepped through the glass doors to go inside.

A cop broke into their group and raised his eyebrows. "Gotta go, man."

"Just a few more minutes," Starr pleaded.

"Sorry, Miss O'Malley." He gave her a compassionate half-smile. "We've stretched out the time all we can." He unhooked his cuffs from his belt. "Sorry, man, gotta do this. Hands behind your back."

Nathan turned away from the cop and put his hands behind him. He forced himself to stare into Starr's Caribbean blue eyes one more time.

She swung her arms around his neck and crashed her mouth into his. Pain exploded in his chest, his shoulder, but damned if he'd have stopped her, even as the cold cuffs snapped around his wrists.

She broke the kiss but didn't loosen her hold on him.

He'd give anything to brush her red hair from her forehead. "Sorry I'm not going to be able to get you that boat."

"I don't care about boats." She rose higher on her tiptoes.

"You should. You deserve it and more. Listen, Starr, I—"

"Don't say it. Don't you dare say it," she whispered into his mouth and then kissed him again. He would never, ever forget the taste of her, the softness of her lips and skin, the flash in her eyes.

His gaze floated over all the people left on the sidewalk. Declan, Luna, Phoenix, and even his parole officer, stood there as if a show of force would change his circumstances. It wouldn't, but a curious sense of belonging overcame him. A crushing sense of loss washed it away just as quickly.

The cop lowered him into the backseat and slammed the door. He searched Starr's face and committed to memory every freckle. He only broke contact with her when the glass of the window went up. He couldn't watch those blue eyes fill up with tears. He faced the front seat, stared at the back of the cop's head, and didn't dare look back again.

48

———

Three Months Later

Welcomed, bright sunlight cut into his eyes. The noisy clank of the chain-link gates closing behind him startled him. He finally stood on the other side of those cold, silver, diamond-shaped twists of metal that had caged him for three months. He drew in the bus fumes and the scent of some distant fire. Burning leaves—it was a beautiful scent.

As if on cue, a leaf skittered across the cracked asphalt, and the distance hum-rattle of a bus accelerating urged him to step forward.

"Hey, handsome. See you still have your beard."

He pivoted to look up the street. His eyes weren't working properly in the sunlight because a voluptuous figure sat on the hood of a white Mustang, leaning back, her hands splayed behind her, her legs swinging a little against the side of the car. Her red hair lifted in the wind.

He hung his head, his gaze falling to the ground and then back up sharply, expecting her to be gone—just gone.

He tapped his bottom lip with his index finger. "Nice car."

"It's not mine—yet." Starr jumped off and leaned against the car. "Declan bought it for Phee, who, of course, refused it. She'd rather drive around in her old VW relic. It's a little cliché but … " She shrugged one shoulder.

And just like that his mind catapulted to Shakedown, the scent of oranges and furniture polish, the clang of beading on costumes, and horns blaring in the music.

Her hair danced in the wind. "Thought you'd walk away without me, didn't you? Good luck with that."

His heartbeat stirred and then built to a furious rhythm. His body took over, thank God, because his mind was useless. The distance between them was gone, and his arms were full of Starr with her cinnamon scent and soft flesh. She'd said she was coming in their last phone call, but he hadn't let himself believe it until now.

"Hey." She grasped both sides of his face. "Guess you missed me?" Her lips came up to his, and for long minutes his world was full of nothing but the moist heat of her mouth.

When they broke their kiss, she pushed him backward. "Declan made me promise." She pulled out a cell phone from the back of her jeans and hit a number.

"I've got him." Her gaze never left his. "Okay … here." She handed him the phone. "He wants to talk to you."

Now? "Hey." He scrubbed his chin.

"Nathan. Welcome home. Look, I know you and Starr have some catching up to do … "

Understatement of the century. He turned away from Starr and stared back toward the prison where he'd been held for the last ninety, untenable days. He swung his gaze back to Starr. Much better view. "S'okay. What's up?"

Starr grasped his free hand with both of hers as if he might run. No fucking way. He knew Declan was saying something, but he couldn't stop staring at Starr. "Uh, say that again."

"Ruark MacKenna. The guy's not getting out of prison for a while. Just got word this morning that his probation hearing was a bust. Wanted you to hear it first."

"How did you hear?" He'd spent considerable time mulling over the fact Carragh had called Declan "cousin."

"He'll be gone for at least another few months. Now tell me you're coming back to work."

So Declan wasn't going to answer his question. There was time, he supposed. Starr was pulling him around to the side of the car.

"What's he saying?" Starr drew so close to the phone Declan had to hear her breathing.

He lifted his chin at her but kept the phone to his ear. "Yeah, I'm coming back, Declan. Thanks." He looked at his smiling angel. She had to be an angel given she'd waited three months for him. "Yeah. Listen, about when we'll be back—"

"Whenever you need to be."

"Thanks. And ... yeah, just thanks." He needed to say more to the man who had basically given him his life back, repeatedly. First a job, then for sticking it out with him when he could have tossed him out on the street. Truth was, he didn't have the words ... not enough words.

"Thank your parole officer. She really went to bat for you. Only three months back inside?"

Yeah, he'd been damn fortunate. "It was worth it, though." He'd have done three more years to save Starr. At least Ruark couldn't get out of his crimes. First time offender status and the best attorneys money could buy didn't counter the roll-over his two hired guys did to them. Ruark would do some serious time—or at least be on the inside until his family could grease enough palms to shorten his sentence.

"I understand." Declan killed the call.

Nathan let himself get lost for a few minutes in Starr's expectant face.

"Well?" Her leg jogged in impatience and broke his trance.

"Ruark will be inside for at least a few more months. Maybe more than a few if he's not a good boy." Or the payouts weren't large enough.

"Something tells me it's going to be more then." Unrestrained glee filled her voice. "Come on. I'll drive."

"Where to?" He slipped into the passenger side.

She'd slammed the door and jogged to the other side. As soon as she settled herself in the driver's side, she inserted the key into the ignition and turned to him. "We are going to Florida."

"Why?"

"To see your daughter."

Jesus. He swallowed thickly.

She shifted to face him. "Then, when you ask me to marry you, I can say yes with zero reservations. I'll only have children with a man who would never abandon a child."

His heartbeat clattered under his ribs—and, for once, it felt damn good. Marriage. Children. A future. "So this is what we have to do? Right now?"

"Yes. I cleared it with Erin. I like her."

Shit. He did have a lot to catch up on. Starr's letters didn't mention any of this. An ambush, perhaps? After what he'd faced in the last few years, however, how hard could this be —seeing Dawn again and his daughter for the first time? How about harder than facing the entire MacKenna clan?

He drew the seatbelt across his chest. "Let's just hope my ex doesn't shoot me on sight."

49

This was a dream. Either that or he had "road head" from traveling one thousand ninety-five miles from Lorton, Maryland to Coral Gables, Florida. He leaned forward to unstick his back from the hot vinyl of the car seat. He couldn't make himself step out of the car onto the parking lot of the older housing complex.

The first day they'd made their way south on 81 through Virginia and then North Carolina, and he'd rather enjoyed Starr's chatter mixing with the wind from the convertible top being down. He was going to have a sunburn from hell, but it was worth it to watch all her red hair lift and wave at him.

He'd had a lot to catch up on. She'd written to him every few days when he was away he'd learned, though he wasn't sure where all the letters had gone. To thoroughly catch him up, she'd recounted everything.

In Virginia, he'd learned their father recovered from his coma and was back in rehab—again. They didn't see or talk to him but got updates, which was as much as the three of them were willing to do. Declan was helping with bills, which made Phee mad, but the man refused to back down from supporting them.

"She secretly loves it," Starr laughed. "She'll cave one day. Oh, and she's adopted Moonlight. The two of them are like best friends."

Perfect. Because he had enough to contend with just relearning how to be on the outside.

Once they crossed the North Carolina line, she'd grown lighter, happier, regaling him with tales of Shakedown. Max was dating a girl who looked as formidable as he did. "Her biceps are as large as my thighs, I swear," she'd laughed. Rachel and Trick were married with a baby on the way. He hadn't remembered she was such a chatterbox, but he'd listen to her forever if it meant he could be this close to her.

It was when they crossed into South Carolina, she grew serious again, making him stop and leave a message for a Dawn Mancuso. Nosy Declan, Max, and the O'Malley sisters had pulled out all the stops to find her, and her phone number, while he was imprisoned.

He was glad she'd dropped his last name—for her sake. Perhaps she'd remarried, though if she had, he might open the door to one angry husband. He'd like to avoid being punched. Somehow, he'd avoided any violence during the last three months in prison. Curious that.

His message had been comprised of some stilted words, but thank God there hadn't been anyone to hang up on him. He couldn't even recall what he'd said. Starr, who listened to his ramblings, reported he did "just fine." He'd dropped words like "it's been a while" and "sorry to call out of the blue" and "I'd like to see my daughter." Starr had told him he'd said those things, anyway.

Halfway through South Carolina, they'd stopped at a cheap motel where his nerves didn't have a chance to take hold because she stripped nude and made him do the same the second they were inside the doorway. Thank God for his greedy, eager girl. She'd pushed him back on the bed, and it wasn't long before he had each of her legs hooked in the crook of his elbows and entered her with a satisfying glide. That earned him one of those throaty moans of hers for which he'd pined for three months. Nerves stood no chance against his love, lust, or respect for this woman.

Now, however, they threatened a rebirth.

He stared through the windshield at the front door of the townhouse where Dawn Mancuso and Madeline Baldwin lived. "I don't know. The MacKennas … "

His words abruptly stopped. Starr had climbed on to his lap.

"You going to make me do this again?" Her freckles stretched a little as her cheeks lifted in a devilish smile. "If I'd known this would be the result, I might have to keep talking."

"How about we skip the talking?"

She planted a kiss on him that made his cock take notice.

She pulled back. "Ready?"

"No."

"Good. Let's go."

"Wait." He stopped her from opening the car door. "Give me a sec."

"Just breathe, Nathan. It's going to be okay."

How could it be? They were showing up at a woman's door who'd divorced him and whom he hadn't seen in ten years. He raked his fingers through his hair as if a delay tactic would put an end to Starr's incessant desire to deal with the past.

She crossed her arms and gave him that *look.* "You're being a pussy," it said.

He placed his hand on the door handle. "You don't have to go in with me."

"I want to. I mean, if you want me to."

"Why?" He turned in his seat. "I mean—"

"Because I love you. That's what people do. They don't leave when things get hard."

He fingered his phone, the picture of him and Starr staring up at him from an overlook they'd stopped at in North Carolina. "I should have been the one to tell you about Dawn and Madeline."

"You're not the only one with secrets, Nathan. Everyone has them. Like me and school. How I paid off my own father. Like ... my real name is Catarina." Her words nearly ran together as if she had to just get them out. "My mom had some Russian fantasy, apparently. We go by our stage names because we wanted to start fresh. We all did."

"Luna? Phoenix?"

"Can't tell you. It's part of our deal."

He'd need a spreadsheet to keep track of those sisters and their deals.

The front door of the home, pale yellow, trimmed in white, stared back at him. *Shit, man, just get it over with.* He cracked open the door and unfolded his cramped legs. He paused for a second, taking in the small bungalows lined up in one long, neat row, like yellow, turquoise, and shrimp-pink candy boxes with jalousie windows, opened to let in the tropical breezes. The whole neighborhood looked like it belonged in a 1950's movie when things were picture-perfect.

Starr stood at the sidewalk leading up to their front door.

He joined her. "I don't belong here." He really, really didn't.

"You're just nervous."

"Maybe."

"Nathan, let me spell it out for you. My father wasted so much time, and part of it was my fault. I've also been think-ing. I know why Dad did what he did, why he left us."

He stilled. Even he knew this was going to be important.

"It was to save us from him. He was ... angry and, well, you know what? I told Phee and Luna what I did when I was seventeen. They forgave me. So, today, it's time you ask for the same. And, here's the final thing." She squared herself to him. "Don't be my father."

It was that exact moment, on the word "father" that the front door opened. A gangly young girl stepped out, a cell phone to her ear. For a long minute, he just stared and watched her smile and talk in that way young girls do—their whole face helping to form words, their arms and hands gesturing as if signing all the enthusiasm they had for the world.

"That's her, isn't it?" Starr smiled at him.

Was it? "I don't know." He held the small picture, crinkled and cracked. Madeline had been a year and a half in that picture—the one and only one Dawn had sent before she stopped writing to him at all and served divorce papers instead.

The girl peered at them. Cocked her head. Suspicion crossed her face, and she frowned. The cell phone lowered in her hand, but she didn't show signs of running back into the house.

"Oh, that's her all right." Starr hooked her arm in his, lowered her voice to a whisper. "Look at those eyes. Same warm brown."

"Well, whoever she is, she doesn't trust us." *Good girl. Don't talk to strangers.* "This isn't a good idea. Let's wait until I can talk to Dawn."

"Half the battle is stepping out onto the stage. Once the lights hit and the music starts, you've got no other choice than to move. Let's move." She stepped forward, and he had no choice but to follow.

This was going to go down one of two ways. He'd be

ordered off the premises, or he'd finally get to meet his daughter. The girl fingered her phone but still didn't turn away as they grew closer. When he was four feet away from the girl, he stopped. No need to scare her. "Uh, hi, you don't know me, but—"

"You're my father, aren't you?"

Whoa. "Yes. How did you know?"

"I have a picture of you. From Grandma."

Grandma? His *mother*? Fuck, his eyes pricked. That was another person he hadn't talked to much over the years.

"Mom said you were coming today." She stepped closer. "You don't look like a hardened criminal."

He swiped under his nose. "Oh, yeah?"

"No." She inclined her head toward Starr who stood back by the curb. "And, you're pretty." She looked back at him. "Is she your girlfriend?"

"She is."

Starr stepped up to them and held out her hand. "Hi, I'm Catarina. I go by Starr, professionally."

"Are you in the movies?" Madeline's interest in them kicked up a hundred notches.

Starr laughed lightly. "Not yet. Dancer."

"Where do you dance?" Madeline only had eyes for Starr. Instantly, he was the interloper in this odd conversation.

"In a club. More cabaret than ballet. Think *Chicago*, you know, the musical?"

"Uh, yeah. Of course." This girl sounded more like twenty than ten.

"You have a good turn-out." She glanced down at the girl's legs.

"Thanks. I'm going to go on pointe soon. Or so, Madame Tremont tells me."

"Good for you for waiting. You don't want to ruin your feet by starting too early."

He stood stunned by the casual way Starr and Madeline had dropped into a conversation.

Madeline looked up at him and scrunched her eyes. "Do you dance?"

He burst out laughing. "I'm afraid I've got two left feet, Madeline."

Her face dropped. What did he say? He scrubbed his hair, words dying in his throat.

"I'd always wondered what it would sound like to hear you say my name." Her voice was so small—fragile.

It was impossible for him to talk because his throat clamped shut like a vault.

Starr sidled closer to him and took his hand, looking toward Madeline. "Is your mom home?"

"She's inside. Come on. She knew you were coming." She cocked her head and trudged up the steps.

He was shocked that Dawn hadn't barreled out the door holding a frying pan, or a Glock, given the times, to beat him backward.

"Oh." Madeline stopped at the doorway. "Don't worry about her. Mom's nice. She basically said you and she were handed a fistful of tough luck."

His limbs froze for a second in shock. The ability to be forgiving wasn't something he remembered about Dawn. But then he could barely remember anything about their time together. They hadn't had the best marriage, a quick ceremony in the heat of some romantic notion due to her sudden pregnancy. After he'd gone to prison, well, he supposed it was a good thing for them, for him to be permanently out of their way.

This strange, self-possessed young girl, ushering him inside, reminded him he also didn't know shit.

Starr hadn't let go of his hand. She didn't let go when he stepped over the threshold straight into an entryway that led to a small living room. God bless her, she still didn't let go when he stood before Dawn for the first time in ten years. She looked a little older, with more lines on her face, but she was still the round-faced girl he remembered. She didn't smile, but she didn't frown, either. She stared at him as if she couldn't quite recall who he was.

A gentle tug on his hand by Starr urged him to step deeper into the small living room.

He swallowed hard. "Dawn."

"Nathan. You've met Madeline." She circled her arm around her daughter's shoulder.

"Mom, Starr's a *dancer*." His daughter smiled at Starr in a slightly reverential way. He understood that look. He was sure he looked like that often in Starr's presence.

That's when it hit him. Madeline did have his eyes.

"Uh, this is Starr, my girlfriend."

Starr dropped his hand and held it out to shake Dawn's. "Hi. It's nice to meet you. Thank you for seeing us so out of the blue."

Dawn merely nodded.

Madeline slipped out of her mother's hold and jogged to the fireplace mantle. She grasped a photograph and brought it to him. "Grandma sent this a long time ago."

"Your mother." Dawn let out an amused puff of air. "She thought it was a good idea for Madeline to have some sense of her father. I got used to it sitting there."

He cleared his throat as he stared down at the picture. It was of him and Dawn with woods in the background. A barbeque, perhaps? Who knew? He had his arm around her shoulder, a red cup dangling from his fingers. Dawn was looking up at him, smiling, happy. He looked directly into the camera, a lazy smile playing on his lips. His forehead held no lines. His eyes held no fear. Of course they didn't.

"Have you seen her? Your mother?"

"Not yet," Starr filled in.

Not *yet*? So his girl had more reunion ideas in her head.

"We can go together." Madeline's energy practically poured into the room. "She has a pool."

"We'll see, Maddy." Dawn gave her a certain look he'd recalled from his own mother. "Do you mind getting us some iced tea?"

Madeline rolled her eyes.

"I'll help," Starr moved toward Madeline.

"Don't say anything important while we're gone." She gestured with her hands before turning the corner to go into what he surmised was the kitchen.

Dawn's face schooled to something neutral, unreadable. "Starr seems nice."

"She is. Madeline is … "

"Amazing? Yeah, she is."

He didn't remember Dawn being so … cool. Of course, he hadn't known her that well, had he? He pressed fingers against the back of his neck trying to loosen the knots there. "Listen, I'm not good at this, but would you be willing to … talk?"

Dawn cracked a smile for the first time. "That's the first time I've ever heard you say you wanted to talk."

"I've changed."

She cocked her head. "I believe you have." She gazed at the hallway where the girls had disappeared. "Starr responsible for some of that?"

"Probably all."

Dawn gestured to the couch. "Then don't let her go."

Like he would ever think of such a thing. "Thank you for letting me come and see Madeline. I'd like to get to know her. I mean, if that's all right."

She sat back. "Then we do have a lot to talk about."

For the first time in over a decade, the urge to talk, to

explain, to learn, crowded his head and made him jittery. He had to learn everything he could about his daughter. He even wanted to know how Dawn had fared.

"Know any good places to buy an engagement ring?" Because why not?

Dawn's face cracked into a large smile. "Take Madeline. She'd love it."

He got the curious sensation that his life was changing as he sat there. He stared at the photo in his hands. A ton of dead weight dissolved into the ether at the thought. He was no longer just the ex-con. He was an ex-husband, father, a son, an employee, a friend, and with any luck—Starr's husband.

Starr rounded the corner carrying a tray of glasses with Madeline behind her holding a large pitcher of iced tea. Glass clinked against glass.

"Mom, Starr has two sisters. They're triplets. Isn't that cool?"

Starr looked at him and winked. His heart about stopped for the millionth time since he'd laid eyes on her—and he hoped it would for a million more. Hope wasn't a strategy, but he was okay with that. He was okay with everything.

Oh, except Starr needed his ring on her fourth finger. Then life would be perfect.

EPILOGUE

Declan stood on the loading dock at the far end of the store-room gazing out over the Patapsco River. His jacket and pant legs ruffled in the wind. In the bright sunshine, the passage of time showed in the lines etched on the side of his face and the salt and pepper dusting of his temples.

Nathan sidled up to the man. "Heard you wanted to talk to me."

Declan glanced his way and then trained his gaze once more on the river, the surface barely rippling in the wind. "Heard you and Starr finally got engaged."

He scrubbed his hair. Fuck, he should have told Declan. Sure, it'd been less than twenty-four hours, but the man deserved to be one of the first. "Hey, sorry, man. I should have told you by now." He glanced backward. He'd left Starr at the front part of the storeroom to sift through some props. They both should have been here to deliver the news.

Declan raised his hand. "Not at all." He squared himself to Nathan. "Congratulations. Really, you and Starr deserve every happiness."

He was beginning to believe it. "She certainly does. I'm not about to get a fatherly talk, am I?"

The guy laughed. "No, I believe you have things under control there. I hope not much else changes, though."

The man thought he'd leave? Fat chance. "We're not going anywhere, in case that's what you're wondering." If he'd learned anything in recent times, it was how important it was to stick together. The whole "stronger together" shit worked. Nearby, her laughter rang out. It was comforting to know she wasn't far away.

"Good." Declan turned to face the river once more. "I have something to tell you, and I wanted you to hear it from me directly."

Worry twisted his gut. "Okay."

"You know the MacKennas and I have a long history."

Yeah, he knew. What was the man getting at? "Right."

Declan hesitated for a second, placed both hands on his cane and pushed down as if trying to drill a hole in the concrete. "What you don't know is that history goes to the very beginning. My mother's maiden name was Kate Louisa MacKenna."

Cold tingled up his spine and across his scalp. "Wait. You're related to the MacKennas."

"Tomas MacKenna was my mother's brother. That makes—"

"Daniel, Ruark, and Carragh, your cousins."

"Yes." He sighed heavily. "It was a recent discovery—"

"How recent?"

Declan scratched his neck with one hand. "You want to hear this story or not?"

The man couldn't expect much patience from him. That family had screwed him over royally—hell screwed *Declan* over royally. "Go on," he said.

"My mother was estranged. Married someone no one in

the family approved of, got pregnant with me, and was disinherited—the usual MacKenna heavy-handedness to prove a point. She didn't care. She'd wanted out of her family, her whole life. Later, after she died, let's just say they came looking for me. They don't like loose ends."

"How were you a loose end?"

"Family means everything to Tomas. When he learned one of his family members was out doing his own thing, uncontrolled, well … "

"I see where Ruark gets his sociopathy from."

"You don't know the half of it."

Did he want to know more? He had to know now, didn't he? "They're never going to stop, are they?"

"We have a truce at the moment. Carragh seems more reasonable."

Nathan let out a disbelieving huff. "He's considered reasonable?"

"Well, the bar is quite low in that family."

Didn't he know it.

"I told you because we need to prepare for another round. Ruark will get out sometime, and knowing them, sooner than we want. Given he will be released *after* you …well, let's say they consider that a loss of face."

"Of what? Pride?" Why did he even have to ask these questions? Nothing that family did made any sense. They believed they could craft their own world with rules and goals most normal people would never consider.

Declan sighed, thumped his cane once on the ground. "The thing is, they don't want any more bloodshed."

"No, they want slavery."

Declan's chin nodded a few times. "That's one way of putting it."

"I've got news for them. I don't care what the fuck your MacKenna relatives think …"

A gasp sounded from behind them. They both turned at the same time. Starr and Phoenix stood there, each holding up a costume to their bodies – Starr with a flapper dress and Phoenix with a Cleopatra get-up.

Starr's mouth had dropped to an "O" as if she'd been struck. He moved to her, and she stepped forward into his arms.

Phoenix, however, stood frozen, her blue eyes growing colder, brighter, as the red blossomed on her cheeks. "You son of a bitch." She threw the garment down to the concrete and sped back into the storeroom.

Declan sighed heavily. "Fuck."

Nathan didn't often hear the man curse, but if anytime called for it, it would be now.

Declan peered at Starr, who slowly shook her head. "We heard wrong, didn't we?" she asked.

The man gazed toward the ground. "I'm afraid not." He turned back to face the water, the veins in his neck growing more pronounced, as if he was holding back strong emotion.

Starr eased herself from Nathan's hold. He let her go. She stepped tentatively up to Declan, touched his arm. "I don't know what's going on, but whatever it is, please tell me—"

"What?" His head swung her way sharply. "That I'm not tied to the family who put you in danger and Nathan in prison? I can't."

It never quit, did it? They just couldn't catch a break for long.

"Are we in danger?" she asked.

At those words, Nathan stepped back to her and banded her against his chest. "Never again, North Star." He placed a kiss on the top of her forehead and glared at Declan over her head.

He glanced up at him, then back to Starr.

"I know what to do, and it does not involve danger to anyone."

Good, and Nathan was going to be all ears once the dust settled. Starr had started to tremble, and he couldn't allow that.

She swallowed. "Then don't give up on her. We trust you."

"Good." He stared back out at the water. "I'd have to be dead before I'd give up on Phoenix."

Nathan held Starr tighter. "That's the problem. Dead is Ruark's specialty."

~

If you loved Tough Luck, you'll love **Tough Break**, the next Shakedown series story.

Declan Phillips, Shakedown's owner, doesn't pine for women. They come to him. Throw themselves at him. No one understands his obsession with cold, angry Phoenix Rising, a dancer in his club. But how could they know what she did for him so long ago? He owes her, and he won't stop until every trace of the hurt and betrayal he sees in her eyes is gone.

Turn the page for a Tough Break excerpt!

TOUGH BREAK (EXCERPT)

Enjoy this short scene from the next Shakedown book. Phoenix and Declan travel far to get to their happily ever after. Some things are worth waiting for.

Phee shoved the door open with her shoulder. Damn back door always stuck.

"You sure you work here?" Naomi gave her the side-eye. It hadn't taken Phee long to find out her real name and that she'd been crashing on one of Maxim's bartender's couches for the last three weeks, not yet finding her own place—one that dealt in cash only and didn't mind dealing with an unemancipated seventeen-year-old.

"Positive. You'll see, come on." She hadn't brought any of the girls she'd pulled from Maxim's street to Shakedown or to her home before, but this girl was in rougher shape than expected. She wasn't only drunk. She was high on something and needed water at least. Crashing for a few hours on the cot in the staff lounge would do her well. Phee couldn't take her back to her apartment, not with her sisters there.

Once the door unjammed, she flicked on lights in the long hallway and urged the girl to follow. Hesitation crossed the girl's eyes but she followed.

Concrete dust, cinnamon, and lemon furniture polish grew stronger as they approached the black curtain separating the unimpressive cinder-block hallway and the main floor. She swiped the curtain back, gestured for Naomi to enter.

"Wow." Naomi stopped short. Her eyes widened. "You weren't shittin' me."

"Look." She pointed at the long row of oil paintings along the back handicapped ramp. "The owner used to deal in antiques, so he commissioned portraits of all his lead dancers. That's Cherry. Aspen. Cortelana. Nicholas-slash-Nikki. And that one is me." Declan and his romantic notions. "Those are my sisters."

"They look like you."

"My sisters and I are triplets."

"Get out." The girl jutted her chin back. "I've never met a triplet before."

"Most people haven't." She turned to face the stage. "That's where we dance." Now that she really looked, Shakedown *was* impressive with its heavy red curtains, velvet booths, white tablecloths, and high-end lighting. When had she lost her awe?

"Where are the poles?"

"No poles. We dance more like cabaret and burlesque."

"Oh, great movie. That Christina chick can belt them out. So, you sing?"

"I don't, but Cherry, the emcee does, and some of the other performers, too. Come on, I got coffee, soda, whatever you want." She headed to the bar, clicking on the espresso machine.

Naomi slid onto a barstool. "I'll have Jack." She pointed to a bottle of Jack Daniels.

"No." Declan's voice rang in the air.

Phee's nerves crackled at his sharp bark. Of all the times, the man was pulling an all-nighter. The tiniest tremble ran through her fingers as she gripped the bar edge. A dose of adrenaline from the male intrusion, that was all.

Naomi swiveled around and held up her hands in surrender. "Look man, she made me come here." She stood. "I don't want no trouble."

Phee pulled out two espresso cups from under the counter. "Don't worry. He's just the owner."

Terror crossed Naomi's face. "Fuck, what did you get me into?" She would be scared. Jones, as an owner, was the polar opposite of Declan. In fact, those bruises on the girl's neck had deepened over the last forty-five minutes. Phee brushed her fingertips over her own throat, the small muscles there remembering the grip of a hand wrapping around it.

The coffee machine hissed, snapping her back to reality. "Want an espresso?" She glared at Declan.

One side of his mouth inched up. "Don't mind if I do." He sauntered over, swinging his cane. The young girl eyed the thing as if it were a taser.

He held out his hand. "Hello, I'm Declan Phillips. I run Shakedown. And you are?"

She didn't return the gesture—another familiar sign. Naomi wasn't about to be yanked toward him and groped, though Declan would never do such a thing.

He dropped his arm, seemingly unbothered by Naomi's suspicions.

"He's not going to hurt you," Phee said over the hiss of steam. "I would know. I've been here for six years."

The muscles around Naomi's eyes relaxed. "I'm happy to audition. My name's Desha-biller." She inched closer, ran her eyes up and down his torso.

He smiled down at her. "Well, Desha-biller—"

"Her name is Naomi."

The ungrateful woman sliced her eyes toward Phee. The girl would learn Phee was not her enemy—eventually.

"Naomi." He cleared his throat and grasped her wrists before her hands landed on his chest. "We don't audition acts like that here. Our dancers do their work on stage—and only on the stage. Here, take a seat. You look like you could use that coffee." He helped her up on a stool. "Hungry?"

"Shit, Phoenix here was right. You are a gentleman."

He cut his eyes to Phee. "Is that what she said about me?"

Damn his smug smile. "Don't let it get to you." She set a small espresso in front of him. "I still meant what I wrote."

"Ah, yes, the napkin." He pulled it out of his suit coat pocket and placed it on the bar.

The girl glanced at the tiny espresso cup. "How much you charge for these tiny things?"

Declan chuckled. "A lot."

She took a sip and wrinkled her nose a little but gulped the whole thing down.

Phoenix inclined her head to the end of the bar. "Got a second, Declan?"

He pocketed her napkin note, took his espresso, and followed her to the end of the bar, his gaze trained on her face over the rim of the cup as he took a leisurely sip. "Decent espresso. A second calling, perhaps?"

"Perhaps."

He set it down, his eyes never leaving hers. "Let me guess where you found her."

Declan knew very well where she had found Naomi.

When Phee first worked for Declan, she often urged girls from Maxim's to audition at Shakedown. "It doesn't matter."

"I told you never to go back there."

Jesus, could the man look any more stern? "You don't get to tell me what to do. I don't work here anymore."

He glanced over at Naomi, who had laid her head on the bar, and then back at Phee. "Tell you what." He reached into his suit jacket, pulling out the napkin. "If you do work here, she can stay."

Blackmail? Over her dead body. "To serve espressos?"

"To dance."

They both glanced over at Naomi, who'd let out a slight moan as she settled into dozing, her face pressed against the bar. Jesus.

He laid her resignation on the bar before her. "Where else is she going to go? Back to Maxim's? You know that place better than anyone."

She scowled. "You would bring that up." He'd once brought a girl back here before—three of them actually: her, Starr, and Luna, two days after they'd met Declan. Back then, Shakedown didn't look like this—it had been more like an abandoned warehouse filled with Declan's dreams of turning it into the swankiest music hall in Baltimore.

"You put yourself in danger like that again and—"

"And what, you don't bring danger?" It felt good to spit that out.

His jaw tensed. He lifted the napkin again. "I burn this. She can stay."

A string of expletives waiting to be unleashed sat on her tongue. She choked them back. "Fine. But only until I find someplace else for us to go." She could find a better club than this place.

"Come on. I'll put her in my office." Declan moved to the sleeping girl. "Okay, beauty, time for rest." She slipped into his arms so easily, just folded into him. With one hand on his cane, the other arm full of Naomi, he eased her toward the back rooms.

"Mmm, smell good." Naomi murmured against his jacket —a vintage Ralph Lauren if Phee wasn't mistaken. She mentally curled a fist around her desire to take a strong inhale of his scent. Her willpower squeezed the life out of it. Damn Declan and his impeccable taste.

She followed them to his office. Declan laid Naomi on his couch and pulled the blanket that always hung off the end over her. She didn't visit Declan's office often, yet she'd always noticed that worn red and blue plaid blanket. She'd wondered if it was sentimental in some way.

When he straightened, he appraised Phee. She squeezed her heart shut in case that warmth in his eyes reached her. She had to stay the course and keep that blood-pumping organ where it belonged—under lock and key. If she didn't, she'd bleed out.

"I'll fill her in when she wakes. Try to place her."

A stab of sorrow arrowed through her chest anyway at his kindness, his immediate acceptance of responsibility for the lost girl.

He gestured to the hallway. "Now, we talk."

"Tomorrow."

He pointed to his door. "Now."

Download or purchase Tough Break from your favorite online retailer or request it from your local library or favorite book store.

ALSO BY ELIZABETH SAFLEUR

Elite

Holiday Ties

Untouchable

Perfect

Riptide

Lucky

Fearless

Invincible

The White House Gets A Spanking

Spanking the Senator

Tough Road

Tough Luck

Tough Break

Tough Love

ABOUT THE AUTHOR

Elizabeth SaFleur writes romance that dares to "go there" from 28 wildlife-filled acres, dances in her spare time and is a certifiable tea snob.

Find out more about Elizabeth on her web site at www. ElizabethSaFleur or join her private Facebook group, Elizabeth's Playroom.

Follow her on Instagram (@ElizabethLoveStory) and TikTok (@ElizabethSaFleurAuthor), too!

www.ingramcontent.com/pod-product-compliance
Lightning Source LLC
Chambersburg PA
CBHW051651180726
48284CB00006B/1952